"You're playing with fire, Emily,"

Rye warned softly. "The kind that you won't find
easy to control."

Emily's heart gave a leap. "Please," she said, "don't
go melodramatic on me."

"There's no way that I'm going to retire to the
sidelines and let you take over as the parent Lindsey
turns to for counsel. You're going to have to contend
with me being around, talking to you in person,
calling you on the phone. Can you handle that?"

"Can *you* handle it?" she responded.

"I'm not sure."

His gaze lowered to her mouth and then farther
down. Emily felt her body's immediate response.
Her heart was pounding and her pulse hammering.

"Well, I'll say good-night," Rye said.

"Goodbye," Emily said firmly.

"Good night," he repeated with soft, steely
emphasis. "Be sure to lock the door."

Emily opened her mouth to tell him to mind his own
business. Then she closed it, knowing what his reply
would be. As long as her house was his daughter's
home, whether or not she locked her doors at night
was his business.

Dear Reader,

Welcome to **Silhouette Special Edition** . . . welcome to romance. Each month, **Silhouette Special Edition** publishes six novels with you in mind—stories of love and life, tales that you can identify with—romance with that little "something special" added in.

And this month, we have a star-spangled surprise for you. To help celebrate the Fourth of July, we have two books that are dedicated to the Navy—and our country's valiant armed services. *Under Fire* by Lindsay McKenna is part of the thrilling WOMEN OF GLORY series—the hero and heroine are both naval pilots. *Navy Woman* by Debbie Macomber is set at a naval submarine base in the state of Washington—the hero is the commander of a vast fleet, and the heroine is a busy naval attorney. Three cheers for the red, white and blue—and the Navy! We're protected in the air as well as by sea! Happy Fourth of July.

Rounding out July are books by Ada Steward, Laura Leone and Carole Halston. And, as an added bonus, July brings the initial story of the compelling series SONNY'S GIRLS—*All Those Years Ago,* by Emilie Richards. The next installments in SONNY'S GIRLS due out in August and September, respectively, are *Don't Look Back* by Celeste Hamilton and *Longer Than . . .* by Erica Spindler. Don't miss these poignant tales!

In each **Silhouette Special Edition**, we're dedicated to bringing you the romances that you dream about—the type of stories that delight as well as bring a tear to the eye. And that's what **Silhouette Special Edition** is all about—special books by special authors for special readers!

I hope you enjoy this book and all of the stories to come.

Sincerely,

Tara Gavin
Senior Editor

CAROLE HALSTON
Yours, Mine and ... Ours

Silhouette Special Edition

Published by Silhouette Books New York

America's Publisher of Contemporary Romance

SILHOUETTE BOOKS
300 East 42nd St., New York, N.Y. 10017

YOURS, MINE AND...OURS

ISBN: 0-373-09682-8

First Silhouette Books printing July 1991

Printed in the U.S.A.

Books by Carole Halston

Silhouette Romance

Stand-In Bride #62
Love Legacy #83
Undercover Girl #152
Sunset in Paradise #208

Silhouette Special Edition

Keys to Daniel's House #8
Collision Course #41
The Marriage Bonus #86
Summer Course in Love #115
A Hard Bargain #139
Something Lost, Something Gained #163
A Common Heritage #211
The Black Knight #223
Almost Heaven #253
Surprise Offense #291
Matched Pair #328
Honeymoon for One #356
The Baby Trap #388
High Bid #423
Intensive Care #461
Compromising Positions #500
Ben's Touch #543
Unfinished Business #567
Courage to Love #642
Yours, Mine and . . . Ours #682

CAROLE HALSTON

is a Louisiana native residing on the north shore of Lake Pontchartrain, near New Orleans. She enjoys traveling with her husband to research less familiar locations for settings, but is always happy to return home to her own unique region, a rich source in itself for romantic stories about warm, wonderful people.

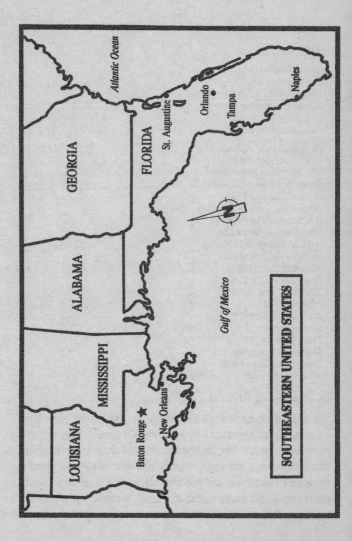

SOUTHEASTERN UNITED STATES

Prologue

Her mother was home. The battered old red van was parked in back of the farmhouse, and there was music coming from Emily's studio in one of the outbuildings. Lindsey listened for a moment, long enough to make out the song, an oldie from the sixties by Crosby, Stills, and Nash.

She hummed the tune as she got two suitcases from the trunk of her car, leaving it open for a return trip. Lugging the suitcases toward the rear screened porch, she sang aloud softly, hearing her own despondent note.

It was no wonder that the melody and the lyrics of the song were as familiar to her as those of any pop favorite of her own, younger generation. The one similarity between the separate households of her divorced parents had been the music of the sixties and early seventies playing in the background.

Going back and forth between such drastically different environments, Lindsey had made the transition more easily thanks to the recorded sounds of the Beatles, Simon and Garfunkel, Bob Dylan and other musical greats from the same era. She had taken heart in the knowledge that there was something akin to a family activity that she and her mother and father might have enjoyed together. They could have sat somewhere or ridden in an automobile and listened to music.

But as long as Lindsey's stepmother, Claire, had been in the picture, even that idea hadn't been feasible. Then, when Lindsey was eight, her father and Claire had split. There had no longer been anything standing in the way of Lindsey's parents becoming friendly acquaintances, at the very least. Nothing prevented her father from delivering her personally to her mother's place every other weekend, rather than having Mrs. Pearson, the housekeeper, act as chauffeur. He could talk to Emily over the phone himself when he wanted to verify arrangements, not have his secretary call.

Lindsey had been convinced life would be simpler if her parents would only start dealing with each other directly. Then, as they carried on conversations and came in contact, they were almost certain to like one another again. They both had such wonderful qualities that made Lindsey adore them.

Perhaps in time they would even fall back in love and get remarried, she had speculated wistfully. They'd both reluctantly admitted that they'd once been deeply in love. Surely love didn't just die, but could be revived.

It was such a wonderful thought that she might live in the same house with her mother and her father, see them both every single day, school days and weekends and holidays. Then neither of them would have to feel lonely for her while she was spending time with the other parent, and she wouldn't be pulled in two directions. The whole notion of custody would no longer apply.

Even at the tender age of eight, Lindsey had known that home for the three of them would have to be a house other than the cottage her mother currently rented or the two-storied house her father owned. She couldn't imagine him sitting comfortably in Emily's living room, which was furnished with an assortment of secondhand furniture. Nor could she picture Emily in the spick-and-span elegance of the home Lindsey shared with her father.

But after love had been renewed, living arrangements could be worked out to everyone's satisfaction. Lindsey had put the troublesome details out of her mind and subscribed to vague optimism as she launched a matchmaking campaign that went on doggedly for several years. Finally, however, she was forced to admit defeat. Whether from force of habit or some deeper reason, both her parents seemed bent on avoiding any face-to-face encounter, any exchange over the telephone. There was no reconciling two people whose lives were like parallel lines that never crossed.

Lindsey might have given up sooner except for a single encouraging sign. Neither parent ever pumped her about the other, but when she voluntarily relayed information, she could detect a grudging interest along with the disapproval. Occasionally there was even underlying concern, especially on her father's part when she reported that Emily had been ill or had suffered some mishap.

By the time she had abandoned hope of a reunited family, Lindsey had grown accustomed to playing diplomat. It had become second nature to present both parents to each other in the best possible light, and she sensed that she had accomplished some small good in improving relations.

Now, for the first time in her life, she was about to become a bone of contention rather than a peacemaker. She would undoubtedly destroy whatever tolerance and sympathy she'd painstakingly nurtured through the years. As much as Lindsey regretted the unpleasantness ahead, she welcomed it in a way. She was tired of walking on eggshells.

It would be a painful kind of relief for her parents to finally talk to each other, even if the conversation was hostile and angry. Maybe her hoped-for family get-together would finally take place. There would be some satisfaction in that, oddly enough, even if the meeting took the form of an ugly confrontation.

Reaching the steps of the porch, she put down one of the suitcases and mounted the bottom step. Instead of opening the screen door, she stood and contemplated it. The door had seen better days. Its wire netting was no longer stretched taut, but ballooned outward. In several places jagged tears had been patched with silver duct tape, exemplifying Emily's version of home maintenance.

But being Emily, Lindsey's mother hadn't just torn off swatches of tape and stuck them on. She'd gone to considerable pains to cut out and assemble recognizable forms, a giant mosquito hawk, a chubby spider, a swooping bird, all enemies of the pesky insects—the main one being mosquitoes—the screen was designed to keep outside.

Lest the insects didn't recognize the shapes of their predators, Emily had drawn in details with a black marking pencil, giving sinister life to the whimsical creations that had been born out of practical need.

A smile tugged at Lindsey's lips even as she breathed a sigh. She could just imagine her father's reaction. He would shake his head, his dark eyes noting in a keen glance how fruitless his ex-wife's makeshift efforts were. The door it-self was out of square, and the door frame out of plumb. There were large triangular cracks at both the top and the bottom. Whole companies of invading insects could enter together with room to spare.

Rye's solution to the problem would be major founda-tion work to level up the farmhouse, under the expert su-pervision of an architect and structural engineer. At the very least he would have replaced the torn screen, for the sake of appearance if nothing else.

It wouldn't matter if he were the only person using the door. Rye Keeler's personal standards would never allow him the latitude to mend a screen door with tape, other than as a temporary, emergency measure. Nor could he live, as Emily did, with tables that only stood solidly on uneven floors thanks to folded envelopes, with a toilet that didn't refill with water unless the handle was jiggled according to a set pattern, with appliances that all had their eccentrici-ties.

How had two people as unsuited for living together as he and Emily ever gotten married in the first place?

Lindsey knew the answer. She would have been able to figure it out for herself, even if her parents hadn't always been honest with her, answering her questions in their own differing styles.

She was the reason, of course. She'd *happened* and messed up their lives. Emily had only been eighteen, Lind-sey's age now, and a college freshman. Rye had been twenty-one, in his junior year.

Except for her, their relationship could have ended when the attraction burned itself out or common sense pre-vailed. They could have gone separate ways with keepsake items as the only tangible evidence of what they'd shared, snapshots of the two of them together, silly presents they'd given each other, mementos from dates, like a rock-concert program—all things that could be thrown away.

Instead Lindsey had come along and forged a permanent connection. If they could just have remained friends after their marriage, it would have made matters so much easier through the years. It would make matters easier now. She might stand a chance of convincing her father that she wasn't rejecting everything he stood for.

The truth was that Lindsey was far more like him than like her mother, in temperament, as well as looks. She couldn't quite imagine herself patching a screen door with tape, either. But she could still be charmed by the sight of Emily's door, which brought back vivid childhood memories of herself seated next to Emily, spellbound by the story her mother was making up and illustrating as she went along. Lindsey treasured those sheafs of illustrations every bit as much as she treasured the library of beautiful children's books that her father had bought for her and read to her himself.

It was only partly from economic necessity that Emily improvised and dealt with life, one day at a time, in her own original fashion. Lindsey didn't have any doubt that her mother would have been just as unconventional if she'd been born to riches. Emily would have been a wealthy eccentric rather than a poor one, and she would have remained every bit as convinced that she was the most practical and logical of people.

But whatever she lacked in common sense, she made up for in bigheartedness. For all the worry and exasperation that she might cause those who cared about her, there was the delight and fascination of knowing Emily, the admiration for her dauntless spirit. Despite everything that Lindsey might have wished had been different about her family background, she had always regarded it as her rare good fortune that Emily was her mother.

Not that Lindsey had ever loved her father any less than her mother. She adored him equally as much and was as close to him, so close that she wondered whether he was truly happy, despite all his success.

He was going to be very unhappy with her during the coming weeks, when, for the first time, she would be acting without his permission. Lindsey hated displeasing him, but it was the thought of how much he would worry about her that almost took away her courage.

"Anybody home?" she inquired bleakly, tugging open the screen door. As she expected, there was no answer. The farmhouse had a deserted air. The energy and exuberance that was the essence of Emily was missing.

But the back porch bore evidence that she lived there. Lindsey stood, looking around at the accumulation of newspapers, cardboard boxes, empty jars, plastic jugs, folded paper bags and plastic grocery bags with others wadded up inside them. There was barely a path to the kitchen door.

Emily didn't dispose of anything reusable, which included most items that other people threw away. Her instinct for saving and recycling wasn't, however, accompanied by any sense of organization.

Straightening the porch wouldn't take Lindsey long. In a matter of a few minutes, she could have the boxes nested inside one another, all the paper bags stuffed into one bag, the newspapers in a neat stack, the empty containers arranged according to size, the plastic jugs strung together and hung on a nail, the bags of plastic bags hung on another nail.

Since she'd been a little girl, she'd periodically tidied up her mother's various back porches on visits and had the whole procedure down to a science. This time would be different from all the others. This time Lindsey hadn't come to visit.

Before she tackled the porch, she would finish unloading her car. Then she would go and find Emily and tell her the news that her daughter was dropping out of college and moving in with her.

Chapter One

"**Y**ou're next," Emily cheerfully informed a large lid-ded stoneware pot, picking it up with gingerly care so as not to damage the chalky glaze coating. "I've reserved the best spot in the kiln for you. Now if you don't mind, you could show your appreciation and come out with some gorgeous flashings."

She carried the pot out to a shed located some twenty feet from the door of the studio, a trip she'd made numerous times already that morning. The shed housed a crude structure made of brick and concrete, Emily's wood-burning kiln that she'd built herself with the help of some potter friends.

It had two chambers, one on a higher level than the other, and both presently open to view because the fronts were unbricked. Kneeling on the hard-packed ground in front of the higher chamber, Emily leaned inside, her arm and shoulder muscles tensed with the strain, and put the pot in place on a kiln shelf.

Gently withdrawing her hands, she edged her body backward and, when she was clear of the opening, rose to her haunches and stood.

"It looks like I've arrived just in time to chop wood."

At the sound of her daughter's voice, Emily whirled around with a little squeal of surprise and flung her arms wide in a gesture of welcome.

"Lindsey! What a marvelous surprise!"

The sight of her offspring brought a rush of maternal love and pride to Emily's breast. This tall, poised, pretty young brunette on the verge of womanhood was her daughter.

No one would ever have guessed the relationship, seeing them together. Lindsey didn't look anything at all like her mother, who was five foot three, with a mop of red-gold hair, blue eyes and a fair, freckled complexion.

Rye's genes had definitely dominated. Lindsey had his height, his dark eyes and fine, dark hair, his sculpted features, even his expressions. For the life of her, Emily couldn't be sorry about the resemblance, even if she felt that nature had played sides, keeping Rye's face ever fresh in her mind while he got off scot-free and could erase her image from memory, which Emily didn't doubt that he'd done.

By the same token, she couldn't even resent the fact that Lindsey was largely her father's daughter in personality, much more in control of her emotions than Emily, logical and neat and efficient. While Emily accepted and liked being the way she was, she wouldn't have wanted to produce a replica of herself.

It pleased her to think that Lindsey was better equipped to cope with life than she was. Emily regarded herself as a basically fortunate person who'd had her share of ups as well as downs, but she hoped Lindsey would know a deeper happiness, a greater sense of fulfillment.

For that reason Emily was glad that Lindsey was in no danger of ever following in her mother's footsteps. Rye had seen to that. He hadn't just determined their daughter's genetic makeup. He'd been in charge of Lindsey's upbringing.

He was a good parent, never giving Emily any grounds to criticize him as a father. And he'd always kept his bargain. In return for her giving him custody without a court fight, he'd always seen to it that Lindsey spent the allotted weekends, holidays and summer vacation time with her mother.

And Lindsey herself was living proof that Rye had been right in relegating Emily to the role of part-time mother. Today, as always, Emily wasn't about to let resentment or regrets about the past spoil her pleasure in a visit from her daughter.

It was unusual for Lindsey to drop in unannounced. She always called and made sure her mother was going to be home before making the hour's drive from Baton Rouge. If Emily hadn't been able to provide her own guilty explanation for Lindsey's atypical behavior, she would have been instantly concerned, detecting the telltale signs that Lindsey was upset beneath her calm.

"I'm sorry, darling!" Emily clapped her hands to her chest in a melodramatic gesture of apology. "I guess you've come all this distance out into the boonies to make sure that I'm alive and well. My phone has been out of order for days, and I didn't realize it until Mabel Peabody came over. She'd been trying to call and kept getting a busy signal. Mabel loves murder mysteries and has a grisly imagination. She was all but certain that I had been murdered in my bed and the phone had been ripped out of the wall. Just in case I was alive, she brought me a dozen yard eggs, the dear.'' Emily shook her head in fond amusement.

Lindsey's smile was wan. ''Is your phone working now?''

''I don't know whether it is or not,'' Emily had to admit. ''Mabel was going to go straight home and report the problem for me. That was yesterday, I believe. But I haven't bothered to try it. It's too early to call anyone when I get up and come out to the studio, and too late by the time I call it quits at night. But what a treat this is to have you drop in on me!''

Flinging her arms wide again, Emily walked eagerly toward her daughter to give her a hug. She didn't expect to get away with dropping the whole subject of telephone service. Lindsey would probably lecture her mother on making sure that her phone was in working order, since it was her link to civilization, and point out again how foolhardy Emily was not to have a phone in her studio for emergencies. Emily lived too far from her neighbors to call out for help.

Probably it was foolish not to worry about harm befalling her, but she didn't. An element of risk was preferable to paranoia, and Emily's chosen life-style didn't include through-bolt locks and burglar alarms. On her income as a potter, she couldn't have afforded them anyway.

''Darling, I wish you wouldn't worry about me!'' she scolded when Lindsey hugged her back with fierce affection. ''I'm safer out here in the country than in the city. But if it will give you peace of mind, I'll have a phone put in my studio as soon as I have the time and extra money.''

''I'll take care of it for you,'' her daughter promised pensively, not visibly cheered by what was a major concession on Emily's part.

"I might as well wait now until after I get back from doing the winter shows in Florida," Emily said.

Lindsey nodded in absent agreement.

"Something else is bothering you, isn't it?" Emily asked, realizing that she'd been on the wrong track. "You have too much common sense to panic because you can't get in touch with me on the phone."

"What you mean is that I have too much of my father in me to overreact." Lindsey sighed. "I haven't tried to call you since I saw you during the Christmas holidays." That had been three weeks ago. "I knew that you'd be frantically busy, getting ready for the Florida shows. By the time I would get in at night, I hated to risk waking you up."

"Any time you need to talk to me, I'd want you to wake me up. But a visit is better than a phone call any day!"

Emily was certain now that her daughter had problems on her mind. Evidently she'd come for a heart-to-heart talk. The best tactic with her was to let her confide in her own way. Even as a child, it hadn't been Lindsey's nature to blurt out her thoughts and feelings.

"I've been needing to go to the grocery store, since the cupboard is almost bare. Thank heaven I put it off again or I might have missed you," Emily said, linking her arm with Lindsey's and starting them in the direction of the farmhouse.

"I have my key, in case you were gone and had happened to lock the door." The note of reproof was a sign of normalcy, but it was only halfhearted. "I'd have gone inside and waited." She hesitated. "I came prepared to spend the night."

"Then this is an unexpected treat!" Emily exclaimed, delighted. "If Mabel hadn't brought those eggs, I wouldn't have anything to offer you for lunch but a peanut butter sandwich. How does an omelet sound?"

"I'm really not very hungry."

Lindsey always lost her appetite whenever she was worried or upset.

"Maybe you'll work up an appetite by the time I've made them," Emily suggested cheerfully. "Did you get the official report on your grades yet?"

"Yes." The answer was glum. "They weren't any better than I was expecting."

Her daughter's downcast expression made Emily think that she had probably hit upon the cause of depression.

"But you were expecting to make a C average. That's nothing to be ashamed of, your first semester. It's a big adjustment from high school to college."

"There's not that big a difference," Lindsey contradicted. "College is just more of the same. Attending classes, taking notes, doing assignments, taking tests. Memorizing meaningless information, reading a lot of dull textbooks, writing papers on subjects that I couldn't care less about. I'm just *tired* of it all."

"Once you get past the basic courses, you'll probably find your studies more interesting," Emily soothed. "In the meantime, enjoy the campus life. There's a lot more to a college education than making the honor roll." Lindsey's father might not share that viewpoint, but it was a valid one nonetheless.

Rye's reaction to his daughter's grades was, without a doubt, a key factor behind her low mood. Earning his approval was of utmost importance to her. He knew that, and it wouldn't hurt him to show some sensitivity and ease off his perfectionist standards for once.

Lindsey glanced over at her mother. "Dad gave me the same pep talk you're giving me," she said with a regretful, knowing tone. "To prove that he's proud of me, he's raised

my clothing allowance. Poor Dad. He runs out of presents
to buy me.''

Poor Dad. Emily managed to swallow her totally unsympathetic echo, but she might as well have spoken it
aloud. Lindsey's expression said that she'd read her mother's thoughts again.

''It's a wonder you aren't spoiled rotten,'' Emily said
fondly. ''But you aren't.''

Lindsey went on, refusing to be sidetracked or cheered.
''For Christmas he'd just given me a new stereo for my
dorm room. It's compact, but has fabulous sound. Sarah
was sick when she learned that I was moving out and taking it with me.''

''You're moving out of the dorm?'' At the solemn nod
of confirmation, Emily breathed a disappointed sigh.
''You've decided to live at home, where you won't be distracted and can study and pull up your grades. It's your
decision, darling, but I think you're making a mistake.''

She had said enough, but seeing that she hadn't made
any impression, she couldn't stop there. ''Whatever you do,
whether you stay in the dorm or live at home, I wish that
you'd do what *you* think is best for your total development of yourself as a person. It's wonderful to set high
goals, but they should be *your* goals, not anyone else's.''
Not your father's, she added silently.

''Mom, I'm not moving back home,'' Lindsey said quietly. ''I am going to do what I think is best for me right
now, and Dad definitely isn't going to approve. He'll be
terribly upset with me. And with you, if you go along,'' she
added.

''I can't imagine that you'd ever do anything to upset
your father *terribly,*'' Emily scoffed. ''You've always been
a model child. Where do you plan to live? In an apartment?''

"I want to live with you."

Emily was taken completely unawares. Her steps faltered. "With me?"

"If it's okay."

"There's no question of whether it would be okay," Emily replied with as little emotion as possible. "You know I would adore having you live with me. But it's an hour's drive to Baton Rouge. That's a long commute to classes and a long way for Eric to come to pick you up for dates. He would have to call long distance just to talk to you on the phone."

"Eric and I have broken it off."

Emily came to a complete standstill with a little cry of sympathy. "I'm so sorry to hear that. I know you like Eric a lot." She hugged Lindsey comfortingly and then started them walking again. "Poor darling. No wonder you're down in the dumps. Did you and Eric have a big fight?"

"No, we just got to the point where we couldn't go out and have fun together. All he seemed to have on his mind was having sex. When and if I do have that kind of relationship with a guy, I don't want it to be because I was pressured into it."

"Good for you," Emily commended.

"Not that I wasn't tempted," Lindsey confided honestly. "Eric really is cute."

"And you're naturally curious to find out what making love is like."

"Yes, especially since so many of my friends aren't virgins and haven't been since high school. Sometimes I wonder, 'why hold out?' Then I go over our conversations on the subject and remember how you've said that I'll know when someone is special enough to take that step with him. That when it happens, I'll be glad that I waited until sex was really an expression of love."

"You will be. And there's no hurry. You have plenty of time. My guess is that Eric will want to make up once he realizes how much he misses your company. Maybe you two could still date, but go out with other people, too."

"I'm not interested in dating anybody for the time being. I'm as fed up with dating as I am with going to school and studying. More than anything else, I'm sick of being *me*, this phony person who puts on a show of being so sure of herself when deep down inside she doesn't know who she is or what she really wants out of life. I just want some time out."

"Then take it, darling," Emily urged. "And don't be hard on yourself because you're feeling strain from all the pressures. It's okay to be human. Maybe you should just drop out of school a semester and give yourself a break. There's no hurry to get a college degree."

"That's exactly what I've decided."

Emily did her best to sound casual instead of hopeful as she asked, "So you are seriously thinking about living with me for a while?"

"I've already moved my things into my bedroom."

In Emily's various rented places of residence, Lindsey had always had her own bedroom. It had been important to Emily that her daughter feel that her mother's home was her home, too, even if just on weekends and holidays and the precious longer visits during the summers.

"Your father knows about your plans?"

"I've told him."

"But he hasn't given his permission."

"He agreed that I take off a semester, as long I do something educational, like traveling. He's willing to send me on a tour of Europe or any other part of the world where it's safe to go."

"What a marvelous opportunity for you." Emily couldn't keep a tinge of bitterness from creeping into her voice. Rye would spend any amount of money to give their daughter an attractive alternative to living temporarily with her mother.

"A few years from now, I'd probably be thrilled over the idea, but I'd much rather go to Florida with you instead." Emily's steps faltered again.

Lindsey hugged her mother's arm against her side as she elaborated enthusiastically. "I think the two of us will have so much fun, traveling in your motor home. It'll be a whole new experience for me, staying in camping grounds, helping you set up for shows, meeting the other artists. Unless I'd cramp your style," she ended up.

"Cramp my style?" Emily chided wistfully. "You'd add a real touch of class, and I'd love to have your company. But it wouldn't be any luxury vacation, like your father is offering you. Believe me, there's nothing glamorous about having a flat tire on the interstate or sitting under a canopy that isn't waterproof and getting drenched when it rains cats and dogs during an outdoor show. In your place, darling, I'd go to London and Paris and Rome."

"It'll be an adventure," Lindsey insisted, unswayed.

"We'd be on the road for hours at a stretch. Annabelle won't go over fifty-five." Annabelle was Emily's aged motor home.

"We'll take turns at the wheel and pass the time talking."

Emily persevered. "On my budget we wouldn't be dining out in better restaurants. For entertainment we'd do exciting things like take in a movie."

"We'll cook outside at the campsites. I bought one of those cute little hibachis to bring along. And I'll chip in on groceries and expenses, Mom. It's *my* money in my bank account, not Dad's,'' she stated firmly when Emily immediately bridled.

"Lindsey he's never going to allow you to leave the state with me.''

"I'm eighteen years old. There's nothing that he can legally do to stop me.''

"He'll forbid you to.''

"He already has.''

The troubled confidence was like a grave forewarning. Emily felt a shiver of dread down her spine, even as anger and resentment welled up. *Rye, you selfish bastard,* she thought. Then the irony sank in, flooding her with ambivalent feelings.

Emily and Rye had both been born out of wedlock. The difference was that she hadn't grown up ashamed of being illegitimate, and he had. Reared by her dear, eccentric great-aunt, Emily saw herself as a love child. Reared in foster homes as a ward of the state of Louisiana, Rye saw himself as an unwanted bastard.

"I'm not leaving for Florida until the middle of February,'' she said. ''That's a whole month away.''

Between now and then, a lot could happen to change Lindsey's mind. Emily wasn't going to get her hopes up.

"I hope you're ready, Mom.''

"A long way from it,'' Emily denied cheerfully. ''There's a hundred and one things to be done.''

"I don't mean ready for the trip.'' Lindsey's glance was a mixture of impatience and compassion. ''Ready to stand up to Dad.''

"This is strictly between you and him. It's better for you if I don't get involved.''

"There's no way that you can stay out of it, I'm afraid. When I don't come home, Dad will try to wear you down.''

"With any luck, maybe the phone will keep malfunctioning," Emily said in a feeble attempt at a joke. "Or we could just unplug the darn thing."

"That would only bring him out from the city a little sooner."

They had almost reached the house. With a sick feeling in the pit of her stomach, Emily stared past it at the unpaved country road that wound for miles before it intersected with another unpaved road that connected eventually with a two-lane rural highway.

"Rye would never come here," she protested.

"I realize that it's been an unwritten rule all these years that you and Dad won't go near one another's home, but, believe me, Dad will break that rule now. When all else fails, he'll come here to have a face-to-face showdown with you."

"Don't give him directions," Emily suggested only half-facetiously. "He'd never find this place without them."

"You don't think for one minute that Dad couldn't pinpoint this farmhouse on a map of the area. He's known the exact location of every place where you've lived."

"Naturally he would, being a conscientious father."

"Try *overprotective*." Lindsey halted a few steps from the back porch, pulling Emily to a stop. "Listen. I think I hear your phone ringing."

Over the beating of her own heart, Emily could detect the faint pealing. "Whoever it is will call back if it's important," she said.

"Whoever it is isn't giving up easily."

"It's probably an employee from the phone company, checking to make sure I have service. Or someone peddling aluminum siding."

"I'll bet it's Dad, tracking me down. He's been in Houston, opening up a new frame shop there, and was due back this morning."

"He's opened up another frame shop in Houston?"

"With the two in Dallas, this makes four altogether in Texas, then the three in Louisiana. He's thinking of branching out into Mississippi and Alabama."

"The phone's stopped ringing," Emily said with relief. "I guess it's safe to go inside now."

No sooner were the words out than the phone started ringing again.

"You can answer that, if you don't mind, while I start cooking our lunch," Emily said as they entered the house.

"I'd rather you answer it, Mom."

"If it is your father, he'll want to speak to you."

"Please."

Emily searched her daughter's face. Along with apology and pleading, she read the need for a deeper assurance. Nodding, she reached up and gave Lindsey's cheek a tender pat.

"Why don't you put a pot of coffee on?" she suggested. "I'm out of any other kind of beverage. You know where everything is."

At the wall phone, she lifted the receiver and reminded over her shoulder, "Remember, darling, the knob has to be turned to Off to start the coffee maker." Speaking into the mouthpiece, she said conversationally, "Hello, this is Emily Barrett."

There was silence, despite her strong intuition that the caller was on the line.

Chapter Two

Rye recovered his lost power of speech.

"Hello, Emily. This is Rye. Is Lindsey there?"

Or was she addressing someone else as "darling" in that warm, loving tone that made his heart ache with an unexpected pain?

"Why, yes, she is. Hold on just a moment, Rye."

Rye drew in a deep breath, mentally shifting gears and preparing for his conversation with his daughter. But then he realized that his ex-wife apparently wasn't summoning Lindsey to the phone.

"Is there enough coffee grounds?" he could hear her inquiring worriedly.

Lindsey answered in the background. "Just barely."

"That's good because I don't have another bag in the pantry. We'll have to go stock up on groceries this afternoon. I'm sorry, Rye." She was back to him.

"I'd like to speak to Lindsey, Emily. Would you please put her on?"

"She's right in the middle of doing something. Would you like for me to ask her to call you back later?"

"No, I'll hold."

"Jiggle it a little."

"What?"

"I was talking to Lindsey," she hastened to explain, and then switched her attention again. "There—that's it. Now you're in business. She's making coffee, and my coffee maker is temperamental."

"It sounds to me like the wiring is faulty."

The last thing Rye wanted was to troubleshoot one of Emily's household appliances via long distance, but that was his daughter operating the damned coffee maker. She was in danger of getting shocked. Through the years, he had never rested easy when Lindsey was visiting her mother. Now the old nagging fears for her physical safety were reborn, exacerbating more serious concerns.

"More than likely," Emily agreed.

"Emily, an electrical short is nothing to fool around with."

"Of course it isn't. To be on the safe side, I always unplug the coffee maker when I leave the house."

Rye squeezed his eyes shut, welcoming the surge of irritation. She hadn't changed. She never would. He might have rarely spoken to her in years, but she could still get under his skin in a matter of seconds. And the hell of it was that he still found that husky timbre of her voice sexy. He had to fight the urge to continue a discussion that would only drive him up a wall and accomplish nothing.

"Emily, I've just arrived back in town. I want to talk to my daughter."

"She's my daughter, too, Rye," she informed him quietly. "She just went to the bathroom. Why don't you call back tonight? She hasn't been here an hour, and I haven't seen her since Christmas. We're about to have lunch."

"I'll call back at six o'clock sharp." Rye hung up the phone, letting his tone convey the rest.

When he called back, he wouldn't be put off. He meant to speak with his daughter before the night was over, one way or another. Damn it, she was *his* daughter, *his* responsibility.

She had been, since the moment he'd learned that he'd gotten Emily pregnant. It had been up to him to insure that his unborn child had the proper prenatal care. Emily's attitude, typically, had been to let nature take its course.

Rye had read the books and pamphlets, accompanied Emily to the doctor's office, seen that she took her vitamins and stuck to a healthy regimen. The last had been anything but easy. Following any kind of schedule was alien to Emily, who thrived on impulse.

He hadn't been able to get through to her either before or after Lindsey was born that being a mother was now her number-one priority, just as his was being a father and provider. It didn't matter that they'd taken on the roles of parents prematurely. They had no choice but to grow up, make whatever sacrifices were necessary, put the needs of their child first.

Deep down, Rye had known when he'd married Emily that she couldn't change. That she would never grow up, but always be a perennial child herself. He'd known that he was going to have to carry the full load of responsibility, make all the important decisions.

He'd been willing to do that, if she'd only made some effort. But it had proved more than he could handle, trying to earn a living and getting no help at all in providing Lindsey with a stable home environment.

Rye could have put up with the disorder and the hit-and-miss meals. But he wanted his daughter to have every advantage in growing up. That included a mother who was more than a playmate.

The deciding factor for him in giving up on his marriage had been doing what was best for Lindsey. In the years since then, every important decision he'd made, including marrying Claire, whom he'd hoped would be the perfect stepmother, had been weighed in terms of how Lindsey would benefit.

His daughter was his joy, his pride. Her happiness and welfare came first with him. His love for his little girl brought out the gentlest side of his nature. It also unleashed his most primitive instincts. He would kill to protect her.

He could be hard and ruthless on her behalf.

He *had* been hard and ruthless in obtaining custody, for he had known the end justified the means. There had never been any question of whether Emily loved Lindsey as much as he did. She just wasn't capable of taking good care of Lindsey.

Rye was.

It had been as simple as that. And nothing had changed, except that parental guidance was perhaps more crucial than ever at this stage in Lindsey's life.

God help him, Rye wasn't going to stand back and let Emily become a formative influence at a time when she could do the most damage. She was the last person he wanted Lindsey turning to for advice.

And when he called back at six o'clock, he would either speak to Lindsey on the phone or else he'd get in his car and go have a talk with her in person.

Emily lived way the hell out in the country. He was in no mood to make that drive tonight. Or any other time, for that matter. He had no desire to see where his ex-wife lived, no curiosity whatever.

He had no desire to see her.

It was distaste at the whole prospect of showing up un-invited at her home and having to confront her that caused the tension in his body. The sensation in the pit of his stomach was caused by dread, not suspense.

There was no suspenseful element where Rye and Emily were concerned. They were history. He was certain she felt exactly the same way.

Year after year she'd avoided any contact with him, just as he'd avoided any with her. They had purposefully kept direct communication to a minimum. Steering clear of each other had been a cooperative effort, ironically. In divorce they'd proved that two totally incompatible personalities could be partners in an endeavor.

If Emily opposed him now and tried to undermine his parental authority, she was just going to have to suffer the unpleasant consequences, along with him, of dealing with him personally.

When Rye called back at six, right on the dot, he was prepared for anything. Lindsey answered.

"Hi, Dad."

She sounded cheerfully apologetic and perfectly normal.

"Hi, baby."

Along with a surge of love and relief, Rye was aware of a little stab of disappointment. He'd been expecting Emily to answer. Had he been spoiling for a fight with her? The thought disturbed him.

"How was Houston?" Lindsey asked.

"Everything went off like clockwork." Rye briefly filled her in, then got down to the important subject at hand, her immediate future. "I have some travel brochures for you to look at. It's possible for you to pick up college credits doing educational travel. Then your semester off won't be wasted. Time is of the essence, though. We need to book reservations."

Her sigh came over the line. "Dad, I'm really not worried about getting college credit. I don't even know what I want to major in."

"That will come," he assured. "You can't go wrong with a liberal arts degree."

Except for her own self-esteem, she didn't have to worry about a career. He would see to it that she had everything material that she required, and more.

"Before I choose any major or set goals for my future, I need to know myself better. Please don't worry about me," she urged. "I'll be fine."

"Sure, you will. At your age you just have so many options that it can be overwhelming." And so many potential mistakes to make. "It'll do you a world of good to see other parts of the world, be exposed to other cultures. You'll get to exchange ideas and broaden your viewpoint."

"Dad, I appreciate the fact that you're willing to put out a lot of money and send me to foreign countries. Honestly I do. But I can broaden my viewpoint right here in the United States and be some company for Mom and a big help to her at the same time."

Rye had hoped to avoid putting his foot down and issuing an ultimatum. He saw that it was going to be necessary.

"Lindsey, I absolutely refuse to give you permission to go off to Florida with your mother next month. You can visit her as often or as long as you like in the meantime. That's my final word.''

"I hope it isn't,'' she replied regretfully. "Because I am planning to go with Mom this year, and I'd rather go with your permission. Another thing, Dad. This isn't a visit. I want to live with Mom until I go back to school."

Rye couldn't trust himself to answer right away. He was too hurt. Braced for tears and pleading and argument, he hadn't been ready for the threat of outright disobedience. Or the added slap in the face that she was rejecting her own home that he'd provided, with every grace and comfort, in favor of moving in with Emily.

Lindsey went on miserably. "Please don't take it wrong. I'm not ungrateful, Dad. I know how lucky I am to have a father like you, who's always given me everything. I'm *not* choosing sides or being critical of you, but I'd like to make things up to Mom just a little, while I can. She's never said so, but I could always tell that it hurt her not having her daughter live with her."

"You couldn't live with both of us, and I was better able financially to give you a good home, clothe and educate you.'' Rye had gotten control of himself. "Plus I felt I was the more stable parent and could provide the emotional security that you needed. I've explained all this to you as you were growing up."

"Yes, and I accepted it. You and Mom both put my welfare first. I know that it would have been far easier for you, paying child support and letting her raise me, just like I know she did the unselfish thing by letting you have custody."

"We both loved you,'' Rye conceded. "It's just as important now that your mother and I continue acting in your best interest."

"Which, translated, means that Mom should go along with what *you* think is best for me."

Rye didn't bother with denials. "I don't claim to be infallible, but where you're concerned, I'd rather err on the side of being overly cautious. I couldn't sleep nights, sweetheart, with you off traveling with your mother in a twenty-year-old motor home. Having flat tires and breakdowns and heaven knows what problems. I'd be against the idea, even if she owned something newer and more reliable. Call me a chauvinist, but it isn't safe for two women to travel and stay in campgrounds without any male protection. Too many things can happen. There're too many dangers out there."

"Mom makes the trip by herself."

"I realize that she does," he said. "In my opinion, it's very unwise of her, but I have no say over what kinds of risks she's willing to take for herself. Just for the record, what is her reaction to all this?"

Rye wanted to know exactly what he was up against.

"She's thrilled at having me spend some time with her, but she doesn't see how I can pass up going to Europe. I guess she's always wanted to go herself. Also I think Mom is afraid to get her hopes up. Deep down, she doesn't believe that you'll let me go to Florida with her or live with her."

"I've always wanted to go to Europe myself," Rye remarked, refraining from responding to the rest of her summation.

"Why haven't you? You could have afforded it."

Whereas her mother couldn't.

"I just haven't had the free time."

"All you do is work and make money, Dad," Lindsey scolded. "You need to spend some of it on enjoying yourself."

"I enjoy myself," he protested. "I have a fairly active social life. I'm involved in civic affairs and have a voice in politics."

"You're a big success story, a self-made millionaire at the age of forty, according to that recent article about you in *Money* magazine. The important thing, though, is to be happy."

"I'm happy." Rye heard his lack of conviction and got the conversation back on track. "It's your happiness that I'm more concerned about. Before you rule out the travel opportunities that I've been gathering information on for you, at least look at the brochures. Tomorrow's Saturday. Come home and we'll talk. I'll take you out to lunch. Oh, and I bought you a little present in Houston."

"Dad, I'm sorry. I can't get away tomorrow. Mom's firing her wood kiln, and I'll need to stay here and help her. We'll be splitting and stacking wood and feeding the firebox in shifts. It'll be late tomorrow night or early Sunday morning before the kiln reaches temperature."

Rye held on to his patience. He managed not to point out that he hadn't sent Lindsey to private schools to prepare her to do rude labor. "There must be some local high school boy she could hire. Pay him yourself, and I'll reimburse you."

"Then I'd miss all the fun. If you'll put the brochures in the mail, I'll look at them. I promise. Now I have to hang up. I'm fixing supper, and it's time to take the casserole out of the oven and get Mom in from the studio."

Rye had surmised that Emily wasn't within hearing range. "Casserole?" he repeated.

"Yes, it's a taco casserole. It has the basic ingredients of a taco, seasoned ground meat, cheese, sour cream, fresh chopped tomatoes, chopped green onions. I saw the recipe in a magazine and clipped it out. Mom's always game to try any dish that I concoct.''

Her words weren't a dig at him, but Rye still felt a sense of slight. ''I hadn't realized that you were interested in cooking,'' he remarked. ''You could certainly have experimented in our kitchen if you'd wanted to.''

''If I'd shown any interest, you'd have had me enrolled in cooking classes,'' she accused only half-teasingly. ''There was never any reason that I should cook at home. By the time that I was old enough, we had someone to do the cooking. And our kitchens have always been so state-of-the-art and spotless.''

Unlike her mother's, which, Rye would bet any amount of money, was neither. ''I tried to see to it that you had meals that were not only nutritious, but varied, to develop your palate.''

''We had delicious meals and ate supper at night in the dining room on nice china with cloth napkins. You took me out to expensive restaurants from the time that I was a little girl, and encouraged me to sample gourmet dishes. As a result, I love fine food. At the other end of the spectrum, Mom couldn't afford a lot of eating out and didn't have any household help. She made a big adventure out of the two of us shopping for food at the grocery store and then getting in the kitchen and fixing ourselves something to eat. I discovered that I like cooking, and Mom gladly turns her kitchen over to me.''

''I hope her stove is in better shape than her coffee maker,'' Rye said.

''It isn't,'' Lindsey admitted. ''The oven thermostat doesn't work, and I have to turn the oven on and off to regulate the temperature.''

''It's a gas stove?''

"Propane gas. She doesn't have natural gas out here in the country."

"Does the pilot light stay lit?"

"No."

Rye smothered a curse. "You mean you have to strike a match to turn the damned oven on. For heaven's sake, Lindsey, get it repaired and have the line from the propane tank into the house checked to make sure there's no gas leak."

"The stove's practically an antique," she demurred. "I doubt that there are spare parts for it."

"Then buy her a new one and while you're at it, buy a new coffee maker, too."

"Dad, Mom knows that I don't have any money of my own, and she won't accept charity from you. Besides, she likes older things that have character."

"Lindsey, I'm not having you stay there if it's a death trap."

"With propane gas, you can always tell if there's a leak because of the strong odor," his daughter soothed. "I'm just about to turn the oven off and won't have to light it again. This moment I'm reaching for the knob. The kitchen phone has a long cord," she explained.

Rye heard a screeching noise. "The oven control knob makes a noise like that when you turn it?" he demanded incredulously.

"No, that was the oven door. My casserole looks heavenly and smells good, too," she reported in a satisfied tone. "Oh, *no!*"

Her cry of dismay filled him with alarm. "Lindsey, what's wrong?"

"The electricity just went off. It's pitch-black in here. There're no streetlights. Dad, I have to hang up."

"Lindsey, if anything happened to you—"

"Don't be paranoid," she scoffed. "Nothing's going to happen to me. Bye, Dad. I'll be talking to you soon."

Rye held the receiver to his ear in an iron grip for seconds after she'd broken the connection. Cursing his helplessness and frustration, he slammed it down, picked it up to dial again and then replaced it with punishing force.

Stumbling around in the darkness, she might forget that the oven door was open and burn herself, answering the phone. Damn Emily and her pride and her oddball sense of values! It was fine for her to eke out an existence, if that was what she wanted out of life. She had every right to live on a run-down old place, miles from nowhere, without modern conveniences or police protection, so long as she was bringing hardship on herself alone and endangering only herself.

But if she meant to go along with Lindsey's plan to move in with her, suddenly Rye had a say in the matter. Anything that seriously affected his daughter's welfare came in the realm of his business.

Tomorrow he was going out there. He wanted to see for himself just how bad Emily's housing conditions were. Based on what he found, he would deal with the situation.

If the farmhouse she rented was as dilapidated as he visualized it and as hazardous as he feared that it was, then she had two options if she wanted Lindsey visiting her. Either she relocated or fixed the place up. Rye was willing to subsidize both plans.

It was time that Emily swallowed her pride and accepted financial support from him, for Lindsey's benefit. Hell, he could easily afford to give his ex-wife an income and see that she had basic amenities.

Even if Lindsey weren't a factor, Rye felt a certain sense of obligation. A man of his means couldn't help being bothered by the thought of his former spouse having to struggle to make ends meet.

For the sake of his conscience, Rye was ready to apply pressure on Emily and force her to let him make her life easier.

The following morning Rye considered calling Lindsey and getting directions, but he decided against it. He was fairly confident that he could find the farmhouse Emily rented. The general location was clearly fixed in his mind, and he would just as soon appear unannounced.

In mid-January the temperature was mild, in the fifties. There hadn't been a hard freeze so far this winter. The sky was overcast, the day promising to be somewhat dreary, but Rye might have enjoyed the drive along rural highways under different circumstances.

He rolled down the window of his car and breathed air that wasn't scented with exhaust fumes, but with country smells. There were whiffs of barnyards as he passed farms. The going got slower when the route took him on graveled roads, and he had glimpses of the Saturday-morning routines of the sparse population. Several times he waved in response to friendly waves.

By the time he arrived at Emily's farmhouse, he was in a relaxed, almost expansive mood. The sight of her mailbox at the side of the road told him that he'd found the right place, even though there was no name or number for identification. It was brightly painted with flowers and birds, also dented, with a flap that didn't close tight enough to keep out driving rain.

Trust Emily to put more emphasis on decoration than function, Rye reflected, turning into the driveway. It was deeply rutted, needing a load or two of gravel, not a major outlay of money.

His view would have been obscured during any other season because of shade trees, but their branches were bare, allowing him to see the whole layout, which had its own bleak charm. The one-story house was painted white. Barns and outbuildings behind it were barn red. Fenced-in fields on either side and to the rear hadn't been plowed in recent years. Saplings had started to convert old furrows back to woods.

There was a general air of benign neglect, but not of abuse or dangerous disrepair. The house was due for re-painting. The old paint had grayed to an oyster white, worn thin and started to peel, he saw as he pulled up into the yard. No doubt a hired handyman would find plenty to do, both inside and out, but the house appeared stoutly built and sound.

Getting out of his car, Rye glanced appreciatively at a large camellia shrub in full bloom, its deep rose-colored petals contrasting with the dark green glossy leaves. There were several other varieties growing in the yard, all covered with waxy flowers. He spotted an abundance of azaleas, too, and beds of lilies. The farmer's wife must have liked flowers. In the springtime and early summer, the place would be quite a sight.

So far it was beginning to seem that Emily might have found herself quite a pleasant location, considering the cheap rent she was paying. He knew the amount, thanks to Lindsey.

Instead of being deeply relieved, as he should have been, Rye was oddly disgruntled. He wondered why. He hadn't wanted to find her living in a hovel so that he could intervene.

Or had he?

Finding his own ambivalence disturbing, Rye started to get back into his car and leave. His alarm of the night before was obviously a case of overreacting on his part. Lindsey wasn't a child. She was eighteen years old and levelheaded, with a great deal of his personality. She probably wasn't in any more physical danger out here with her mother than in the city. As difficult as it was to accept, Rye couldn't insure her safety every moment.

There was still the matter of her wanting to accompany Emily to Florida. His objections there were definitely not a case of overreacting, but he had a month in which to overrule the notion, which might die on its own. Since he'd driven all the way out here, he might as well see the condition of Emily's motor home, though. Plus he'd brought along the travel brochures for Lindsey. And he would like to say hello to his daughter.

Rye debated with himself and found reason enough to carry through with his visit and intrude on Emily's privacy. What it really came down to, he knew, was that his urge to stay was stronger than his logic.

Carrying the fat folder of brochures, he walked up onto the front porch and knocked. When there was no answer, he went around to the back of the house. Lindsey's bright red, sporty car, a high-school graduation present from him, was parked next to Emily's Volkswagen van, which was much the same vintage as her motor home. About a 1969 model, Rye would guess. Its tires didn't look much newer from a distance, especially compared to the brand-spanking-new whitewalls on Lindsey's car.

"Hello," Rye called, approaching the steps of the rear screened porch. The door, like the mailbox, was more evidence that Emily lived here. Rye gave his head a little shake, marveling at the time and patience expended in creating elaborate patches out of silver duct tape. The stuff was sticky and had to have been a bitch to work with.

Part of Emily's inefficiency had been her ability to focus painstakingly on minor tasks. She might spend a whole day turning a toilet-paper holder into a work of art and never get around to cleaning the bathroom.

Rye rapped on the door frame, banishing an unexpected and totally unwelcome wave of nostalgia. Once again there was no response. He hesitated and then opened the screen door and laid the folder of brochures on the floor just inside.

He could still leave. Lindsey and her mother evidently were both outside, apparently oblivious to his presence. A curl of smoke rose beyond one of the outbuildings, which he assumed was Emily's studio. It must be blocking her kiln and the activity from his view.

A whiff of burning wood seemed to remove any indecision. Rye headed toward the outbuilding. Halfway to it, he glanced toward the barn. Open doors afforded him a glimpse of Emily's motor home. It was painted canary yellow, a color as conspicuous as it was cheery. He shuddered at a mental picture of the gaudy vehicle pulled over to the side of an interstate highway, his brunette daughter and red-haired ex-wife standing by it and trying to flag down help.

A ripple of laughter dispelled the vision. Emily's laughter—which had a husky quality, like her voice. The sound was incredibly familiar, considering that he hadn't heard it in years. Rye walked slower, hearing chopping noises and the murmur of conversation as he neared the building.

"Lindsey?" he called, wanting to give them advance warning. One or the other had an axe in her hands and didn't need to be startled.

"Dad?" Lindsey called after a second.

Then there was total silence. Rye rounded the corner and took in the scene. Emily had been the one wielding the axe. She stood frozen, a stunned look on her face. Lindsey, down on her haunches, had been tending the firebox of the wood kiln under a nearby shed. Her eyes were for her mother.

So were his.

Emily wore old jeans and a kelly green sweatshirt, both stained. She hadn't bothered with any makeup. She might not have combed her hair. It was impossible to tell, since she'd had her red-gold tresses permed into one of those kinked, frizzed styles that he didn't particularly like. In short, she looked a mess.

Rye was attracted to women who dressed smartly and were well-groomed. Yet his gut male reaction to Emily's appearance was a jolt of approval.

It didn't make sense that he would find her appealing and sexy. It never had made sense.

"Hello, Emily." He greeted her politely. "Excuse me for barging in like this uninvited."

She let the axe drop to the ground and stood very erect, her shoulders squared. The dignified posture lifted her breasts and thrust them forward. It wasn't likely that she was wearing a bra under the sweatshirt, Rye knew and he detected no need for support. Her breasts were still ripe and high.

"Hello, Rye. This is quite a surprise." Emily's response was guarded. He noticed that her eyes were vividly blue against the ivory pallor of her complexion.

"I came to see Lindsey and bring her some travel brochures." Rye managed to force his gaze away from his ex-wife, over to his daughter, who rose to her feet. Her expression was anxious, but oddly interested. "Hi, honey," he said warmly.

"Hi, Dad," she answered warily. "Mom, do you want to take over here while I go get the brochures from Dad?"

"I left them on the back porch of the house, just inside the door," Rye said, addressing the words to both of them.

Lindsey replied, "Oh. Okay. I'll get them later, then."

"While I'm here, I'd like a few words with your mother about you." It was a spur-of-the-moment idea.

"Whatever you want to say to Mom, you can say in front of me, Dad," Lindsey stated.

Rye ignored his daughter, letting his ex-wife speak for herself.

"This is hardly the time or place for a discussion, Rye," she rebuked him. "You knew that I was firing today. Lindsey mentioned that she'd told you. There's two months of work at stake."

"I apologize for the inconvenience," he said, standing his ground. "But Lindsey's future is of urgent interest to both of us."

Spots of angry color bloomed in Emily's cheeks, and her blue eyes went wide with indignation. Even her hair color seemed to intensify and become more vibrant as she demanded, "Since when have you ever deemed it necessary to discuss Lindsey's future with me? When have you ever consulted me about what schools she should attend or about any matter concerning her development and health and happiness? You haven't come here to 'discuss,' Rye, but to dictate and intimidate. At least do me the courtesy of being honest."

"You never made any effort to consult with me." Rye made the best defense that he could in the face of the truth. "If you questioned my judgment as a father, you were free to criticize and object."

"Believe me, I would have if you'd ever given me reason," she assured him bitterly. "But you've been a model father. You haven't left me any room for thinking that I was wrong to let you have custody of our child." She cast an appalled glance over at Lindsey, as though suddenly aware that she was there, looking on and listening.

"It's okay for me to hear how you feel, Mom. Don't hold back on my account," Lindsey urged with a gentle note. "The same goes for you, Dad," she told Rye, dropping down to her haunches again. "I'm old enough that you two don't have to put up a civilized front anymore."

"Your mother and I agreed when we divorced that we wouldn't belittle one another and be at cross-purposes as parents."

"I gathered as much. Neither one of you ever said bad things about the other. Although I could always tell that you both were biting your tongues and had things you'd have liked to say," Lindsey added candidly. "Not to sound unappreciative, but I almost would have rather you hadn't kept your comments to yourselves. It would have been a kind of relief if there'd been an occasional row over me. Maybe I messed up," she mused to herself, seeming lost in thought as she fed small pieces of wood into the firebox of the kiln.

Emily reached down and picked up her axe to resume her interrupted task, too. Rye considered leaving, for a third time since he'd arrived. Instead he walked over closer and resumed his conversation with Emily.

"I was true to my word and fair with you," he said. "You had Lindsey two weekends out of the month. Plus she spent an additional Saturday or Sunday with you and a total of six weeks during the summer. We alternated big holidays and her birthday."

"Yes, you did keep your word, right to the letter," Emily concurred. "I never had any doubt that you would. It would have meant that you were less than perfect if you had gone back on it. I'm sure you had serious qualms about trusting Lindsey in my care."

She chopped viciously into a slice of junk wood, sinking the axe, pulled it free and chopped again, splintering off a portion.

"Yes, I did have qualms," he admitted, managing not to point out that her job would be easier with a sharpened axe. "You haven't lived in the best neighborhoods, for one thing."

She lifted the axe and brought it down hard again as she declared, "The neighborhoods I've lived in have all been *respectable.*" The axe lifted and descended with the rest of her reply. "Just because people have modest *means*—that doesn't make them criminals. It was good for Lindsey to have *contact*—with the ordinary working class. I take some credit for the fact that she isn't a *snob.*"

To his relief, she stood, taking a breather.

"It wasn't her contact with the ordinary working class that concerned me. Most artists don't exactly fit into that category."

"No, we don't. We have a sense of values that doesn't put primary emphasis on money and status symbols, like owning big houses in the right neighborhoods and driving expensive cars. Otherwise more of us would compromise our artistic beliefs and commercialize our art. Or deny our talent in favor of doing something more lucrative, as you did." She recommenced her chopping.

"I didn't deny my talent. I accepted the necessity of supporting my wife and child and discovered in the process that I had other talents, too. Talents just as vital to our society as producing art."

Putting the axe aside, she stooped down to gather up the scattered kindling. "I disagree. But as long as you have no regrets, that's the important thing."

Rye picked up the axe to examine the edge. "Of course I have regrets, but none about being a businessman. With hindsight I can see that I wouldn't have been happy or successful if I'd stuck with my ambition to pursue art as a career."

Emily dropped her bundle and stood up, small bits of wood clinging to her sweatshirt. "Words like *ambition* just don't apply to choosing a career in art!" she objected passionately. "Nor do the conventional measures of success. Art is all about self-expression and translating ideas and emotions into tangible forms and images."

"I know all the vocabulary and idealistic phraseology, Emily," he reminded her. "I was an art major and have a degree in art."

"You were an honor student and graduated cum laude. How can you honestly say that you wouldn't have been a successful artist when you impressed the whole faculty? Then you just threw all that innate ability away."

"I was a good all-around student because I was highly motivated to make something of myself. Some of that ability was the result of self-discipline and plain old hard work."

"You were gifted," she insisted. "There were other art majors with as much dedication who plugged away and just didn't have your talent."

"Gosh, Mom. You make it sound like Dad could have been a modern Michelangelo," Lindsey put in from the sidelines.

Rye had all but forgotten that she was there. So had Emily, he saw. Her startled glance at Lindsey told him that she had been just as involved in their exchange and shared his own ambivalence about the interruption. It was both welcome and unwelcome.

"Go on with your conversation," Lindsey urged. "I'm finding it very enlightening. Was that a real bone of contention between you two, that Dad went into management and became a business entrepreneur instead of an artist? I was under the impression that you couldn't make a go of it because your personalities were too different and you just weren't meant to be married to each other.''

"I didn't exactly 'go into management,'" Rye said. "I took the best job that I could get as the assistant manager of a frame shop."

"We could have gotten by on a smaller salary, but your father insisted on taking a demanding job that didn't leave him with any spare time or creative energy for his art. He had to be a martyr."

"I wasn't a martyr, damn it! I was a man with a family and wanted a decent standard of living for myself, my wife and child."

Emily continued to address Lindsey. "Rye wouldn't hear of letting me get a job. I would willingly have dropped out of college or continued as a part-time student. He refused to consider any options that wouldn't have required him to change the whole direction of his life."

"And you refused to give me any moral support or take a single step with me on the chance that it might not be a bad direction."

"I couldn't do anything to please you, no matter how hard I tried. And goodness knows I did try. Our apartment was never clean and tidy enough to suit you. The meals I fixed weren't well balanced. I couldn't even iron your shirts right. You ironed them yourself."

"Dad ironed his own shirts?" Lindsey marveled, sounding delighted and intrigued.

"It was either that or wear scorched shirts," Rye said, realizing guiltily that he'd temporarily forgotten all about his main objective for being there, safeguarding Lindsey's future.

"I had never ironed," Emily defended herself. "My great-aunt didn't even own an iron. She gave hers away when permanent-press clothes first came on the market."

"Your great-aunt sounds like such a character. I wish I'd gotten to know her," Lindsey mused regretfully.

"I wish you had, too. She was a dear." Emily held out her hand for the axe, signaling an end to the reminiscences.

Rye tested the cutting edge again before giving the axe to her. "It seems a little dull," he observed.

"It's very dull," she agreed. "I bought it secondhand and haven't had it sharpened."

He hesitated. "But wouldn't a sharp axe be better for splitting wood?"

"Yes, but a sharp axe is also dangerous. I'd rather put out more effort and be on the safe side. It's the same principle as using a dull knife."

He drew in a deep breath before he trusted himself to reply. "I can see the similar logic."

"You'd better stand back," she warned.

Rye took her advice and backed off several steps as she set to work, sending chips flying.

"If you have nothing better to do, why don't you stick around a while, Dad, and help?" Lindsey suggested in a kind tone.

Emily chopped more vigorously, not seconding the invitation.

"No, I'm going," Rye announced. "I can see that this is not a good time to discuss your plans." His only reason for staying, he purposely implied. "Either I'll come back, or else you and your mother can drive in to Baton Rouge one day next week. Meanwhile we'll talk on the phone."

"Okay, Dad," she said. "Have a nice weekend. Do something fun."

Emily said nothing.

Rye had no choice but to leave.

Chapter Three

"Mom, why don't you take a rest? Dad has had time to get ten miles down the road."

Lindsey's voice penetrated, and Emily was suddenly drained of strength. The axe was embedded in a piece of wood. Too weak to pull it free, she unclenched her grip on the handle and stood, sucking air into her lungs. Her heart pounded with the exertion. She felt the same kind of shakiness that she'd experienced once when she narrowly escaped an automobile accident.

It disturbed her that she was this unsettled over having Rye suddenly show up. She did see him occasionally. She'd seen him last June at Lindsey's graduation. In a suit, he'd looked distinguished, as well as virile and handsome. But today he was wearing jeans. When he'd walked up close to her, his masculinity had been a clean, irresistible force.

"I don't have to tell you that that was quite an *unpleasant* shock," she said, the emphasis for her own benefit.

"Your father was the last person I would have expected to make a drop-in visit. The next time you predict what he's likely to do, I'll pay more attention."

"He took me by surprise today, too," Lindsey admitted. "I was expecting him to come out here as a kind of last resort. I think he would have stayed and helped us if you'd given him the least bit of encouragement."

"Lindsey, I don't *want* your father's help, in any shape or form." Emily began gathering up an armload of the split wood. "Maybe it's potter's superstition, but the human vibes affect how a wood firing goes."

"If Dad had stayed, the fire would definitely have burned hot," Emily's daughter mused. "I could feel the electricity between you two. It almost gave me goose bumps."

"That wasn't electricity. It was tension and repressed hostility."

"Today for the first time, I could actually believe my parents had once been a married couple." The comment was wistful, as well as reflective. "I had this flash of insight. Remember how I tried to be a matchmaker after Dad and Claire divorced? If I hadn't been so dumb, I would have become a problem child. Then you and Dad would have been forced to have some contact with each other."

"You still would have ended up disappointed. Your father and I weren't happily married. There was never any chance of a reconciliation."

"It would have been nice if you'd been friendly toward each other, if nothing else. It would be nice now," she added, sounding wistful again.

Emily had her arms full of small pieces of firewood. She carried the load to the shed and deposited it on the stack, then knelt down next to her daughter and put her arm around her shoulders.

"Yes, it would be nice for you if your parents liked each other," she agreed gently. "But the truth is, darling, that they don't. Very few divorced people can ever be friends. The whole process of breaking up destroys what brought them together in the first place."

"Dad and Claire don't seem to have any hard feelings. I've been with him when we would run into her. He was never in love with her, though. Maybe that's the difference."

"That's just your interpretation," Emily demurred, interested in spite of herself.

"No, I asked Dad and he told me as much. He said he'd admired Claire and believed when he married her that a deeper affection would develop. But the relationship ended up not being satisfactory for either of them." Lindsey smiled. "Naturally Dad turned the conversation into one of his object lessons, telling me to learn by his mistakes and not take a husband unless my heart *and* my head told me that I'd found a man who was right for me."

"It's wise advice." Apparently Rye hadn't gotten the dual messages from his heart and his head since his and Claire's divorce. He had been single now for at least ten years.

"Have you followed that advice yourself, Mom?" Lindsey asked. "Is that why you haven't ever remarried?"

"Marriage is not for everyone. To find a man who's right, you have to want a husband, I guess."

"And you haven't wanted one after Dad?"

"No," Emily answered truthfully. "Nor have I felt a strong-enough urge to try again at being a wife."

"Being married to Dad was such a bad experience that you swore off marriage," Lindsey summed up, her face mirroring regret.

"In fairness to him, he tried very hard. He just had very definite concepts of 'husband' and 'wife,' 'father' and 'mother.' I couldn't fit myself into his mold."

"You're too much of an individual."

"I'm me." Emily's gesture conveyed a simple acceptance. "To be happy, I have to be true to my own nature, just like your father has to be true to his. We were too different to be compatible."

Lindsey had been steadily feeding pieces of wood into the firebox through an opening the size of several bricks. There was a brief, absorbed silence while she seemed to be mulling over Emily's words.

"But you and I get along well together, despite the fact that I'm so much like Dad," she pointed out. "When I get on your case, you take it good-naturedly."

"I know that you love me and mean well."

"Dad loved you, and you loved him. The fact that he got you pregnant and had to marry you didn't change the way you two felt about each other, did it?"

Emily sighed. "It gets very complicated, darling."

"Is there more to the whole story than you've told me?"

"Yes. But I guess you're old enough to hear it now. Your dad can't be blamed for getting me pregnant. He was very careful to take precautions. After we had become lovers, I went on the Pill, at my suggestion. Once he'd agreed to let me take responsibility for birth control, he worried and would remind me. Occasionally I would still slip up and forget, but I wouldn't mention it to him."

"You were afraid that he'd be mad at you."

"Exactly. Plus I didn't have sense enough to worry. Science was never a favorite subject, and I figured the pills probably had residual effect. Then I missed a period and had to confess."

"Dad must have been furious."

"He was, but more so at himself, for relying on me. I felt terrible on his account, not on mine. For me it wasn't a tragic situation. In fact, deep down I was thrilled. He only got more upset when I tried to convince him that our lives didn't have to change drastically because there was a baby to consider. We had talked about our backgrounds. I knew that he had been raised in foster homes and hadn't had a secure, happy childhood. It came out that he looked upon bringing a child into the world as an act that carried the heaviest possible obligations. He was conscience bound to provide for his daughter or son all that he hadn't been given, regardless of the personal cost or sacrifices."

"Poor Mom!" Lindsey cried softly. "What a guilt trip for you. I never fully understood before why you let Dad have custody of me without fighting him. It was your fault that he was a father."

The explanation wasn't that simple, but Emily had revealed enough. Rye had used every method of intimidation to get custody of their daughter, including undermining Emily's confidence in her mothering ability.

"I would have fought him," she said, "if he hadn't been such a loving, devoted father."

Lindsey leaned over and kissed her mother on the cheek. "You've been a good mother, too, Mom. Sometimes I wonder if you give yourself all the credit you deserve."

Emily had to blink hard at a glaze of tears. "Thank you, darling. What a sweet thing to say. You've been a joy to me."

The emotional moment passed as they let the discussion drop, by unspoken consent, and went on to talk of other matters. But the closeness didn't dissipate.

Throughout the day and on into the night, Emily was conscious of being happy as she and Lindsey worked as a team, raising the kiln to temperature. It occurred to her that

Rye had done his part, however unintentionally, in making this firing a very special event.

He had provoked the confidence between mother and daughter, caused Emily to unlock memory and ease the old pain in her heart.

Maybe she and Rye could finally let bygones be bygones for Lindsey's sake, she found herself thinking.

It was after two o'clock Sunday morning when she finally fell into bed, bone tired but with a feeling of deep satisfaction. The firing had been a good one. She just *knew* it. After the kiln had cooled for at least twenty-four hours, there would be the drama and excitement of unbricking the doors and unloading the finished wares, one by one. The only thing that could compare was being a child on Christmas morning and waking to see what Santa had brought.

The knowledge that Lindsey would be there, sharing the gifts of the kiln, heightened Emily's usual anticipation. She dropped off to sleep, smiling.

On the table next to her bed was an electric alarm clock that served little purpose other than emitting a restful hum. It was rarely set to the correct time, because of frequent power outages, and Emily detested waking up to an alarm. Normally she slept until she had had enough sleep and was rested.

Also on the table was a phone that she kept disconnected, since she also disliked being jolted out of a peaceful slumber by the ringing of a telephone, especially when the callers were pranksters or drunks who'd gotten the wrong number.

When the phone came shrilly to life, she had no perception of the time and was confused about the source of the irritating, insistent sound. Without opening her eyes, she groped for the alarm clock, then, realizing that it wasn't the culprit, fumbled for the phone and dislodged the receiver.

With the horrid noise stopped, she burrowed her head into her pillow again.

Lindsey must have used the phone and left it connected, she reasoned sleepily. With that mystery solved, she gave her first thought to the unknown person responsible for disturbing her sleep.

Reaching over, with her eyes still closed, she picked up the receiver with lax fingers. A faint male voice was saying repeatedly, "Hello."

Emily brought the receiver to her cheek. "Hello," she mumbled, the greeting partially muffled by her pillow.

"Did I wake you? I thought it was late enough to call."

"Rye." She breathed out his name on a sigh as her fuzzy brain supplied his identity.

"Shall I call back later, in the afternoon?" he inquired brusquely after a pause.

Emily turned over on her back and opened her eyes. It was fully daylight. "What time is it?" she asked. Her vocal cords weren't warmed up, and her voice came out a husky whisper.

"A quarter to twelve."

"That late?"

"You don't have a clock by your bed?"

"I do, but it's electric." She yawned, stretching.

"Does it have a bad cord?" he asked after a moment.

Finding the question odd, Emily took her own moment to answer. "The clock works fine. But the electricity goes off, and it loses time."

"Oh. I thought maybe it had faulty wiring, like your coffee maker."

"No, its wiring is okay. When the phone rang just now, I thought the alarm was going off on its own. I keep the phone unplugged," she explained, pushing up into a lounging position. "Last night when I went to bed—or actually this morning—I didn't notice that Lindsey had left the cord connected." Emily glanced over and added indulgently, "I see that she set the clock, too. She always does. She's so much like you."

"Just out of curiosity, why do you have the clock by your bed if you can't depend on it to tell you the correct time? Why not get a wind-up clock or one operated by batteries?"

"A tick-tock clock would drive me crazy, and I didn't realize that they made clocks that worked with batteries." It was only the partial truth. When he didn't say anything, she confessed sheepishly, "I've had this clock for umpteen years. It's like an old friend, and it makes a little humming noise that I've gotten used to. I can hear Lindsey stirring around in the kitchen. Hold on and I'll go and tell her you're on the line." Emily was embarrassed by her own note of reluctance.

"No, wait—"

There was a low, urgent note to the command. Emily's heartbeat speeded up and all her drowsiness vanished.

"I wanted to talk to you, anyway," he said, his tone more matter-of-fact. "First I'd like to apologize for barging in uninvited yesterday at a bad time."

"There was no harm done," she assured him, striving to sound casual. "You probably called and didn't get an answer. I can empathize with your position, Rye. You're very concerned about Lindsey's getting safely through this phase that she's entered."

"I didn't try to call before I came out there," he stated. "To be honest, I wanted to see where you lived. The place hasn't been as well maintained as it might have been, but judging from the outside, it could be a nice home with a little money invested."

Emily really didn't know how to respond. "It's a plain, old-fashioned house, but I like it," she said. "Also the rent is low. The owner is a doctor and lives in California. This was his parents' farm, and he doesn't want to sell, for sentimental reasons, which is another plus. I don't have to worry about being evicted."

"Does he hire someone local to do necessary repairs?"

"No, our arrangement is that I'm responsible for having small repairs made myself. If a tree fell on the house or something of that nature, I'd notify him, but a broken toilet, for example, is my problem."

"What about carpentry jobs like rebuilding your screen door on your back porch? And having the outside of the house painted?"

"He's willing to go halves on cosmetic improvements and deduct my portion from the rent. The only thing he insists on is keeping the character of the house the same."

"That's a good deal for you," Rye remarked, sounding thoroughly pleased on her behalf. "You'd just need a long-term lease for protection."

"I trust him to keep his word, but when the time comes, I'll mention a lease," Emily said agreeably. "At the present, I don't have a lot of extra cash, so I'll have to put off improvements. You'll probably think it's un-American, but I make it a policy not to go into debt."

"You would need collateral to get a loan from a bank. Since the house isn't your property, you couldn't take out a mortgage on it. You'd have to have a cosigner."

"There's no one I would ask..." Suddenly it dawned on Emily what he might be leading up to. "Rye, if you're about to offer to help me get a loan, please save your breath. Number one, I don't want to borrow any money, and number two, I'd be very leery of accepting any favors from you."

"I wasn't thinking about helping you get a loan, Emily. I can make you a personal loan."

"That's very generous of you," she said. "But no, thanks. My house could be falling down on my head, and I'd manage some other method of financing."

He'd tried to offer her financial aid in the past, but always through his attorney, never directly. Somehow this was even more insulting.

"I was your husband and never paid you a nickel of alimony. I feel a sense of obligation."

"Well, don't. I didn't want any alimony. I was fully capable of supporting myself. I still am," she asserted proudly.

A muffled curse came over the line. "Aren't you being selfish as well as vindictive?" he demanded.

The question took her off guard. She sputtered indignantly, "Selfish? Vindictive? Because I won't let you salve your conscience by playing the generous ex-husband?"

"Yes, selfish. How do you think it makes Lindsey feel for her mother to be living in a house with peeling paint and torn screen? To be driving a dilapidated old van with worn-out tires while she's driving a new car? If you don't care about your own quality of life, give some consideration to her."

"My quality of life is not suffering because I don't have a lot of surplus money to spend!" Emily blazed hotly, tears of anger coming to her eyes. "For you to suggest that my own daughter pities me is playing dirty pool, Rye! I'm not listening to any more of this!" She slammed down the receiver.

Sitting on the edge of the bed, she jerked the cord free from the phone. Rage seemed a better alternative than breaking down and crying.

"Mom?" Lindsey tapped on Emily's bedroom door. "I brought you some coffee, unless you want to go back to sleep."

"No, I'm getting up. Come on in, darling," Emily invited, trying to compose herself.

Lindsey entered, bearing two steaming mugs, and sat down on the edge of the bed. "Was that Dad on the phone?" she asked.

Emily took a sip of hot coffee. "Hmm. That tastes good," she said gratefully before replying, "Yes, it was your father." *Not a pleasant way to start off a Sunday morning,* she started to add and then didn't, because the statement wouldn't be entirely truthful.

In actuality she hadn't found talking to Rye on the phone at all unpleasant those first few minutes while she was half-asleep. Quite the opposite. The realization was very disturbing.

"I started to come and tell you that I was up, in case it was him, but then I figured that you could hear me in the kitchen." Lindsey's voice held curiosity, as well as apology. "You had quite a long conversation with him," she noted. "I assume that I was the topic."

"You entered in," Emily said.

"I really don't get it," Lindsey mused. "Most of the time I can read Dad like a book, but he isn't using the strategy I expected. Instead of reasoning with me, he's obviously decided to work on you. What was his tactic, Mom? That you should be an unselfish mother and put my interest first by going along with his best judgment?"

Emily bought time, sipping her coffee. "I'm not quite sure what his tactic was," she admitted. "Unless he has in mind getting on your good side by taking me on as a charity project."

"Did Dad offer to buy you a new stove?" Lindsey asked ruefully.

"No, he didn't get around to suggesting that I should replace all my appliances at his expense," Emily retorted.

Lindsey raised her eyebrows, silently encouraging her mother to explain. Her expression grew more and more intrigued as Emily gave a recap of her phone conversation with Rye, trying to be as objective as she could.

Emily's injured pride got the best of her as she ended up, "I certainly hope you don't get depressed because your poor down-and-out mother lives in a hovel and drives a rattletrap ready for the junkyard!"

"Of course I don't get depressed," Lindsey chided. "Just the opposite. You always give me a lift." She sipped her coffee thoughtfully and suggested, "If Dad does feel a sense of obligation, like he said, you'd think his conscience would have bothered him before now."

"This isn't the first time that he's offered to raise my standard of living," Emily's innate honesty and fairness compelled her to say. "Every few years Rye's lawyer has contacted me. Once, I started getting monthly checks in the mail."

"What did you do with them?"

"I sent them back, of course."

"When was this exactly?" Lindsey asked.

"Let's see." Emily thought. "It must have been about seven years ago. My finances were a little tight at the time. I'd had some doctor bills, and my electric kiln had bit the dust." She grimaced, remembering. "It took some moral fortitude not to cash those checks."

"Poor Dad! How frustrating for him!"

"He wasn't 'poor dad' by then," Emily pointed out, totally without sympathy. "He could well afford to spare the money. That was what made it twice as hard to hold on to my self-respect."

"Were you afraid that there would be strings attached?" Lindsey asked. "That if you accepted money from Dad, he would infringe on your freedom?"

"No."

"If he had been anyone else, a distant wealthy relative, a patron of the arts, would you have been too proud to let him help you through a rough period until you were on your feet again?"

"No," Emily had to admit again. "Actually I did have to turn to friends and ask them to cosign for a loan to tide me over. Then, out of the blue I got a nice commission to do a large tile mosaic installation for a new office building."

"Yes, I remember. I wonder..." Lindsey's voice drifted off.

"You wonder what?"

"Oh, nothing. You've gotten some other good commissions, haven't you?"

"Yes. I've been very fortunate."

Lindsey reached over and patted her mother's arm. "You're a talented artist, Mom. If it weren't against your principles to make a lot of money, you could have a fat bank account. Every time you've started developing a reputation in one area of ceramics, you'd change to another one."

"I would also start getting stale. But thanks for the compliment, darling. Now, why don't we go out to the kitchen and have some breakfast?"

"Sounds good."

Emily had recovered from her phone conversation with Rye and was feeling cheerful. Now that she'd calmed down, losing her temper and hanging up on him seemed the best thing that could have happened.

Yesterday she had entertained the idea of being friends with Rye. But it wasn't possible. She didn't want Rye in her life. She didn't want his help or his interference.

In the event that he had been toying with the idea of being friends with her, he would now also abandon the whole notion. Emily hoped that he'd been thoroughly irritated by her response to his interest in her personal affairs, irritated enough to swear off making her any more generous offers for at least another ten or fifteen years.

By then Lindsey would be married and a mother. Rye and Emily would be grandparents. They would bury the hatchet in order that they could both enjoy holidays with their daughter and her family.

History would repeat itself, after a fashion. Emily sighed philosophically, breaking eggs into a bowl and thinking, as she whisked vigorously, of how Rye would play the wealthy, indulgent grandfather, arriving with expensive, lavish gifts that would overshadow her presents that she'd made or purchased for their whimsical value.

"Mom, are you making scrambled eggs—or a soufflé?" Lindsey asked, bringing her mother back to the present.

But Emily's thoughts kept drifting to her future fantasy during the breakfast preparations. Rye would make a handsome, distinguished patriarch. She could imagine him with touches of white at his temples and an air of dignity.

Her mental image stirred a wifely pride that was perfectly absurd. To banish it, Emily conjured a gracious, chic woman whom he'd married in the meanwhile, the third Mrs. Rye Keeler. The sudden flare of jealousy she felt was just as unsettling as the earlier possessiveness.

"You're a thousand miles away," Lindsey accused in an interested tone of voice. "One moment you're smiling, and the next you're frowning."

"I was time traveling," Emily admitted sheepishly, relieved at the interruption. While they ate, she gave her daughter an entertaining account of her visionary trip.

After the meal, they lingered over coffee, then cleared the table and put the dishes in the sink to soak. The big, old-fashioned kitchen wasn't equipped with a dishwasher.

By now the kiln was drawing Emily outside, even though it wouldn't have cooled enough for her to risk unplugging a peephole. Thermal shock was too much of a danger to the cooling wares. Still, she felt the urge to go back and see that all the bricks were in place.

Lindsey's immediate plans for the day were to read through the brochures that her father had brought and then give him a call if he hadn't called first.

"I'll be out in the studio puttering," Emily said, leaving her daughter the full privacy of the house. It surprised her and hurt her feelings slightly that Lindsey hadn't so much as mentioned wanting her mother to read the brochures. Evidently she didn't require any input from Emily.

Father and daughter would hash over travel options and decide on an itinerary. Emily wasn't counting on her daughter's accompanying her to Florida. Rye would win out.

As soon as her mother was gone, Lindsey went into action. Humming lightheartedly, she washed the breakfast dishes, wiped the stove and the kitchen table. Then she got the folder of travel information from her room and gave the contents a cursory reading, occasionally looking more closely at a picture.

Her father was offering her a truly marvelous opportunity to visit far-off places that she would love to see someday. But even if this were a once-in-a-lifetime chance, she wouldn't take it. Before yesterday, she might have, but thanks to him, not now.

Lindsey smiled to think of how her shrewd and decisive dad had unknowingly defeated his very purpose by rashly confronting her mother, who didn't realize, either, that she was going to have the upper hand. Nothing might come of the next few months, but Lindsey was about to shake the status quo.

Her parents might arrive at a new stalemate, but there would be some interaction first. Judging from yesterday's scene and her mother's state this morning, following the phone conversation with Lindsey's father, the sparks would fly.

Almost as if on cue, the wall phone in the kitchen rang just as Lindsey was closing the folder and pushing back her chair. She could tell at the sound of her father's voice that he had been stewing and fuming for the past hour and an half.

Sorry, Dad. You're going to have a bad day, she commiserated silently before unloading on him.

"I was just about to call you and tell you that I've looked at the travel brochures, like I promised. All the trips look interesting, but I'd still rather go to Florida with Mom. Dad, let me finish, please," she requested when he tried to interrupt.

"Go on," he said grimly.

"This semester off from school isn't a vacation or time for goofing off. Don't think that I'm looking upon it as that. I'm just at a stage in my life when I'm very confused and need to learn who I am and what's important for *my* happiness, not what's important for yours or someone else's. It will do me good to take the silver spoon out of my mouth and rough it for a change, see what it's like to be a woman relying completely on herself, like Mom.''

Lindsey felt a stab of compunction as she went on, sensing that her father was exerting all his self-control to keep from exploding. Thus far she'd outlined some of her actual motives, the selfish ones. Now she deliberately and gently baited him.

''I need to experience the struggle for day-to-day existence and the hardships that an artist faces if I'm going to even consider choosing art as a career. And that is an option. Neither you nor Mom has ever encouraged me in that direction, but my whole problem may be that I'm trying to deny my creative genes that I inherited from both of you. By traveling to the winter art shows with Mom and meeting lots of artists, I should have some basis for deciding whether I want to switch my major to art. Also I'll get exposure to different media.''

''You would get exposure all right.'' Her father gritted out the words between his teeth, his steely tone communicating, *Over my dead body*. ''This is all nonsense that you're talking, Lindsey. You took art courses in high school. Other than a flair for drawing, you showed no particular artistic talent. Your favorite courses were science and math. You put considerably more effort into your science projects than you did into art assignments.''

''I didn't like the art teacher. Besides, there's a great deal of technology involved in art.''

''If you want to change your major to art, then do. You're free to switch fields of study until you find one that truly suits you. You can transfer to another university. I was in favor of your choosing an out-of-state school rather than staying in Baton Rouge and attending LSU,'' he reminded.

"I'm all for your exploring career options. But you aren't cut out to be an artist."

"Maybe not, but I would have to find that out for myself, Dad."

"Then go to Paris and Rome. I'll look into art-study travel programs for you."

"Please *don't.* You'll only be wasting your time. I'm going to Florida with Mom."

His frustrated opposition seemed to come at her over the line in strong, battering waves. If nothing else, Lindsey could appreciate what her mother had been up against years earlier when she'd relinquished custody.

"Lindsey, I will *not* consent, and that's final."

"Dad, I'll understand if you cut off my allowance."

"Who said anything about that?" he demanded. "When have I ever resorted to bribery or threats of any kind in my dealings with you as a father? When has providing for you ever been conditional?"

Lindsey had to harden herself against the hurt note in his voice. "Never," she said quickly. "I'm sorry if I seemed to imply that you might try to bribe or threaten me now. I promise that I'll call often and check in with you while Mom and I are on the road, Dad. Before we leave, I'll give you an itinerary. Maybe you could even take a few days off and come over to Florida for one of the shows."

"Let me talk to your mother," he instructed brusquely.

"Mom is outside."

"I'll hold while you go and get her. She can decide on whether she'd prefer for me to come out there or for the two of you to drive into the city. Before this goes any further, the three of us are going to sit down and lay our cards on the table."

"She isn't feeling too kindly toward you after talking to you on the phone earlier," Lindsey warned ruefully. "Why

don't you and I just go ahead and set something up? Mom
will go along. Tonight would be too soon. By tomorrow she
should be cooled down. We'll be unloading the kiln in the
afternoon, and that should put her in a good mood. How
about coming for dinner tomorrow night?''

"I'll pass on dinner, since what I have in mind isn't a social get-together.''

The stern refusal didn't come as quickly as it might have.
Lindsey urged lightly, ''It would be your chance to eat a
meal I'd cooked.''

"What time?'' he asked gruffly.

"Oh, about seven. You might like to drive out earlier
while it's still daylight. We could use an extra pair of hands,
I'm sure, unloading the kiln. It's really a neat experience,
and Mom will probably be too excited to be hostile. Well,
goodbye, Dad. See you tomorrow.''

Lindsey signed off cheerfully, leaving it up to him what
time he arrived at the farmhouse. Hanging up the phone,
she grinned at her own thought: *Maybe I should think
about becoming an actress or a double agent.*

Chapter Four

Rye wasn't worried about losing his way, but it would be easier finding the farmhouse in the daylight. And he admitted to a certain interest in seeing Emily's wood-fired pottery.

In his high-school art classes, he had been introduced to working with clay himself and taken a couple of ceramics courses as a college art major. Clay hadn't been his medium, but he appreciated the potter's art, which ranged from functional pottery to sculptural and avant-garde forms to architectural installations.

Among his own personal art collection, Rye had some fine examples of clay art. He also had a whole assortment of hand-thrown mugs that he used, among them one that Emily had made for him and given him as a present when they were both students.

After their divorce, he'd tried to bring himself to throw it away, then had stuck it out of sight instead, taken it out years later and started to use it again. It was his only piece of her work, although Lindsey had numerous pieces that she displayed in other rooms of the house as well as in her bedroom. Rye had never objected, once Claire's feelings were no longer a consideration.

He had to admire Emily's versatility, if not her instinct for supporting herself. She had gone from one technique to another, from wheel-thrown to hand-built vessels to those that combined the two techniques. She had experimented with size and scale, running the gamut from miniature to mammoth.

If she had ever operated by any rule of thumb, it was to challenge the fashion of the day. When earth pottery had been all the thing, Emily had glazed with brilliant color. Now that color was popular, she was doing wood-firing, the method for producing plain, rugged pottery in the Japanese tradition.

Rye had little doubt that her current output was good, but he did doubt seriously that it was commercial. And she insisted on a nonelitist marketing approach, if "marketing approach" were even a part of her vocabulary. Rather than selling through galleries, where her wholesale price would be doubled, she preferred to do art-and-craft shows and sell directly to buyers.

With a good agent/business-manager, Emily could have been successful. Even without one, she had had her chances to build a reputation as a ceramist and support herself well on good commissions from corporations. Unbeknownst to her, Rye had used his connections on a number of occasions to open doors.

But Emily being Emily, she had walked through and right back out again. Each time, Rye had sworn that this time he washed his hands of her.

Except for his daughter, he might have been blessed with ignorance of Emily's career and her life. Instead he'd kept abreast. He knew more than enough to give him nightmares at the thought of Lindsey casting lots with her mother for the next six months, taking to the road with a wing and a prayer.

It was a miracle that Emily hadn't been mugged or murdered before now. Rye wasn't taking the chance that her luck was about to run out. He wasn't going to sit on the sidelines, developing ulcers, while Emily endangered his daughter and filled her head with the idealistic credo by which Emily herself had lived.

In this determined frame of mind, Rye turned into Emily's driveway past her decorated mailbox at four o'clock, with another hour of daylight remaining. Before getting out, he lightly tooted his horn.

Lindsey shortly emerged from behind Emily's studio, waved broadly and then walked to meet him. Even from a distance of perhaps a hundred yards, Rye could tell that she was unusually animated.

As father and daughter came nearer, he noted that she wasn't her well-groomed self. Her shoulder-length hair was pulled back into a ponytail, and her cheeks were streaked with soot, as were her designer jeans and pullover sweater.

"Dad! I'm glad you came early!" she called out, and opened out her arms when she was several steps away. The gesture was pure Emily. Lindsey tended to be reserved like him.

"I'll take a rain check on the hug," he said. "Otherwise I'll look like a chimney sweep, too."

"My hands are dirty," she agreed cheerfully, and grimaced as she lowered them and held them out in front of her, coming to a stop. "Don't they look awful? Only three nails have managed to survive, and I guess I may as well trim them off before I break them.''

''They don't even look like your hands,'' Rye observed, frowning. She always kept her nails beautifully manicured. Now there was no polish on them, and she wasn't wearing any rings, her favorite jewelry.

''Feel the calluses on my palms from chopping wood.''

He explored her palms with his fingertips, and his frown deepened. ''You should have used gloves,'' he scolded.

''Mom didn't have any except big mitts. It's just as well. My skin needs to toughen up.''

''Your hands don't need to be tough,'' Rye growled.

She ignored his fatherly consternation and kissed him on the cheek before urging, ''Come on back, Dad. Mom is in seventh heaven so far over the results of our firing.''

Lindsey had never been a chatterbox, but she talked a steady stream as she matched her long-legged stride to his. It was difficult to keep from softening in response to her obvious eagerness to include him.

''Unloading the kiln is a slow process,'' she explained. ''From Mom's reaction, you'd almost think that she was opening up presents. She has to examine every single piece, as though she wouldn't want to hurt anyone's feelings by not giving equal attention.''

Rye had come prepared for this second face-to-face encounter with Emily on her turf. Today he wouldn't allow himself to be distracted from his purpose. He wouldn't engage in a pointless rehashing of the past and get himself all in a turmoil, as he had done on Saturday.

Today he wouldn't let his masculine reactions take him unawares. He knew that the old physical attraction was still there, ready to flare up along with hostile emotions.

Rounding the corner of Emily's studio, he expected her to be standing and waiting to get the greeting over with.

She'd be composed and dignified, he thought, as on her guard as he was.

If Rye had learned anything at all about Emily, it was that she could be depended upon not to act as most normal people would. He felt a spurt of annoyance at himself, as well as at her, as he saw that she wasn't treating his arrival as anything more than a casual event, but was proceeding with unloading the kiln.

She was down on her knees on the ground, her whole upper body hidden from sight, giving him a view of her bottom, snugly encased in her jeans. It wasn't any less shapely than he remembered, a fact that didn't put him in any better temper.

He slowed his steps and didn't follow Lindsey up as close as she went. Still, what was he to do, other than watch Emily back out slowly with little side-to-side motions of her hips? Being a man, he found the sight damned provocative, which only made him that much more annoyed.

Annoyance was his best protection against the memory of how thoroughly familiar his hands had once been with Emily's derriere, covered with various textures of cloth; the rough denim of her jeans, the silky nylon of her panties, the cotton knit of his T-shirts that she'd worn for nightshirts. He well remembered, too, that her bare skin underneath had been soft and smooth and supple.

It only irked Rye that Emily was obviously innocent of any seductive intention. When she finally rose to her feet and turned slowly around, she spared him only an absent glance and said, "Oh, hi, Rye." All her attention was for the large lidded jar that she held reverently.

"Mom, that's *beautiful!*" Lindsey praised.

Emily just gazed, an awed expression on her face. Then a smile broke out. "Isn't it incredible?" she breathed. "I've got goose bumps all over me. Just look at the flashings."

Leaving them to follow behind, she walked very carefully toward the studio, bearing her prize as though it were an excavated treasure. Her back was ramrod straight beneath her sweatshirt, which had pulled up around her waist. Rye had another unobstructed view of her pert bottom.

Rather than fight his natural male instinct, he searched for evidence that she had put on a few pounds and lost some of her muscle tone. Her hips were slightly fuller, but her buttocks were still firm and rounded.

Inside the studio she set the jar on a table that held the other pottery that had been removed from the kiln. Tenderly she wiped it with a damp cloth and stood back, admiring it.

"That really is nice," Rye complimented sincerely, glad to focus on something besides her figure. "The shape is graceful and yet robust. The glaze and flashings of color from the flame complement the form itself perfectly."

"Perfectly," Emily repeated happily, nodding.

Rye glanced over at her. Her red hair stood out on end, forming a riotous halo of kinky waves and curls. She wasn't wearing any makeup, not even lipstick. With sooty smudges on her face and clothes, she looked even more a mess today than she had two days ago, and yet he wanted to feast his eyes on her.

The color of her hair was all the more vivid because her redhead's complexion was delicate and fine, saved from being too pale by a lavish sprinkling of tannish gold freckles. Her eyes were so blue that he felt a little shock tremor when he made eye contact with her. Her mouth was shell pink, sensuously full-lipped and yet sensitive.

"How will you price it?" he asked, tearing his gaze away.

"Expensive enough so that maybe no one will buy it," she answered with a rueful sigh.

"Why don't you keep it, Mom?" Lindsey suggested.

"I could just display it in my booth and put Not For Sale on it," she mused, and then clapped her hands, postponing a decision. "There's still half a kiln to unload, and it'll be dark in another hour. Rye, you can wait for us at the house if you'd prefer. Help yourself to a beer in the refrigerator."

"Heck with that. Dad can help," Lindsey declared.

Rather than look inquiringly at Rye for his own decision in the matter, Emily ran her gaze over him, starting at his neck. Rye's body responded to the inspection.

"He's dressed too nicely. He'll get his clothes all sooty," she said to Lindsey, not him.

"Those aren't good clothes he's wearing," Lindsey argued. "Dad dresses like that for lounging around the house."

Rye had changed from his business attire and wore fawn-colored corduroy slacks, a long-sleeved cotton shirt unbuttoned at the throat and a pullover sweater. He had just reached into the closet and pulled out the individual garments, giving no thought to putting together a coordinated outfit. He had to stop and think which shirt he'd put on.

"They look like clothes that have to be dry-cleaned," Emily pointed out, giving him another throat-to-feet glance.

"Do I get a vote?" Rye asked.

"He can express an opinion, anyway, huh, Mom?" Lindsey answered laughingly.

Emily didn't smile or take her daughter's playful cue. She finally spoke directly to him, much as Rye had expected her to greet him on his arrival, without friendliness or antagonism.

"It really isn't necessary for you to help us. The work isn't heavy, and we can finish it ourselves."

"I wouldn't mind helping, unless you'd rather that I didn't." He kept his voice just as neutral as hers had been.

"Meanwhile it's getting darker by the minute," Lindsey reported cheerfully. "I say let Dad do a little honest labor for a change. We can load up ware-boards, and he can carry them and not even have to get his hands dirty. Come on, crew."

Emily and Rye both watched her as she marched around the studio, collecting the boards that were used as a kind of rude tray for transporting pottery.

"I take it you're the supervisor," mother remarked to daughter.

"Somebody has to do the job."

"It was only a matter of time before she organized this whole operation," Emily said to Rye. "She is so much like you."

"Up to just recently, I've thought so," he replied.

"You had your own lapses into being a fallible human being," she reminded. "After all, you got involved with me."

"Is that supposed to ease my mind about her?" Rye asked.

"We can talk while we work," Lindsey interrupted, breezing by them with an armload of boards.

After a tense, reluctant moment, they followed.

"Shall we leave this discussion until later?" he suggested.

"We can postpone it indefinitely. I can't see that there's anything to be gained from continuing it. Can you?"

"No."

"Lindsey knows our whole unfortunate story and can benefit from our mistakes. We've spared her growing up with divorced parents who fight and haggle in front of her. Why start now?"

"I agree completely."

"Then let's both show a little adult restraint."

"Let's," Rye said shortly.

At the kiln he had to stand by while she crawled in. He averted his gaze, his teeth on edge because he had to exert so much willpower to keep from watching.

Lindsey crouched in readiness for taking the pottery from her mother's hands, but Emily backed all the way out to examine the two Japanese-style tea bowls that she held before handing them over. She could just as easily have placed them on the ware-board herself, Rye observed, but he kept the observation to himself.

For something to do, he dropped to a squatting position for a closer look at the tea bowls. Immediately he realized his mistake. He had placed himself almost at eye level with Emily's posterior as she crawled back into the kiln. Out of sheer stubbornness, he stayed there.

"You have longer arms," he commented to Lindsey, who took the hint.

"Mom, would you like to trade places?" she inquired when Emily had edged out again.

"I think I'd better do this," Emily refused. "It's like a cave in there, and I'm relying a lot on memory and feel."

"Then if no one objects, I'll go on to the house and clean myself up and set the table for supper. I'm not really needed here."

They both looked hard at her, expressing strong silent objection, but she sprang up lightly anyway. "With me out of hearing, you can be really nasty with one another and get it out of your system," she tossed back over her shoulder as she left them, walking with her leggy, coltish grace. In no time at all she had disappeared around the studio, leaving them alone.

"I can finish unloading the kiln tomorrow morning," Emily said, depositing the two pieces she held. "You go to the house with Lindsey, and I'll be along soon."

"No, you won't. You'll finish unloading it now, once you've gotten rid of me."

Her face was a confession. She shrugged. "This isn't exactly a dignified process. I feel at a definite disadvantage, exposing my rear end to you."

"Don't feel at a disadvantage," he said with revealing fervor. Carefully he picked up the board and got to his feet before adding, "You've kept yourself in good shape."

"You haven't exactly gone to pot," she replied.

"I'm about ten pounds heavier."

She nodded and complimented grudgingly, "You look very trim and fit."

"I have to work at getting exercise. I belong to an athletic club."

"Yes, I know. Lindsey has kept me posted on you."

"She's kept me well-informed about you, too. I'll take these inside the studio. Why don't you take advantage of my absence?" he suggested.

"You can just set the board down." She addressed his back after he had gone eight or ten steps.

"I won't leave permanent fingerprints on your pottery if I handle it," he countered.

She didn't answer.

Inside the studio he added the four pieces to the others on the table. Then he killed some time, admiring the assemblage. Pottery invited touching, and he yielded to the temptation to pick up several pieces that particularly drew his eye.

The large jar that she had carried inside was a beauty. Rye lifted it, noting its balanced weight, took off the lid and replaced it. If she were going to sell the jar, he might buy it himself, he reflected, and was struck suddenly by one of those inspired realizations that had served him well in business.

There wouldn't be any reason for Emily to go to the Florida shows if a wholesale buyer came along and purchased her whole inventory of pottery. If Lindsey couldn't be swayed from accompanying her mother, Rye would tackle the problem from the angle of circumventing the whole trip.

He'd be doing Emily a favor by keeping her off the road, whether she'd ever concede the fact or not.

Her studio was well lighted with fluorescent lights. When Rye went back outside, he saw that dusk was rapidly falling. Emily had been busy and had two ware-boards loaded.

She didn't comment on the length of time he'd been gone or make another attempt to get rid of him. Instead she asked whether he would bring her a flashlight when he came back out.

"Where will I find it?" Rye inquired.

"Probably in the storeroom where I keep my glaze chemicals," she replied as though he should logically have guessed. "It should be in plain sight. It's orange."

Rye located the flashlight, mentally shaking his head at the clutter and general untidiness. Not surprisingly, the batteries in the flashlight were weak, and he doubted seriously that she had replacement ones on hand.

With the faint beam switched on, he took the flashlight out to her, refraining from anything more than a noncommittal, "Here you are."

She thanked him absently and began smacking the flashlight hard against her palm, muttering, "These darned batteries are almost dead."

"Bruising your hand isn't going to bring them back to life," Rye pointed out. "If you have spare batteries, I'll get them."

"I don't ever buy new batteries until I need them. They last a short-enough time as it is without having them lose their power in the package."

She was crawling inside the kiln as she delivered that bit of economic and scientific wisdom. Rye opened his mouth to state that good batteries, properly stored, had a long shelf life, but said instead, "I have a flashlight in my car."

"You would," came the muffled, disgusted reply.

They both dispensed with conversation. It was full dark when the kiln was finally emptied. A light misting rain began to fall as they walked together toward the house, their path illuminated inadequately by the flashlight. Emily had already thanked him formally for his help, and just as formally, Rye had assured her that she was welcome.

"That cold front that the weathermen are forecasting must be coming through," she said.

"It's supposed to get down to freezing by morning," Rye replied.

"To be on the safe side, I'd better turn all my faucets on tonight to protect the pipes."

"Your pipes aren't wrapped with insulation above the ground?" The ground seldom froze this far south.

"No, unfortunately. One of these days I'm going to have that done. Before you offer to lend me the money, that wasn't a hint," she added quickly. "Let's get one thing straight here and now, Rye. I'd starve to death before I accepted the price of a loaf of bread from you."

"Are you afraid that there would be some stipulation about what kind of bread you bought and whether you made sandwiches with it or not?" he demanded.

"Without a doubt. I'm sure you wouldn't trust me to pick out my own grocery store."

He bit back a retort, hanging on to his patience. "Just answer me truthfully. Do you honestly think that I have an ulterior motive in offering to help you out financially? Do you suspect that I want to put you under some obligation to me?"

Her silence was more stubborn than reflective.

"No, probably not," she said finally.

He waited for her to elaborate, his exasperation building. "Well?"

"Well, what? I answered both your questions. The fact is that I would *feel* under obligation. My independence happens to mean more to me than letting you act the good Samaritan. There are lots of better charitable causes out there. Donate money to them."

"Have some consideration for Lindsey, for heaven's sake! She worries about you and would like for her mother to have the amenities!"

"What you're really concerned about, Rye, is that you might look bad in her eyes. Now isn't that the whole crux of the matter?"

"No, it isn't!" he denied hotly. "She knows the situation, that I couldn't afford a lot of alimony when we divorced and you refused any support at all. I've never mentioned to her that I've tried to give you supplemental income at various times, although I'd like to have made a public announcement in the newspaper. It's a hell of an embarrassment for me as a man for my ex-wife to live like an indigent."

"Nobody even knows that I'm your ex-wife, unless you tell them!" she blazed back, almost shouting. "I sure don't broadcast the fact that I was married to you! I go by my maiden name!"

"*I* know that you were married to me, if nobody else does!" Rye thundered. He lowered his voice with an effort. "You are, without doubt, the most stubborn, maddening woman I've ever known."

"And you are the most rigid, domineering man that I've had the misfortune to know. You're so utterly convinced that you're right about everything. It must be wonderful not to have any human failings."

They had reached the back door of the house. Lindsey had turned on the porch light. In hostile silence they both reached to open the screen door. Some perverse instinct kept Rye from drawing his hand back, and he closed his fingers over Emily's.

Fighting a battle of wills, they stood there, glaring at each other angrily, neither of them pulling the door open.

"Let go," Emily said, a note of bravado in her husky, sexy voice.

Rye's heart was already beating faster than normal. Now it began to thud in his breast. His fingers tightened on hers, not in a show of force, but because he wanted to let go and take her into his arms.

"No. You let go," he replied in a strained voice.

They stared at each other, engaged in a whole new battle as hot attraction flared up. His desire for her was a sharp, throbbing ache that spread throughout his body, but concentrated in his chest and in his loins.

"You're hurting me," she complained barely above a whisper.

Her voice acted on him like a caress, setting off shivers of sensation. He tensed against the pleasure and muttered between his teeth, "Sorry. Let me open the damned door. I'm the man."

"It's my door. You're only here as my guest."

Rye sucked in an audible breath. "This is ridiculous."

"Yes, it is."

They both relaxed their grips on the handle. He could feel the tremor in her fingers and then wondered if he wasn't feeling the unsteadiness of his own hand. Now he couldn't bring himself to draw it away because he didn't want to lose the warm, intimate connection with her body.

"This is ridiculous," he said again, his gruff tone betraying him.

"Like a bad scene in a movie," she agreed breathlessly. "Any moment now you'll grab me and kiss me into submission."

"I tried that years ago, and it never worked."

"Didn't it? I seem to remember turning into putty."

"I'd just as soon not remember," he said harshly. "Nothing was ever solved for us in the bedroom."

"Nothing whatsoever." She sighed.

Rye took his hand away abruptly, and just as abruptly she let hers fall. Disappointment and anticlimax were so strong as to be palpable.

They both stood there.

"Be my guest," she said.

"You go ahead." Rye's hands were clenched.

The door to the kitchen opened. Lindsey peered out curiously. "Are you two reaching a truce out there?" she inquired. "I heard loud voices a few minutes ago."

"Not exactly a truce," Rye denied.

"More of a standoff," Emily added.

There was a fleeting moment of shared relief and mutual awkwardness. Emily pulled the screen door open briskly, and Rye held it, waiting until she had climbed the steps before he followed her up onto the back porch. There he paused for a glance around at the collection of cardboard boxes, newspapers, plastic jugs and other throwaway items. The orderliness surprised him.

Emily seemed to read his mind. "No, I haven't changed and gotten neater," she informed him. "Lindsey straightened up."

"Mom's back porches are her own personal recycling centers," Lindsey remarked cheerfully. "But hurry up and come on in, you two. Supper's ready, and I'm starving."

The kitchen was redolent with appetizing aromas. The source was a big pot simmering on the old-fashioned white porcelain stove. The kitchen table, a massive, round, oak pedestal affair, was set with three place mats, no two alike. The pottery bowls and bread plates weren't a set, nor was the stainless dinnerware.

Lindsey had probably used her mother's company best. It would be typical of Emily not to own a matching set of anything. Rye had to admit that the overall effect of the table setting was haphazardly charming, just as the plain country kitchen itself was cozy and inviting. He felt himself relaxing.

"Something smells very good," he commented appreciatively to his daughter, who looked clean scrubbed and yet chic in a fresh pair of designer jeans and fashionably oversize sweater.

"It not only smells good. It tastes good," she declared with a complacent smile. "I sampled it. We're having homemade beef-vegetable soup."

"You cooked it yourself?"

"From scratch. Not a single ingredient is from a can."

"Did you follow a recipe?"

"No, I just more or less made up my own."

"Don't worry, Rye." Emily spoke up in a knowing tone. "You'll like Lindsey's cooking. She has a real knack in the kitchen, unlike her mother at the same age."

Rye couldn't help himself. She'd left herself wide open. "You mean I can expect to find beef and vegetables in my bowl of soup? Not fruit?"

"Did you really put fruit in vegetable soup, Mom?" Lindsey asked, looking from one of them to the other.

Emily shot him a scathing glance before she pointedly ignored him. "No, but I did put apple in spaghetti sauce once, and you'd have thought I tried to poison him. Your father's idea of gourmet food was a plate lunch served in a cafeteria. All he wanted me to cook was the same boring dishes."

"My tastes in food were limited," Rye conceded. "But it was in the interest of survival that I encouraged you to prepare easy, simple meals. As I recall, you also put raisins in that spaghetti sauce. And brown sugar, wasn't it?"

"Ugh. That does sound awful, Mom. Where did you get the idea?"

"I'd still like to know the answer to that myself," he commented mildly. "I asked that same question and never got an answer."

"Dad, stop needling her," Lindsey scolded.

"You were lucky that I didn't dump that whole pot of sauce on your head," Emily told him before directing her explanation to their daughter. "I was eating an apple while I was cooking. I was pregnant with you, and Rye harped at me constantly to eat fruit. After I'd started making the sauce, I discovered that my onions had rotted and that I was out of garlic. I chopped up an apple and added it first, then brown sugar and finally the raisins. The stuff kept tasting worse and worse," she admitted, allowing herself a pained smile of reminiscence.

Rye could tell that she was trying not to let her sense of humor undermine the resentment that she'd nourished. He made his own wry confession that he hadn't made years ago: "The reason that you were out of garlic was that I had thrown it away."

"Why did you do that?" Lindsey asked in amazement. "You like garlicky food."

"Now I do. I didn't then. And your mother was very heavy-handed with seasonings, her theory being that if a little was good, a lot would be that much better."

"Mom grew up in New Orleans and likes a lot of seasoning," Lindsey explained indulgently, as though Rye didn't know Emily's background. Then she explained, for her mother's benefit, "Dad was accustomed to a much blander diet, growing up in the northern part of the state. Now he'll try anything on the menu. You wouldn't find cooking for him nearly so dull."

"I'll take your word for it, darling," Emily said. "Quite frankly it's a moot point. I have no intention of ever cooking another meal for him myself. The only reason he's sitting down to my table in my home is that this is your home, too, and you've invited him. Now, if you'll both excuse me, I'm going to take a bath and change."

She concluded her speech and, without another glance at Rye, marched out of the kitchen, her head held high.

"I'll be heating the bread, Mom," an unperturbed Lindsey said cheerfully to her back. "So don't take your time soaking in the tub." She lowered her voice, disclosing in a confidential tone after her mother was gone, "We just have one of those big, old claw-footed tubs. There isn't a shower."

To hide his expression, Rye went over to the stove to lift the lid off the pot. He could visualize a bathroom as old-fashioned as the kitchen. He could visualize Emily, peeling off her soiled clothes, stepping naked into a tub of steaming hot water.

Her only insurance of privacy was their daughter's presence at the farmhouse. If Lindsey hadn't been there, Rye would have gone searching for the bathroom....

He cut off the crazy, disruptive line of thought. Or, not thought. Fantasy. If Lindsey weren't here, he wouldn't have any wish to be here, either, he told himself firmly. The only reason he'd come was concern about her.

"Well, what's the verdict?"

"Verdict?" Rye realized that he was gazing blindly into the pot. "The verdict is that this soup looks like a savory concoction if I've ever seen one."

He heard his own note of false heartiness.

Chapter Five

It made Emily furious that she was actually hesitant about shampooing her hair. Damn it! Her hair needed washing, and she was going to wash it and go to the dinner table with wet hair the way she would do if Rye weren't there.

She collected her clothes, in the same spirit of defiance, one of her most ragged pairs of old jeans and a men's flannel shirt that was a couple of sizes too big for her. She'd picked it up at a rummage sale for a quarter.

The water pressure at the farmhouse was low. Although she'd turned on the taps to draw her bath on her way past the bathroom, the tub was still only about a third full as she got in. Sinking to her knees, she shampooed her hair, scratching her scalp vigorously. A handy, simple attachment made out of rubber, which clamped on to the taps and funnelled the flow of hot and cold water through a flexible hose, made a thorough rinsing possible.

With her hair squeaky clean, Emily lay back, still letting the water run. The tub was half-full now, with steam rising. She liked a hot bath in the winter. Sighing deeply, she closed her eyes and relinquished herself to the sensual pleasure of being immersed. The tension in her body ebbed. Along with it, her irritation seemed to dissolve.

In her newly relaxed state, Rye's presence in her house didn't seem all that great a threat. She let his face loom up on a mental screen. Devilment had gleamed in those dark eyes of his just now in the kitchen. He had been enjoying poking fun at her.

Emily felt a smile twitching her lips and slid down deeper into the tub. The smile faded as she became aware that her nipples were tingling and her thighs were easing open in a womanly response to a delicate curl of sensation between her legs.

She sat up so abruptly that water splashed on the floor. "Damn you, Rye!" she muttered, grabbing a washcloth.

Roughly she washed herself, got out of the tub, splashing more water on the floor, and roughly toweled off, fuming the whole time. Righteous indignation and lack of gentleness with her own body didn't ease her vague physical dissatisfaction, though.

Along with everything else that he'd done to disrupt her peaceful existence, Rye had stimulated her sexually. It was too humiliating for words that she could still be so strongly attracted to him.

She uttered a little sound of frustration as she bent over from the waist, shook her head and used her fingers to muss her wet mop of hair into its permed style. Then she put on her clothes, yanking up her panties, jerking up the zipper of her jeans and tying the tails of her flannel shirt into a knot with a vicious motion.

Maybe he had left, she thought. But when she opened the bathroom door, she could hear voices coming from the kitchen.

"You couldn't get so lucky," she murmured to herself disgustedly.

The fact that she had to steel her nerve to make her entrance set off fresh waves of resentment toward Rye.

"Feel better?" Lindsey inquired with a smile of warm welcome for her mother.

Rye didn't say anything, just looked her over critically, those dark eyes of his missing nothing. He almost scowled with his masculine disapproval of her appearance as he noted her men's shirt.

"*Much* better," Emily declared, holding her head a little higher. "I hope I didn't delay supper too long. My bath was so relaxing that I nearly fell asleep. I just hope that I can keep my eyes open long enough to eat supper."

She didn't sound in the least relaxed or sleepy, but more as if she could crunch bullets.

"You weren't gone more than fifteen minutes," Lindsey reassured. "That's a record time for you. Dad was catching me up on his recent trip to Houston. Sit down," she urged both her parents. "I'll serve the soup."

"How nice to be waited on," Emily remarked, picking a place and heading for it.

Rye was there before her, pulling out her chair. "Allow me," he said when she hesitated, disconcerted.

"Thank you," she said stiffly, and plopped herself in the chair. It had to be her imagination, but she would swear that he touched a tendril of her wet hair before he moved to take his own place.

Emily's stomach felt empty, but she was much too tense to be hungry. As appetizing as the food aromas were, she just wanted to do justice to Lindsey's cooking and get the meal over.

"Did you see that issue of *Time* with the article on Vince Gabrelli?" Rye asked.

"Yes, I saw it. I'm so pleased for him. He's recognized now as one of America's most talented sculptors."

"Judging from the commentary and the photographs of his exhibition that's making the rounds of the big galleries, he's still very much convinced that art should make a political statement."

Lindsey set a tureen in the middle of the table on a tile trivet. Both tureen and trivet were handmade pottery, like the bowls and plates and all of Emily's dishes.

"You showed me that article in *Time,* Mom," she recalled. "Vince Gabrelli was a classmate of yours at LSU."

"Did your mother also mention that Vince was an old boyfriend?" Rye asked.

"No, I didn't mention that," Emily answered for her. "Because it wouldn't have been true. I never even dated him."

"He followed you around like a sick calf."

"You weren't very nice to him."

Listening interestedly, Lindsey had been busy ladling soup into the bowls. "It sounds as though you were jealous of Vince, Dad," she commented as she sat down and passed a wicker breadbasket to her mother.

"Of course I was jealous," he admitted. He took the breadbasket from Emily and helped himself to a chunk of crusty French bread. "Just think," he said to her. "If you hadn't gotten messed up with me, you could have married Vince. Then you'd have been the wife of a nationally known artist."

"I could have been that anyway," Emily replied. "You were just as talented as Vince."

"Frankly I'm just as glad you got 'messed up' with each other," Lindsey put in. "If you hadn't, you wouldn't be eating this scrumptious meal prepared by yours truly."

"This soup is delicious," Emily praised.

Rye added his hearty compliments, and Lindsey beamed.

He ended up eating three bowls, and Emily had two herself with several pieces of French bread. She lost count of the number of pieces Rye ate. He seemed ravenous and made himself quite at home, refilling his own bowl after the first helping.

It apparently wasn't in the least awkward for him to be dining in her company in her kitchen. From his manner he might have been a frequent supper guest. Rather than being annoyed, Emily found herself relaxing and enjoying the meal. For one thing, her sense of hospitality was ingrained, and also the occasion was so obviously a rare treat for Lindsey, who'd been cheated of a normal family life.

Emily just hoped that her daughter understood that this was not setting a precedent, but was a rare, *one-time* occasion, with both parents making an effort for her sake.

Lindsey refused any help from her mother in clearing the dishes. She served coffee and for dessert put out a plate of cookies and sliced fresh fruit. When she sat back down, she smiled complacently and said, "Now, hasn't this been nice?" in the same tone she might have used with two youngsters who were baby-sitting charges and had behaved exceptionally well. Then she said, "Shall we begin our family conference now?"

Emily and Rye exchanged suspicious glances and confirmed that each had been taken off guard. There was no conspiracy afoot.

"We might as well," he answered their daughter, sounding no more eager for controversy than Emily was feeling at that moment.

"Yes, let's all make our positions clear," Emily stated. "Why don't I go first?"

"Good idea, Mom. Then I'll go, and Dad will speak his piece last. Is that agreeable?" she asked, sounding like a chairman of the board outlining the meeting procedure.

Emily sat up straighter, taking a moment to organize her thoughts. Noticing that Rye's gaze had dropped to the front of her shirt, she looked down and saw that a button had come undone. The shirt wasn't gaping open indecently, but unceremoniously she rebuttoned it.

"One of you should have told me that I was coming undressed," she said dryly to cover the fact that she was ridiculously flustered. Her nipples had popped out hard as rocks.

"It hadn't caught my eye," Lindsey replied, biting into a cookie.

"You were about to state your position," Rye reminded curtly, pushing his chair back a few inches from the table.

The atmosphere was no longer relaxed and friendly. The small interruption had turned Rye and Emily back into no-holds-barred adversaries.

"If I come across as somewhat uneasy and resentful with this whole forum," Emily opened up with a cutting edge in her voice, "it's because I've had very little experience with having any say where Lindsey's concerned. You've had custody, Rye, and haven't sought my advice as her mother. It goes against your grain for me to take any stand in this particular instance."

"I never sought your advice because I didn't trust your judgment, and I especially don't in this instance. I don't expect you to realize that by being supportive, you'll ultimately be harming her. But go on," he ordered.

"Your mind is completely closed," Emily accused, feeling the angry color rise in her cheeks. "You haven't even *heard* my views yet."

"I'm hoping to, eventually."

"Dad, you'll get your turn. Let Mom talk," Lindsey chided. "Mom, don't let Dad get your goat."

"That's very difficult not to do. He's such an insufferable know-it-all." Emily drew in a deep breath, composing herself. She directed her words to Lindsey, pointedly ignoring Rye. "Unlike him, I can get past personalities. I do respect his judgment and wisdom as a father. Otherwise I would never have given him custody of you without a fight. My feeling is that you could make better use of your time off from school than traveling to Florida with me, although I would like nothing better in the world than to have your company. I've already told you this and only repeat it for his benefit."

Emily silenced Rye with a glare as he shifted in his chair and opened his mouth to speak. "I'm not finished." She continued, once again addressing Lindsey. "On the other hand, you're not a child who can be told what to do. You're eighteen years old and have always been very responsible. If you've reached the stage where you feel that you can exercise your own independent judgment, then I trust you not to act foolishly."

"You're behind me all the way if I want to go to Florida with you next month." Lindsey spelled out the bottom line.

Emily took in a breath. "Yes."

"No surprises there," Rye bit out grimly. "You've just demonstrated why I never consulted you, Emily. You're the classic example of a permissive parent. That whole speech you made just now is nothing but a lot of rationalization on your part to disguise the fact that you'd rather evade taking the right stand as a parent. Out of weakness and self-ishness, you'll allow Lindsey to waste a portion of her life.''

"You're the one who had better do some soul-searching, Rye. Are you sure that you don't just begrudge me the joy of sharing a short portion of her life when she isn't under your thumb?''

Rye scraped back his chair and stood up. "I can see that this isn't going to accomplish a thing, just turn into a mud-slinging match.''

"Dad, that's copping out,'' Lindsey protested. "I haven't had my chance to state my position, and Mom hasn't heard you state yours.''

Reluctantly he sat back down, but didn't pull his chair up to the table. "I'm listening,'' he said tersely.

"Would you like to go before me?'' Lindsey offered.

"It won't matter either way,'' Emily couldn't keep herself from putting in. "His views are etched in stone.''

Lindsey admonished her mother with a mild glance. "Before I start, would anyone else like more coffee?'' They both refused and had to wait while she got up and refilled her cup. "The funny thing about all the furor that I've caused,'' she mused, "is that my mental state has improved about four hundred percent since I left Baton Rouge in a state of depression three days ago. I felt so uptight and pressured because I didn't know what I wanted to do with my life. It seemed that I had to decide and formulate some goals and start working toward them. There wasn't a minute to lose.

"Well, I *don't* have to decide right away. I have some time that I can take between being a minor and an adult. I plan to use that time living with Mom and traveling to Florida with her in her motor home. It's just not a crisis situation, Dad, even though you're treating it like it is. Just think. I could be wanting to hitchhike across the country or go touring on a motorcycle with a boyfriend. Now your turn," she told him in a gently compassionate tone.

Emily almost felt sorry for Rye herself. His whole posture, as well as his expression, reflected his inner struggle to conquer his frustration and conceal his hurt. It obviously cut to the quick that Lindsey was prepared to disregard his wishes and act without his permission.

"I would agree to your living here with your mother, but I'm absolutely opposed to your traveling with her in her motor home," he said sternly. "Number one, it isn't a reliable vehicle in good repair. Number two, you wouldn't be safe even if it were. There are too many risks involved in two women traveling without male protection."

"There are risks in my driving with a girlfriend around Baton Rouge in my new car," Lindsey pointed out. "Life has risks, Dad."

"My other objection to your plans also pertains to danger of a more insidious nature," he went on. "The way to cope with a problem is not to postpone dealing with it. If you're having difficulty making the transition from high school to college, there are underlying reasons that will still be there in six months."

"I'll cope with them then."

He gestured in defeat and got up abruptly again. Emily and Lindsey both stood up, too.

"Why don't you see your father to the front door?" Emily suggested.

"Why don't you?" Rye said soberly.

"Bye, Dad." Lindsey came around the table and kissed him on the cheek. "Drive carefully and take care of yourself."

"Bye, baby." He gave her a hug and complimented gruffly, "Your dinner was good."

Emily was braced for attack as she led the way, but he was silent and seemingly in no hurry. She guessed that while he was there, he wanted to get a look at more of the layout of the farmhouse. No doubt he was mentally shaking his head at the idea that Lindsey would choose to live here even temporarily.

"I haven't improved my housekeeping," she said as he paused to glance around the living room on their way through. "Things normally aren't this neat. Lindsey has been tidying up."

"Who would have thought she'd have a domestic streak," he commented. "She's never had any household chores to do."

"I certainly never tried to turn her into a housemaid when she visited me," Emily hastened to inform him.

"I didn't think that you had." He walked over to a wall that was almost solidly hung with artwork.

She realized what had caught his eye, one of his watercolor paintings. Mustering her defenses, she went over to stand near him.

"You accused me of never being able to part with anything once I'd added it to my junk collection. 'Junk' being your word for my worldly possessions."

"I said that partly out of jealousy. You attached sentimental value to things that other people had given you, including old boyfriends."

"I happen to be a sentimental person. In the case of your painting, though, I had to divorce the object from any associations or I couldn't have kept it." She gazed at the painting. "I just enjoy it purely because it's wonderful art."

"It really isn't too bad," Rye said with a hint of pride.

"I can't tell you how many of my artist friends have remarked on how good it is. There should be laws against not developing a talent like yours."

"You make it sound as though I was a budding Van Gogh or Picasso," he scoffed. "In all honesty, I do think I had some talent, but not genius. If I had been destined to be a great artist, I would have felt a compulsion to paint. I wouldn't have been able to give it up."

"Haven't you felt the urge, the *need* to pick up a brush?"

"Of course. A time or two I have gotten out my easel and paraphernalia. But I didn't find painting relaxing. I would get frustrated because I was out of practice and the total concentration wasn't there. My main focus was on other things."

"You had sold out," Emily said sadly. "Your focus was on being a big business success and making lots of money."

"Don't sound so tragic," Rye protested. "From your tone of voice, you could be speaking at my memorial service. If I had it to do over again, I'd go the same route. I don't expect you to ever understand, but being in the business world is highly stimulating and challenging, as well as financially rewarding."

"No, I won't ever understand," she agreed.

"If I still wanted to be an artist, I could now. And I wouldn't even have to worry about selling my paintings. I'm only forty. Whatever ability I had when I was younger isn't gone."

"It's the creative desire that you've lost, the vision. You'll never want to be an artist again."

"Probably you're right."

Emily hadn't been hoping that he'd argue with her, but his quietly reflective agreement was deeply disappointing. She sighed, turning away to end the conversation and hurry his departure.

At the front door he stopped her before she could open it, putting his hand over hers on the knob.

"Just a minute."

She quickly drew her hand free and took a half step back, feeling ill-prepared for battle. "Please, Rye, I'm tired and have nothing to add to what I said just now in the kitchen. It's a whole month before I leave for Florida. If you'll just back off, Lindsey could very well change her own mind before then."

He shook his head. "No, she won't, and it's not in my power to prevent her from making that trip with you."

"Unless you can manipulate me somehow into ganging up with you against her. Forget the whole idea, Rye. I'm through feeling guilty because I messed up your future. I've paid the price all these years for being irresponsible. As far as I'm concerned, the slate is clean. You and I are both equally concerned parents, and I'm going with my instincts, not yours."

"You're playing with fire, Emily," he warned softly. "The kind that you won't find easy to control once it rises to cone temperature."

Emily's heart gave a leap that was more than fright. "Please," she said sarcastically. "Don't go melodramatic on me."

"There's no way that I'm going to retire to the sidelines and let you take over as the parent Lindsey turns to for advice and counsel. You're going to have to contend with me being around, talking to you like this in person, calling you on the phone. Can you handle that?"

"Can you handle it?" she blustered.

"I'm not sure."

His gaze lowered to her mouth and then down farther to her breasts. Emily felt her body's immediate response. Her heart was pounding and her pulse hammering. She glanced down, attempting to be matter-of-fact as she asked, "Has my shirt come unbuttoned again?"

He didn't bother to answer her question. "It fits you like a damned tent," he observed, sounding resentful, "and yet I can still tell that you aren't wearing a bra underneath it. Whose shirt is that, anyway?"

"Whose shirt?" Emily repeated, folding her arms over her chest. "Why, it's mine. I bought it at a rummage sale for a quarter. The reason I put it on tonight is that it's comfortable. And because it's the least attractive shirt I own," she informed him bluntly. "Not for anything would I want you to get the wrong notion that I care whether you like the way I look."

"I naturally assumed that you wore the shirt deliberately to rub it in that you'd had other men."

"You assumed wrong."

"But there have been other men."

"Of course. At the present, I have no man in my life, Rye, if that's what all this interrogation is about. If there were, I wouldn't be inviting him to stay overnight with me while Lindsey is here."

"I give you more credit than that," he answered, indirectly denying that Lindsey had anything to do with his inquisitiveness. "Well, I'll say good night."

"Goodbye," she said firmly. "Lindsey will be keeping in touch, I'm sure."

"Good night," he repeated with soft, steely emphasis. "Be sure to lock the door."

Emily opened her mouth to tell him to mind his own business and not give her orders in her own house. Then she closed it, knowing what his reply would be.

As long as her house was Lindsey's home, whether or not she locked her doors at night was his business.

Rye drove through his affluent neighborhood in Baton Rouge, mentally contrasting it with the rural environs of

Emily's farmhouse. Through beveled-glass doors he glimpsed the subdued glitter of chandeliers. Floodlights illuminated professional landscaping while discouraging lurking intruders. An attempt at forced entry into any one of the large, handsome houses would activate a sophisticated burglar alarm, serviced by a company that would immediately notify the police.

At his own house, a two-story Georgian built of white brick, strategically placed floodlights highlighted the formal hedging and sculptured shrubbery. Brass carriage lamps mounted on either side of the tall front door shed a bright glow. They had been turned on by the same timer that operated the floods and would extinguish all the outside lights at dawn.

A separate timer was responsible for the diffused glow in rooms throughout the house. A stranger driving along the street could only surmise that the occupants were home.

The word was *occupant,* singular, Rye reflected as he opened the garage door from the street with the electronic remote control and turned into the driveway. Inside he would be met with silence until he switched on his state-of-the-art stereo system that played music in any room of the house or turned the whole house, upstairs and down, into a concert hall.

Last year Lindsey's aged Labrador had had to be put to sleep. Rye missed the old guy and would get another dog for company, except that he was out of town so much that a pet would end up spending half the time or more in a kennel.

People's sympathy was all for women who suffered empty-nest syndrome, but he had a full-fledged case of it. He missed like hell not having his daughter living at home.

At least when she was enrolled in LSU and staying in the dormitory, she had come and gone in the house. He'd seen her at least once or twice a week, taken her to lunch and out to dinner, talked to her on the phone. Now she seemed miles from nowhere out at Emily's farm, inaccessible to him.

It was only nine o'clock, too early to retire, but too late to make last-minute plans for going out. Rye felt like a lot more time had elapsed than five hours since he'd pulled up at Emily's farmhouse and Lindsey had come to meet him.

Each minute had been intense, whether awkward or pleasurable or infuriating. He'd been hit by what seemed the full range of emotions, and had been forced to struggle all the while to maintain perspective and stay in control of himself.

The problem was that part of him wanted to kick the traces, toss the reins, go with the flow. Any one of a dozen trite metaphors would do. Emily had brought out the same urge in him years before. She'd affected him exactly the same way, delighting while she annoyed, drawing him like a magnet, arousing him.

Rye was having trouble believing that simple physical proximity to his ex-wife took him back to being twenty-one again, stripped him of his hard-won maturity. No wonder Lindsey had blinked and stared with amazement at his lapses into behaving like a callow youth.

How could he expect to impress upon her the seriousness of her actions if he didn't retain his dignity in her eyes? If she got the wrong idea that his thinking could be influenced by old resentments and petty conflicts between him and her mother, Rye would lose his credibility as a thoughtful, rational parent.

He honestly didn't begrudge Emily the joy of being close to their daughter, as Emily had accused. He wasn't that selfish or hard-hearted. If he were, he wouldn't have been so scrupulously fair in seeing to it that Lindsey visited her mother. Rye could easily have not kept his bargain with

Emily to the letter. He could have capitalized on her inability to stick to a regimen or schedule.

But he hadn't. He'd suffered the uneasiness and worry for the sake of his conscience and for Lindsey's sake.

And for Emily's sake.

When his daughter was growing up, Rye's anxieties had all centered around her physical safety when she was with her mother. Lindsey hadn't ever shown any signs of developing Emily's attitudes or personality traits.

Now when decisions were crucial, Lindsey was rejecting his advice and seeking Emily's. She was turning her back on the highly respectable niche in society, the affluence that Rye had been so committed to providing for her and for himself.

He was definitely feeling a sense of hurt along with apprehension.

How could she choose to live in that run-down old farmhouse furnished with odds and ends of furniture over this house whose rooms looked like photographs out of *Good Housekeeping*? Rye asked himself as he sat on a stool in his kitchen, drinking a glass of milk that he'd poured himself after a long deliberation, gazing into the refrigerator. Not your ordinary refrigerator that you purchased in an appliance store, but a built-in model with a wood-paneled door that matched the cabinetry.

He visualized Emily's refrigerator—on its last legs, about to expire anytime. It was the same vintage as the stove. The door was rounded, rather than squared like modern refrigerators. Rye doubted that the refrigerator was even the self-defrosting kind.

The thought triggered his memory, and he had a clear mental picture of the cramped, ugly little kitchen in the apartment he and Emily had rented after they'd gotten married. The miniature freezer compartment of the small refrigerator would freeze up within a week, making it impossible to get out ice trays or retrieve packages of frozen food.

Rye had hated that damned refrigerator, but not Emily. Even back then she'd accepted malfunctions as a manifestation of the nature of a nonliving thing. With no malevolence, she'd hacked away with an ice pick and a hammer, her alternative to frequent defrosting. Somehow, despite all his dire warnings, she'd never hurt herself or put the freezer out of commission.

Gulping down the last few swallows of his milk, Rye got up and rinsed the glass before leaving it in the sink. At the door, with his hand on the light switch, he gave one last glance around the kitchen. It was larger than the kitchen in the farmhouse, designed for efficiency, equipped to handle every type of food preparation, attractively decorated and yet...sterile.

In comparison, Emily's old-fashioned kitchen was stamped all over with the message that it had seen use, that it *was* used. Lindsey wasn't immune to the homey atmosphere any more than he had been himself.

Rye had never credited Emily with having any homemaker's abilities. In his mind her deficiencies as a housekeeper had loomed too large. He'd found fault with her taste, too, which she'd described as "eclectic" and he'd labeled "atrocious."

But based on what he'd seen of the farmhouse, she did have a homemaker's touch. Her living room would be a decorator's nightmare, but it had an undeniable charm, a fresh originality that his own rather formal living room lacked.

He could appreciate that charm and originality now. He was secure enough that the approval of the world at large was no longer quite so important. Outward appearances didn't matter as much as they once had.

But they still mattered. The good opinion of his neighbors, the respect of his business associates mattered to Rye. He could never march to his own drummer the way Emily did. He would always be influenced to some extent by the knowledge that he was a member of society.

He couldn't live in Emily's farmhouse in its present state of neglect. Nor could she live in his house or fit into his life.

Disturbed that he was even thinking along those lines, Rye went to his study. He spent most of his waking time at home there, now that Lindsey had moved out. The room, more than his Mercedes or membership in the most exclusive country club in the city or ownership of a house in this neighborhood, was a source of pride and pleasure.

Sometimes it was still hard to believe that it was *his* study, not the private retreat of some other successful, important man. The paneling and built-in cabinets were cherry wood, the couch and chairs upholstered in leather. The end tables and several other pieces of furniture, like his desk, were English antiques. On the floor was a richly patterned Oriental rug. Original paintings hung on the walls.

Seated at his desk, Rye opened up his briefcase, but didn't take out any of the folders or paper-clipped sheaves of papers. He picked up a pencil and held it, staring off into space. Or not exactly into space, but across the room at the double doors of a spacious storage closet.

Inside the closet he had all his art paraphernalia packed away. Emily's face rose clearly before his eyes, her expression troubled and accusing. He replayed in his mind her husky voice as she questioned him about whether the artist in him had died.

Had it?

Rye tossed the pencil down and got up, leaving his brief-case open. He found an unused sketch pad and his wooden box of drawing pencils in the closet.

Settled back in his favorite reading chair, one ankle crossed comfortably over his other knee, he rested the pad in his lap and began to draw freestyle with rapid strokes. He drew the farmhouse from several different angles. Then, letting his mind drift, he sketched Lindsey coming to meet him as he'd arrived that afternoon. Next he sketched Emily's kiln with her backside framed enticingly in the brick opening of one of the twin chambers.

Page after page, Rye recreated scenes from recent memory. He even used himself as a subject. It was good therapy, if nothing else.

With his hand moving almost on its own, he ventured into fantasy and drew Emily in her bathroom, taking off her clothes, stepping into the tub, immersed in bathwater. He took care not to depict her body as that of the nubile eighteen-year-old who had once posed nude for him. She was thirty-seven, and there was bound to be some slight sagging to her breasts, some loss of muscle tone that her clothing hid.

Despite his efforts at realism, Rye could feel himself becoming physically aroused. He closed the sketch pad and put it aside, doubtful that he'd proved anything by the drawing session other than what he already knew.

As far as he was concerned, Emily had lost none of her sex appeal.

Chapter Six

"I don't know *why* I'm doing this," Emily said for the third or fourth time since she'd gotten into Lindsey's car. It was Thursday afternoon, and they were headed into Baton Rouge.

"Because I asked you to ride with me and keep me company." Lindsey took one hand from the wheel to pat her mother's hand reassuringly. "Dad isn't going to come home unexpectedly and find you at his house. If he did, so what? He's been out to the farmhouse twice."

"Yes, but I was there when he came."

"We could stop and call Dad and ask him to be on hand to greet us," Lindsey suggested teasingly, and got a reproving look. "Come on, Mom, relax. It won't take me long. I just want to get a few clothes and things and pick up my mail."

"If you had come by yourself, you could have gone to the campus and visited some of your college classmates," Emily pointed out, still not happy.

"Yes, and taken the chance of running into Eric. No, thanks. You needed some supplies from Southern Pottery anyway, so we're killing two birds with one stone. Dad and Claire were long divorced when we moved into this house," Lindsey said, as though that concern was the source of Emily's reservations. "None of the furniture is even the same that we had when they were together."

"Even if it were the same furniture and the same house, that wouldn't make any difference. Claire wasn't in the picture when Rye and I split up. She was welcome to him," Emily declared.

From her daughter's quick look, she knew that it hadn't escaped notice that Emily hadn't out-and-out said, *I was never jealous of Claire.*

"I wish Dad would marry again. He's not too old to have a second family."

Emily felt some response seemed expected of her. "No, he isn't," she agreed. "Forty isn't over the hill."

"It would be fun to have a little sister and brother to spoil rotten. Plus I could do with less attention." Lindsey flashed Emily a rueful smile. "Right now, though, Dad doesn't even have a prospect for a wife. Oh, he takes women out, and he gets tons of invitations to dinner parties where he's paired up with a female friend of the host and hostess. But there's no special woman in his life."

"Maybe he doesn't want one. Maybe he enjoys being a bachelor," Emily said. *Maybe he has good reason to doubt his aptitude for being a husband, after having struck out twice,* she thought. She fiddled with the radio, managing to keep such a totally unsympathetic hypothesis to herself.

"No, I think Dad was cut out to be a family man. Having a home means so much to him. And look at the kind of car he drives. Not a Porsche or a Ferrari, but a stodgy four-door Mercedes sedan."

That cost more than the average family man would earn in two or three years. A Mercedes wasn't transportation. It was a status symbol on wheels. Rye might just want the most sheet metal for his money.

Emily kept her cynical thoughts to herself, saying instead with careful indifference, "I'm sure he has a logical explanation for choosing that particular automobile."

"Undoubtedly he does. But I've read enough pop psychology to know that we all rationalize our actions. The explanations we give ourselves aren't always our hidden motives."

"That's getting too deep for me," Emily protested. "I have no interest in psychoanalyzing myself or anyone else. As far as I'm concerned, liking the color of a car is reason enough for buying it."

"What would be your reaction if you learned that Dad had walked into the Mercedes dealership, saw his car on the showroom floor and bought it on the spot?"

"I'd think it was a case of mistaken identification."

Lindsey smiled at Emily's wry quip, but prodded, "You would be surprised, wouldn't you, because he was acting out of character."

"Especially after I'd seen his car. It's not my idea of an automobile that would bring on an uncontrollable urge for ownership."

"There would have to be more to the story, you'd assume. Other factors that led him to make a hasty purchase."

"Is all this leading up to pointing out that we expect people we know to act in character?" Emily asked. "Okay,

I confess that I'm as guilty as the next person of playing amateur psychologist. Satisfied?''

Lindsey nodded, but obviously still had more to say. ''Sometimes it takes an outsider to make us realize that people who are very close to us aren't behaving normally. For example, after my roommate Sarah had met you and Dad separately, and had been filled in on the background, she found it hard to believe that the relations between you two were so strained that you still avoided one another like the plague after being divorced since I was a toddler. She insisted that it either had to be just ingrained habit or else the flame hadn't died and you didn't trust yourselves to be in one another's company. Sarah's a real romantic and reads romance novels by the dozen,'' she added.

''Your father and I have simply acted like adults and spared ourselves and you a lot of unpleasantness,'' Emily stated firmly.

Lindsey ignored her interpolation. ''Sarah built quite a case for the latter possibility. She made a lot over the fact that neither you nor Dad had ever found anyone else. She was all for plotting ways to bring you together.''

''It sounds as though Sarah should try her hand at writing her own romance novels. She has quite an imagination.''

''Those were almost my exact words to her. I told her that I'd given up long ago on my parents' ever getting back together. What I was getting at, telling you all this, is that her habit theory did open my eyes. I realized that it was about time for you and Dad to bury the hatchet. There's just no reason that the three of us can't occasionally have dinner together or celebrate a special event, like my birthday.'' She met Emily's glance directly and asked gently, ''Now, is there?''

"No reason other than risking a case of indigestion. Monday night was hardly a relaxed, pleasant meal."

"I enjoyed it. And you and Dad didn't appear to be all that uncomfortable. Was it really such an ordeal?"

Emily sighed. "I guess not. But mainly because it was fairly obvious that you were having a good time. If it will make you happy, I'll go out to dinner with you and your father on your birthday this year, providing he's willing."

"He'll be willing, for the same reason you are. To make me happy." She kept her eyes on the road as she made the confident, pat answer.

"I suppose I am a little curious to see for myself how Rye lives now that he's made his million," Emily confessed. "Otherwise I never would have let you talk me into coming with you today. But you'd already figured that out for yourself."

Lindsey grinned. "I'll give you a guided tour, including closets. In case you feel nosy, Dad even managed to get a peek into your pantry while you were in the bathroom Monday night."

She had shown her mother snapshots of the house some years ago when she and her father had first moved into the elite residential neighborhood near the LSU campus. Emily had been tempted to drive down the street, but had curbed the impulse, not willing to take the chance of having Rye glimpse her.

"I'm impressed," she admitted as Lindsey braked in front of a stately two-story Georgian house. "It's too formal for my taste, but certainly very handsome and beautifully well kept."

"The inside matches the outside," Lindsey stated matter-of-factly, pulling into the driveway.

Inside she showed her mother all the rooms on the ground floor, ending with Rye's study. There Emily detected the first item that seemed out of place, jarring the perfect order and harmony. A sketch pad lay on a table next to a leather easy chair. On top of it was a wooden pencil box that brought a jolt of recognition.

Rye had kept his drawing pencils in the box. It was one of his few possessions, other than clothes, that he'd brought with him from north Louisiana. He had insisted that it had no sentimental value, but simply served a practical purpose.

Emily checked herself to keep from going over and picking it up. "This room looks more lived-in than the others," she commented, letting her gaze rest on the sketch pad. She would like to see what Rye had drawn.

Lindsey ushered her mother from the room, confiding, "Dad loves his study. I think it was the deciding factor in his buying the house, whether he realizes it or not."

"If it was, I'm sure he realizes it." Emily's patience was growing short with probing hidden motivations.

Upstairs she declined continuing the tour, which would include Rye's bedroom. "I've seen enough," she said. "Let's just pack your things and go."

Lindsey didn't argue.

In her lovely bedroom with its connecting private bath, Emily perched on the edge of one of the twin beds while her daughter consulted a list she'd compiled and got articles of clothing out of bureau drawers and took hanging garments from a huge walk-in closet. *She's so much like Rye,* Emily thought, noting the economy of movement and concentration on the task at hand.

True to her word, Lindsey didn't take long. She crumpled her list when she'd finished, crossed over to her desk and tossed the small wad into a wastebasket.

"I'll just take my mail and read it while you're driving, if you don't mind." She gathered up a small stack of envelopes. "I have a letter from Janet Paxton that I'm just dying to open."

"Why don't you go ahead and read your mail?" Emily suggested. "I'll take this suitcase downstairs."

"Would you mind?"

"Not at all. Take your time. I'll just take a closer look at some of the artwork I noticed earlier."

Lindsey was tearing open a pink envelope. "Please do," she urged absently.

Emily fought with her conscience as she descended the stairs, but, putting the suitcase down, she headed straight for Rye's study. After all, he had been present when she was unloading her kiln. He'd touched her new-fired pottery. What could be more personal and private than that?

Picking up the pencil box, she held it in her hands for a moment before she slid the lid open. Were those the same pencils that he had used years ago as an art student? she wondered. They probably were.

Slowly she slid the lid closed again and set the box aside. Then, with a disquieting blend of eagerness and dread, she lifted the sketch pad and opened it to the first page. Surprised only by her own lack of surprise, she gazed at a drawing of her farmhouse. On the next page was a different view of it, drawn with pencil strokes that were already surer.

From the following page, Lindsey's face smiled at her. Emily smiled back, feeling a pain in her heart. *Damn him and his talent.* Her eyes widened, and she gasped indignantly as she turned to the next page and saw her own backside framed in the chamber opening of her kiln. What presumption to turn her into his model!

Scene by scene, her emotions changed. Rye had captured nuances. The rendering was bold and yet so delicately true that he might have looked through the lens of a camera and snapped candid close-up shots of Lindsey and herself. But then there were revealing sketches of himself, too. Emily examined them long and hard, reading awkwardness, anger, frustration.

He had drawn a picture narrative more eloquent than words. His technique was rusty, but the talent was definitely still there. *What a tragic waste,* she reflected, sighing as she flipped over a page.

A little shocked sound came from her throat as she stared down at herself in the act of shedding her clothes in an old-fashioned bathroom disconcertingly similar to hers. Emily's mouth dropped open, and she uttered sounds that expressed not only shock, but outrage at the liberties Rye had taken with his pencil.

If he were going to undress her and parade her naked on a blank page, he could at least not be so unflattering. For his information, her breasts weren't that droopy or her stomach muscles that flabby.

Emily snapped the sketch pad closed, started to put it back exactly where it had been and then plopped it down on the seat of the leather chair instead. Before she could pick it up again and rip out the pages or do something equally impulsive, such as write him a nasty message, she left the study.

Lindsey was coming down the stairs. Fortunately she didn't notice anything amiss. Her mind was clearly on her letter from her high-school chum, and she passed along the gist of it on the way to Southern Pottery, which sold clay and glaze chemicals and various other pottery supplies.

Emily paid scant attention. Once she'd stopped seething, she still couldn't brush aside the knowledge that Rye had sat there in his study and made those erotic drawings of her.

Because they were highly erotic, unflattering though they might be.

Emily yawned, closing the latest issue of *Ceramics Monthly* she'd been thumbing through, while mentally she turned the pages of that blankety-blank sketch pad of Rye's and kept coming to those drawings of her. Putting the magazine aside, she stood and bade her daughter good night. Wearing a fleecy cream-colored robe over teal blue pajamas, Lindsey sat cross-legged on the sofa, writing a letter in answer to the one she'd received from her girlfriend.

"Night, Mom." Lindsey looked up and smiled absently. "As soon as I finish this letter, I'm going to bed, too. I'll put the screen over the fireplace. The doors are locked."

Emily hid a fond smile at the hint of cheerful reminder. It was the same tone a kindergarten teacher might use with her pupils as she taught by example. *Now, boys and girls, I'll look both ways before I cross the street.*

"Maybe I'd better double-check the doors to be on the safe side," Emily said, tongue-in-cheek, and was rewarded with a sheepish grin.

"Don't be so paranoid," Lindsey quipped. "Next thing you'll be installing a burglar alarm."

Mother and daughter smiled at each other in one of those moments of mutual appreciation and tolerance. It was shattered by the ringing of the telephone out in the kitchen.

They both glanced at their watches. Emily's ran slow and even it indicated the hour as nearing eleven o'clock, late for a phone call.

"Dad wouldn't be calling this late," Lindsey mused with faint alarm, unfolding her legs and rising with a swift movement.

"It's probably just a wrong number," Emily suggested.

She took several steps after Lindsey, whose long legs took her quickly into the kitchen. At the sound of a note of panic in her daughter's voice, she stopped, listening.

"Dad! Is anything wrong—"

It was Rye calling. Emily felt her own private sense of panic as Lindsey carried on in relieved conversation.

"No, Mom and I weren't in bed yet. We were just saying good night.... Why, yes, I was in Baton Rouge today. Mom and I drove in together.... Yes, we picked up some of my things at the house. How did you know that we had gone by there?"

Emily strained to hear, as though she could pick up the answer herself. Was he telling Lindsey that the sketch pad had been moved? She bit her lip in frustration when Lindsey's next words didn't give her a clue.

"I tried to give you a call to say hi before we left, but the line was busy.... That's great that business is so good with the economy no healthier than it is.... I'm fine. I've been playing chemist, helping Mom mix glazes. She had run out of a couple of ingredients, so we went by Southern Pottery today, too.... Yes, Dad, I know about the dangers of inhaling silica dust. I wear a mask and use rubber gloves.... No, you guess wrong. Mom is a real stickler for following safe studio procedure."

Realizing that she was eavesdropping, Emily went to the door of the kitchen and mouthed "good night" to Lindsey, who smiled and nodded. In her bedroom Emily got into bed, any former drowsiness gone. She was wide awake, thanks to Rye's lack of consideration.

For the sake of economy as well as preference, she didn't keep her bedroom warm. Her hands would get cold if she read in bed, she reflected sourly, but she wasn't going to lie there and think about Rye. He had already occupied her thoughts for hours. Now he was giving her a case of insomnia.

Fuming, Emily propped herself on pillows, pulled her covers up high, and was reaching to the bedside table when it occurred to her that she had left the magazine she'd been reading out in the living room. She didn't have any reading material within arm's reach. Somehow that seemed Rye's fault, too.

"Mom?" After knocking, Lindsey had opened the door to stick her head inside. Emily struggled to look tranquil rather than irritated. "Dad would like to speak to you."

"Now?" she blurted, jerking the cover up to her chin. "What does he want?"

"He didn't say."

"Tell him I've gone to bed."

"I did tell him that. He wants to take us both to dinner Saturday night. He has some 'business proposition' for you. That's all the explanation he would give me. I assume he wants to get your RSVP on the dinner invitation."

"Business proposition," Emily repeated suspiciously.

Lindsey gestured toward her mother's nightstand as though to say, *Pick up the phone and ask him for yourself.* Emily turned her head to gaze at the telephone with grim distaste, summoning her nerve and her dignity. Quietly the bedroom door closed.

"Hello, Rye. What did you want?" she inquired, holding the receiver tightly.

"Hello, Emily. I guess I'd like to know if I should have a red face."

Her own face warmed at his embarrassed, hesitant manner of speaking. "Am I supposed to understand what you're talking about?" she blustered.

"Is Lindsey there, listening?"

"No. She went to hang up the phone in the kitchen."

A click sounded, right on cue.

"Good." He sounded relieved. "When I walked into my study tonight and saw evidence that someone had been there, the only likely person was Lindsey, since my cleaning lady doesn't come on Thursdays. I was mortified." He paused for her response.

"You should have been," Emily said indignantly. "Thank heaven she isn't more curious and didn't pay any attention to that sketch pad of yours, lying in open sight. Goodness knows what she would have thought! She insisted on giving me a guided tour of the downstairs," she added for his information.

"So she didn't look at the sketch pad?"

"No."

He blew out his breath. "I had my fingers crossed. She didn't give off any signals."

"It was very careless of you not to put it away if it wasn't meant for her to see," Emily criticized sharply.

He rallied to his own defense. "Under ordinary circumstances, she would never have gone into my study. Needless to say, I didn't anticipate that she'd be bringing you here and showing you the house."

"Believe me, I regretted letting her persuade me. I can do without such insults to my modesty and my female ego. It's embarrassing to think that your cleaning lady might have given in to curiosity and gotten an eyeful."

"My drawings might not be especially skilled, but they aren't pornographic," Rye protested. "I wouldn't have objected to Lindsey's seeing them if the model hadn't been you. Although the poses are somewhat...suggestive."

Not just Emily's face was hot, but her whole body. She was able to surmise that he was looking at the drawings while he was talking to her.

"I think you owe me an apology," she said primly.

"Since when have you ever objected to nudity in art? Or felt any embarrassment about your body? You posed nude for me when I was an art student," he reminded.

"We were also lovers at the time."

"Later we were husband and wife. It isn't as though I had to rely on a lewd imagination."

"More like a satiric imagination." As soon as the words were out, Emily wished she could call them back. She felt exposed during the split second of silence and added with heavy scorn, "I don't have the body of an eighteen-year-old anymore, but I haven't gone completely to pot, either."

He didn't reply at once, and when he did, his tone was disarmingly sheepish. "I feel like a damned teenager who's been caught masturbating. Monday night when I got home, some impulse came over me, and I got out my pencils and this sketch pad and just started to draw. As a kind of therapy, I guess you'd say. I'll tear the pages out and put the pad away."

"Don't tear *all* the pages out," she objected. "Just those last ones of me. Lindsey might like to have the other sketches. The facial expressions are quite good. The news media are missing a bet. With no practice, you could still be one of those artists who sit in courtrooms and sketch trial proceedings." Her praise was grudgingly sincere.

"I always enjoyed drawing for itself. It wasn't just a preliminary step to painting," Rye reflected. "Monday night the pencil felt foreign in my hand at first, but then it started feeling a little like it once did, an extension of my fingers." Emily could hear a faint, whispery sound. Apparently he was turning the pages of the sketch pad while he talked.

"It was obvious that you got more confident as you went along," she said.

"My perspective and scale leave a lot to be desired." His self-criticism was matter-of-fact, not regretful. "But purely from the standpoint of drawing technique, these drawings of you really aren't half-bad."

"I'm afraid I lost my objectivity at that point." Emily's sarcasm was pure defense. "My reaction wouldn't have been much different if I'd opened up a girlie magazine and seen myself on the centerfold. Quite frankly I was shocked and offended."

"I do apologize. If it's any consolation, I was thoroughly annoyed at myself and at you."

"At me!"

"Yes, at you. You're the last woman on earth that I would want to stir up my libido."

"You're the last man whose libido I would *want* to stir up!" Emily informed him indignantly. "Good Lord, I came to the supper table with wet hair and looking about as unsexy as it's possible for me to look."

"I can't argue with that. I guess it was just the tension and antagonism. Although wearing a man's shirt and letting it come unbuttoned didn't help."

Emily was seething. "I didn't *let* it come unbuttoned. It came unbuttoned. I wish that I had taken it off so that you could see that my breasts don't sag down to my knees."

He didn't answer, and the silence was suddenly provocative. She could feel her heart beating fast, also feel the heaviness of her breasts beneath her flannel nightgown, feel the hardness of her nipples.

"This is enough of this conversation," she said, cringing at her hint of breathlessness. "I shouldn't have been so nosy today at your house. It serves me right, I suppose, for giving in to my curiosity and going there with Lindsey in the first place. You can rest assured that I won't do so again. In return, you can give me your word that you won't come out here again. We can both rest easy and go back to ignoring one another's existence."

"I think you and I both know that that state of affairs is in the past," Rye observed quietly. "Whether we like it or not, Lindsey has moved the three of us into a new phase. I'm not giving up my daughter, Emily. She means everything to me. If being a part of her life means being mixed up in yours, so be it."

"She means everything to me, too. It's terribly unfair of you not to give me this time with her without you interfering."

"I'm agreeable to letting her stay with you out at your place while she's taking a semester break from college. As long as I can see her with some frequency and talk to her on the phone, I can live with that situation."

"Rye, you can't possibly expect me to cancel my trip to Florida! I've paid exhibiting fees. My reputation is on the line, and I need the income. I make my living as a studio potter."

"The sponsors of the shows undoubtedly have a list of backup artists whose applications were turned down."

"They do. Next year my application would be among them. It's out of the question," Emily stated. "I'm going to Florida and taking Lindsey with me if she chooses to accompany me."

"What if I told you that I have an interested buyer who would purchase your whole inventory of pottery, saving you the trouble and expense of a trip to Florida?"

"A buyer?" she repeated skeptically. "Who?"

"I prefer to go over the particulars in person, rather than on the phone. I've made dinner reservations at one of Lindsey's favorite restaurants here in town for Saturday evening. I'd like for you and her to be my guests. We could meet here at my house and go in my car."

"I'm *not* coming to your house or riding in your car."

"As you wish. I'll meet the two of you at the restaurant, then." He mentioned time and place, as though the matter were settled, said good night and hung up.

Emily was left sitting there helplessly, holding the receiver with her mouth open to say, *you might meet Lindsey, but you won't meet me. I don't want to be your dinner guest, period.*

She banged the receiver down, turned out the lamp and lay tensely in the darkness. Fresh waves of irritation washed through her as she realized that she was thinking about how she would dress for Saturday night if she were going.

Chapter Seven

"What was Dad's 'business proposition'?" Lindsey asked curiously the next morning. She and Emily were both bundled in their robes and wearing socks and slippers. A layer of frost lay on the ground outside, and it was chilly in the kitchen, where they were having breakfast. The high-ceilinged farmhouse was cool in the summer, but also drafty in the winter.

"He made vague reference to some wholesale buyer for my pottery, but he refused to go into specifics. I think his business proposition is mainly a come-on to lure us both into Baton Rouge for another round of pointless debate," Emily answered, yawning. She hadn't slept worth a darn, dreaming crazy dreams and thrashing about restlessly. From the state of her covers, she might have fought off an abductor during the night.

"A wholesale buyer?" Lindsey repeated interestedly.

"Yes, his theory being that if I sold all my pottery, I wouldn't have any to sell at the winter shows in Florida."

"Ingenious," Lindsey declared, nodding. "You can bet it's not just a come-on, Mom, or a half-baked scheme. Dad hasn't been written up as a business entrepreneur without good reason. He'll present you with an offer you can't refuse."

"I can and will refuse it. I don't sell wholesale. By eliminating a middleman, I can make my pottery affordable to more people while still getting a reasonable price for my work."

"You put so much of yourself into producing your pottery that selling a piece is more like finding a good owner than a commercial transaction," Lindsey suggested.

"Exactly. Rye could never understand that, of course. You can try explaining it to him tomorrow night, when you tell him that I'm not interested in any business propositions he has."

"I've already decided that if you don't go, I won't either. For one thing, Dad would insist that I spend the night in Baton Rouge, not drive back out here late at night by myself."

"I would be in favor of your staying overnight in the city, too," Emily admitted. "You have your own room."

"Yes, but then on Sunday, Dad would make it hard for me to leave. And the whole time he'd be exerting pressure on me."

"He isn't going to be happy if you don't have dinner with him. One way or another, he'll manage to see you this weekend, if he has to camp on our doorstep."

Lindsey smiled apologetically. "Sorry for hiding behind your skirt like a mousy little kid, Mom. Three more weeks, and we can at least put some distance between Dad and us."

"Florida's not that far away," Emily observed, struck by a new, dismaying thought that made her heart sink.

"You're right. It's not. I wouldn't be at all surprised if Dad doesn't pop over on weekends. Can you stand that?" Lindsey asked regretfully.

"Of course I can," Emily stated bravely. "As for Saturday night, maybe we should reconsider."

"Having dinner with Dad in town might be better than the alternative." Lindsey followed easily, almost *too* easily. "A couple of hours in a restaurant, with other people around, as opposed to having him invite himself out here."

"We can leave with no argument about driving home."

"Less argument anyway. Don't expect Dad to be thrilled over the idea of the two of us being on the road at night," she warned, and then flashed a confidential smile. "I was kind of hoping that you'd agree to go. My mouth is watering for my favorite appetizer on the menu, escargots, and Dad and I usually order Caesar salad. Not only is the food good, but it's a fancy restaurant, and I'm in the mood for getting all dressed up. What shall I wear? Maybe my new red skirt and blouse with boots..."

She discussed the many possibilities in her large, fashionable wardrobe, bought with the generous clothing allowance that Rye gave her. Emily got a normal mother's pleasure from seeing the anticipation in her pretty daughter's face and hearing the eagerness in her voice.

But it was Rye who was responsible for the eagerness and anticipation, and Emily couldn't help feeling resentful toward him. He would use any ploy to intrude upon the time that Lindsey was spending with her mother. He had deliberately dangled a dinner invitation to a posh restaurant that Emily couldn't afford.

If it weren't for embarrassing her daughter, Emily was tempted to show up as a bag lady Saturday night. The idea had such wicked appeal that it put her in a better humor.

"You look fantastic, Mom! I love that gorgeous multicolored shawl over the black dress with the black boots. It's such an ultrasophisticated effect."

"I'm glad you approve. I was striving for 'ultrasomething,'" Emily quipped, smiling her own approval for her daughter's appearance. "You look fantastic yourself in that red outfit."

"Ensemble," Lindsey corrected, feigning haughtiness.

"Oh, how gauche of me," Emily hastened to apologize. "You look chic in that crimson ensemble."

Lindsey threw back her head and laughed. "Isn't this fun?" she demanded. "The two of us getting dressed up and going out on the town together?"

It was fun. Rye's underhanded ploy had backfired on him, Emily reflected with smug satisfaction. Mother and daughter were having a ball, allies who would stick together. The fact that he would be picking up the bill tonight didn't even bother her a great deal.

Emily enjoyed a taste of luxury now and then. She had nothing per se against dining in a fine restaurant with elegant atmosphere. Nothing against living a more affluent life-style than hers, for that matter, as long as compromising her values wasn't involved.

In a self-indulgent mood, she made a dash to Lindsey's car in the drizzling rain and got in on the passenger's side for the ride into Baton Rouge. The forecast was for freezing temperatures by morning. They would be back before there was any danger of the road icing up or the water pipes in the farmhouse freezing, but Emily had left the faucets dripping just as a precaution.

"Br-r-r. That wind is from the North Pole!" Lindsey exclaimed as she started up the engine. "I hope this rain doesn't turn into sleet."

"It won't," Emily assured her complacently. By the time they were pulling out onto the gravel road, the heater was blasting warm air. She sat back with no misgivings, enjoying the warmth, enjoying the comfort of the plush upholstery.

The restaurant had valet parking. Lindsey pulled under the portico sheltering the entrance. Rye had already arrived and was waiting inside. He looked handsome and clean-cut and distinguished in a dark suit, pale blue shirt and conservative maroon-and-navy-patterned tie.

Lindsey offered him her cheek to kiss and smiled radiantly at his compliments on her appearance. When his dark gaze switched to her, Emily offered him her hand and greeted him affably before he could speak.

"Hello, Rye. How are you this evening?"

His expression was quizzical as he hesitated briefly and then clasped her hand, holding it as he said, "Hello, Emily. I couldn't be better, under the circumstances. It's not often that I have two such attractive dates."

She pulled her hand free. "It's not often that I have such a polished, well-heeled escort."

Lindsey put in, "This is a pleasant switch. You two sound like a mutual admiration society."

"Your father's relieved that I'm actually presentable," Emily explained. "He was expecting me to show up looking tacky. That used to be your favorite word to describe my fashion sense, if I remember correctly, Rye."

"One would hope that I have a larger vocabulary now," he demurred. "And a little more sensitivity."

Rather than going on the defensive and retaliating, he seemed uncomfortable, even apologetic. Emily didn't know quite how to deal with his reaction. The approach of the maître d' came as a welcome interruption.

She recovered her poise on the way to their table, finding herself the object of polite scrutiny as acquaintances of Rye's and Lindsey's nodded or waved at them from half a dozen tables.

"Everyone's wondering who you are, Mom," Lindsey commented when they were seated. The maître d' had held her chair, and Rye had performed the courtesy for Emily. "By tomorrow the news will be all over town that Dad was out with his daughter and a glamorous redhead."

"I guess it would create quite a sensation if I lost my temper and threw a roll at him," Emily said.

Lindsey laughed, and a cautiously amused smile tugged at Rye's lips.

"Relax, Rye," Emily told him. "I'll behave like a perfect lady. I'll even take the chip off my shoulder for a few hours and give my shoulder a much-needed rest." As long as he followed suit and made a similar effort.

Rye nodded hesitantly, making the pact with her. Something about his hint of reluctance made Emily's heart beat faster with a sense of new danger. Without the antagonism and the shield of old grievances, they would have to raise some other barrier, she realized.

And he realized it, too.

"This is sounding like a boring evening," Lindsey proclaimed lightly. "I was all set for the usual fireworks."

Emily and Rye both smiled at her indulgently. Emily kept her fond maternal expression on her face as she deliberated on choosing a before-dinner drink, as she perused the menu, as she sipped her cocktail, as she sampled her first course. All it took to renew her mother's role was a glance over at Lindsey.

Whether he followed Emily's example or came up with his own line of defense, Rye played the proud father. He and Emily communicated strictly on the level of parents, not as man and woman, and carefully included their daughter in every conversation, steering clear of controversy. She cooperated beautifully, with only an occasional telltale blandness revealing that she wasn't oblivious.

Over coffee and dessert, she said, "We're going to have to do this kind of thing more often, since it's no pain or strain."

Involuntarily Emily and Rye exchanged a glance. It had been a strain.

"Every five or ten years, anyway," Emily said dryly. When Rye said nothing, she suggested, "Could we go ahead now and get down to the purpose of this evening? It's getting late, and Lindsey and I need to head back to the hinterland. You mentioned a 'business proposition,' Rye."

He pushed his dessert plate aside, frowning slightly. "Instead of making that long drive tonight in this bad weather, the sensible thing would be to spend the night."

"The driving conditions aren't dangerous," she stated firmly. "Are they, Lindsey?"

"No, the roads weren't all that slick," Lindsey backed her mother up. "And I've only had two glasses of wine. This cup of coffee should keep me awake."

She smiled a mellow smile, looking none too alert.

"I can drive," Emily said. "I'm not in the least bit sleepy."

"You had a cocktail in addition to two glasses of wine," Rye pointed out sternly. "That's too much alcohol in your system."

"You also had a cocktail," she reminded him. "Are you planning to take a taxi?"

"No, but I'm only driving a short distance. For heaven's sake, don't be so stubborn. Think of Lindsey's safety if you're not concerned about your own."

"It may have stopped raining altogether by now," Lindsey pointed out.

"Yes, and it may be sleeting," Rye said.

"Just where do you have in mind our spending the night?" Emily inquired. "Surely not at your house."

"That would be the logical place, since there are two spare bedrooms, but I'll gladly pay for a motel room."

"I have nightclothes and extra toothbrushes and things at the house. If it is sleeting outside, we could go by and pack an overnight bag, Mom," Lindsey said, working out the practical details. "Luckily we left all your faucets dripping."

Luckily, Emily thought with a kind of despairing irony. She sighed. "I guess it won't kill me to sleep under your roof, Rye. Just don't ever try to pull this same trick again. Now, was there any business proposition or was that just a pretext?"

"I hardly have any control over the weather, Emily," he snapped irritably. "If you think that I'm any happier than you are at having you sleep under my roof, then you're greatly mistaken. I'll pack an overnight bag and go to a damned motel myself."

"Dad, don't be silly," Lindsey chided.

"Yes, you're acting very childishly," Emily said critically. "And you still haven't answered my question."

Somehow his anger and annoyance seemed to put her in the driver's seat.

Lindsey spoke up quickly, "Mom's question was pertaining to that wholesale buyer for her pottery that you mentioned to her."

"Does he really exist?" Emily asked skeptically.

"He exists, all right," Rye assured her grimly. "But he would prefer to remain anonymous. All you have to do is make up a list of inventory with prices, and he'll write you out a check."

"He's someone you know personally?"

"About as well as I know anyone."

Emily raised her eyebrows at his curt tone. "What does he plan to do with my pottery?"

"He's a collector and would probably keep some pieces. The rest he would place with galleries on consignment. He is familiar with your work and thinks you price it too low."

"Well, tell him that I'm flattered. I've never had a more generous offer, but it's not possible for me to accept it at this time."

He nodded abruptly as though to say that it was her decision. Emily was a little nonplussed. She had expected some argument.

"You certainly aren't representing him very well," she remarked.

"I'm not representing anyone, Emily."

"You mean this *was* just a hoax!"

"No, just an exercise in futility, like any endeavor to deal with you to your advantage."

"Dad was your buyer, Mom," Lindsey said calmly.

"You?" Emily blurted. She stared at Rye, waiting for him to deny it. When he didn't, she shook her head in disbelief. "What a sneaky, underhanded, *selfish* scheme!"

Rye made an impatient sound as he shifted in his chair. "'Selfish'"? he repeated. "I'm acting selfishly by paying you premium price for your pottery and saving you from miles of tiring travel and expense?"

"I happen to enjoy doing the winter shows! I enjoy the travel and the interaction with my fellow artists. There's more than a profit motive, but I certainly don't expect you to understand that!''

"I understand perfectly that you're totally irresponsible and expect me to stand by while you take my daughter on the road with you in an old rattletrap of a motor home."

"If we're finished with our dessert, maybe we should finish this discussion at home," Lindsey suggested.

"It's already finished," Emily said.

"There's no having a 'discussion' with your mother," Rye said, signaling their waiter. "A discussion is carried on by rational humans with open minds."

"According to that definition, I doubt you've had many discussions in your lifetime," Emily told him. "No one could ever accuse you of having an open mind."

"Here comes our waiter with the bill," Lindsey announced. "Poor guy looks a little nervous."

Rye barely glanced at the bill, discreetly presented in an embossed leather folder. He paid with cash, taking bills out of his wallet and jamming them inside. Emily found his anger gratifying, just as she had earlier.

"Aren't you going to get a receipt?" she asked.

"Why would I want a receipt?" he countered with his own question.

"I was under the impression that businessmen were able to write off big restaurant tabs on their income tax."

"When they're entertaining clients, they can, but tonight wasn't business. Don't ask me what category it comes under," he added.

"I can think of several, but they have nothing to do with income tax," Emily said.

"Well, are we all set?" Lindsey inquired.

Outside, the rain had turned into sleet. Driving back to the farmhouse would definitely be hazardous, with bridges

freezing over. There was no question that staying overnight in the city was the wise thing to do.

Adaptable by nature, Emily accepted the inevitable.
What bothered her more than anything else about sleeping
in Rye's house was that she didn't find the prospect as re-
pugnant as she should have. She was tense and filled with
an odd sense of dread that was shamefully akin to exhila-
ration.

Her main concern was winding down and being able to
fall asleep. She was wide awake and had the keyed-up feeling that the night was young.

Rye followed behind Lindsey's car, but then didn't turn
into the driveway, instead driving past.

"You don't think that he's going to a motel after all?"
Emily asked, disgruntled rather than relieved that there
wouldn't be an awkward scene where all three of them
trooped into the house.

"No, he may have a date, but probably he's just killing
time and giving us a chance to go in by ourselves. He realizes that the situation is very uncomfortable for you."

"That's considerate of him," Emily said shortly.

"Dad is considerate like that," Lindsey replied, not
seeming to notice her mother's tone. "He really is a very
thoughtful person, even if he is a little overbearing at
times."

She took Emily straight upstairs to her bedroom, where
she got out nightgowns and robes for both of them, com-
menting, "We can just lounge around and watch my TV.
If you'd like something to drink, hot chocolate or a glass
of wine or whatever, I'll go down and get it."

It wouldn't be necessary for Emily to encounter Rye
again tonight, in other words.

"Am I sleeping in one of your twin beds?" Emily inquired.

"Unless you'd rather have a bedroom to yourself. You won't hurt my feelings," Lindsey insisted when Emily hesitated.

"To be honest, I probably would prefer it."

There was no explaining her faint stir of guilt. She certainly had nothing clandestine in mind. Rye wouldn't even know which bedroom she was occupying, and if he did, she wouldn't have to worry about locking her door to keep him out.

Lindsey was drowsy within an hour and apologetic about pooping out on her mother in the middle of the movie they had been watching on a cable channel. "Mom, why don't you sleep in here, and I'll sleep in one of the spare rooms," she suggested. "That way you can watch TV without worrying about disturbing me."

Emily allowed herself to be persuaded. She wasn't engrossed in the movie, but she wasn't at all sleepy, either.

Alone, Emily thought about Lindsey's earlier offer to get her a cup of hot chocolate or a glass of wine from downstairs. Was there a bottle of wine open in the refrigerator? she wondered. If not, Rye surely had a well-stocked liquor cabinet. A glass of sherry would be nice, and the alcohol might have a lulling effect.

Dared she ease downstairs and quietly help herself?

Even as she posed the question, Emily was getting up and tightening the sash of her borrowed robe. Her bare feet sank into the thick carpet. With her hand on the doorknob, she paused and listened to a muffled sound.

Was it footsteps?

Noiselessly she twisted the knob and opened the door. Rye stood just beyond the threshold, wearing a dark bathrobe, his arm raised and his hand poised to knock. He stared blankly at Emily while she gasped and stared back at him, both of them equally startled by the sight of the other.

"Rye! You scared me to death!" she murmured.

He lowered his arm. "Sorry," he muttered. "I came to tell Lindsey good night."

"She let me have her room since it has a TV set," Emily explained in an undertone. He was wearing pajama bottoms, but no top. His chest was bare beneath his robe. In the V she could see dark curly body hair. "She's asleep in one of your spare rooms."

He was making his own inspection of her. Lindsey had lent her a pretty pale pink nightgown made of thin, soft cotton with a matching robe of a slightly heavier material, trimmed with eyelet lace. The robe was lined, but didn't seem a very substantial covering under his dark gaze. Emily had to remind herself that she was modestly clothed.

"Do you need anything?" he asked, keeping his voice low, too. His quizzical expression asked a different question: *Where had she been going so stealthily?*

She answered the second question. "I was on my way downstairs to raid your liquor cabinet."

He raised his eyebrows slightly.

"No, I don't have a drinking problem," Emily informed him. "Although you may drive me to drink and turn me into an insomniac at the rate things are going."

"What would you like?" he asked.

"What would I like? I'd like things to return to the way they were, with you living your upscale life and allowing me to live my life without any advice or interference."

"I meant what would you like to drink?" he explained patiently. "I was going to offer to go and get it for you."

"Oh. I wouldn't want to put you to any trouble. Just tell me where your liquor supply is and go on to bed. I promise not to snoop around in your study, so don't lie awake worrying about that."

"It's no trouble, and I'm not ready to go to bed."

"Just forget it," Emily said. "I'm about out of the notion, anyway."

He shook his head. "You're so damned contrary. I could shake you—" Stepping over the threshold, he was reaching for her when he stopped himself. Slowly he lowered his hands.

Emily stood her ground, her heart pounding and her knees quaking. "Don't you *dare* try to manhandle me!"

"Don't push me, Emily," he warned softly. "My self-control has limits."

"That's a disillusioning thought," she jeered sarcastically. "Don't you threaten me, Rye. I'm not afraid of you."

"You get a real sense of power from frustrating the hell out of me, don't you?" he demanded.

"Yes, I do." Her admission was defiant, as well as honest.

"What is it that you're really after? Are you trying to provoke me into something physical? Because I just may oblige you."

Emily sputtered, "Why, of all the colossal *nerve!* This whole conversation sounds like a Grade Z movie! 'Oblige' me, indeed! If you so much as touched me, I'd scream my head off and wake up Lindsey."

"Then you'd better scream and save us both." He took another half step so that their bodies were almost touching.

"Rye, don't..." Emily whispered protestingly as he framed her face with his hands and tilted it upward.

"Your best bet is not to say a word," he murmured, caressing her bottom lip with his thumb. "Especially not my name in that tone of voice. That affects me the same way it always did, as though you were unzipping my pants."

An act Emily had performed boldly and with pleasure countless times. The memory of slipping her hand inside his pants and discovering him, hard and aroused, brought a sharp ache of desire.

"You were right on the mark, Rye," she confessed, squeezing her eyes tightly closed. Her voice was desperate as well as ashamed. "Without realizing it, I must have been trying to provoke you into accosting me sexually. It won't happen again. I promise."

"That doesn't solve the problem of tonight," he replied from close distance, his breath warm on her face. Then his mouth was on hers, the hungry pressure incredibly familiar. Emily gripped the lapels of his robe, hanging on and kissing him back, inhaling his scent, tasting his passion as they coupled tongues, deepening the kiss.

When one of his hands found its way inside her robe, cupped and squeezed a breast, his low groan of satisfaction mingled with Emily's softer moan of pleasure.

"Don't let me do this, Emily," he begged, pulling his hand free and wrapping both arms around her in a crushing embrace. "For God's sake, stop me before I make love to you."

"I'll try," she promised, her arms wound tightly around his neck. "Sex was our whole downfall. It was all we had going for us. If only we hadn't been so good together in bed..."

"And on the floor, on the grass, in the shower, in the backseat of a car—" Rye broke off with a groan.

"We tried out every possible position, all right. But afterward we were just as wrong for each other. You even resented me because you had gotten so turned on, as though I was some kind of vamp," Emily reminded accusingly.

"I remember."

His arms loosened slightly, and they pulled back enough for them to look at each other.

"Imagine how much you would resent me now," she said. It was difficult to sound convincing when their hips were still touching intimately and she could feel his tumescent body through the layers of clothing. "Imagine how disgusted you would be with yourself tomorrow morning."

"We probably wouldn't be nearly as good together."

"Probably not." Emily closed her eyes on a wave of weak pleasure as he slid his palms down her back and fondled her buttocks. Somehow she managed not to writhe against him in seductive invitation. Reaching back, she grasped his hands and held them while she eased apart from him reluctantly.

When he let his fingers go lax and put up no resistance, Emily felt ridiculously rejected. "No, I doubt either of us would be very satisfied," she said, releasing him and stepping back. "Sex between us would be empty, like it's bound to be when there's no affection."

Rye turned around, and for a moment she thought that he was leaving her without a further word. But he spoke over his shoulder.

"Who're you kidding, Emily? If either one of us believed it would be empty sex, I'd be inside you by now."

Chapter Eight

"Ten o'clock and not a peep out of Dad tonight, not even a phone call." Lindsey sipped her hot chocolate, her smooth brow furrowed. She was sitting cross-legged on the sofa, and Emily was curled in an armchair, both of them occupying their favorite places and wearing warm night-gowns and robes and heavy socks that they would be leaving behind when they left the following morning for Florida.

Emily lifted her own mug to her mouth as she gazed into the fireplace. The fire, her last fire of the winter, had burned down to molten red-orange.

"There's still time for him to call," she said, an edge of resentment in her voice. Rye was managing to spoil what should be a special evening for mother and daughter.

By all rights they should be focusing on their own senti-ments, sharing their feelings as one phase of the time they were spending together came to an end and another phase began. They should be reminiscing about the days just past, smiling over mishaps and setbacks, talking plans and anticipating tomorrow and the weeks ahead.

Instead Rye was dominating their thoughts, as much an intrusion as if he were there in person.

"No, I don't think he will call this late. You can relax, Mom." Lindsey cast her mother a sympathetic glance and went on musingly, "He has something up his sleeve, though. I'm convinced of it."

"What could he possibly do at this point? Have the state police put up roadblocks out on the highway?" Emily purposefully changed the subject away from Rye. "The motor home is all loaded and ready to go. Tomorrow we'll get an early start and have breakfast somewhere in Mississippi. Mabel Peabody's husband will be over later in the day to turn off the water and drain the pipes and the pump. The post office will hold my mail. The phone bill and the electrical bill have been prepaid, so that I won't be disconnected. Everything's all set."

Lindsey nodded in satisfied agreement, but she obviously was still pondering her father's behavior.

"It's just not like Dad not to tell me goodbye, and not to be at home so that I could call and tell him goodbye. He's been so low-key the past few weeks, ever since the weekend that we had dinner with him and you and I spent the night. Oh, he's kept up the pressure, but nothing like I was prepared for."

Emily had curled up tighter, a little shiver running through her at the mention of that awful weekend. She had tried hard to block it from her memory altogether.

"Maybe Rye just realized that he was fighting a losing battle," she suggested.

"I find that hard to believe. A leopard doesn't suddenly lose its spots. If Dad had thrown in the towel, he would have been up-front about it. No, he was just implementing Plan C, when Plan A and Plan B weren't successful.''

"Plan A being the attempt to entice you to make better use of your semester off and travel to exotic, far-off places.''

"Right. And Plan B the offer to buy up all your pottery and eliminate our selling trip. Now, what could Plan C be?''

"Whatever it is, it won't work, either,'' Emily promised her daughter stoutly. "Aside from kidnapping you and locking you up somewhere, I can't think of any way that Rye could put a hitch in our plans.''

"I can't, either. He wouldn't stoop to sabotaging the motor home. That wouldn't be Dad's style.''

From Lindsey's tone, she'd actually mulled over the possibility, to Emily's utter amazement. Desperate to salvage something of the evening, she said in a playful vein, "Let's put our thinking caps on. Rye has said all along that his main concern is your safety. What if he's contracted with a security company to keep you under guard at all times? Can't you just see us tooling down the interstate in the motor home with an armored car following behind us? I'm not serious!'' she protested when Lindsey sat up straighter, a look of startled concentration on her face.

"Maybe you should be serious, Mom,'' she said slowly. "You may just have hit upon Plan C. It passed through my mind that Dad could arrange for police escorts. But then he still wouldn't rest easy, knowing we were at campgrounds on our own, without a man's protection. He's too busy to take off himself for a couple of months and come with us—'' She broke off to regard her mother concernedly as Emily sloshed hot chocolate on her robe. "Did you burn yourself?''

"No, but it annoys me to be clumsy like that," Emily muttered.

"I didn't mean to give you heart failure by mentioning the possibility of Dad inviting himself along," Lindsey apologized. "There's not much danger that he'll show up in the morning with his suitcases all packed to travel in tandem with us and keep us safe. But it's not too far-fetched that he would hire a dependable type to do that very thing, a retired policeman or a private investigator."

"You're not joking," Emily protested, becoming vaguely horrified despite her skepticism.

"No, I'm not," her daughter admitted. "All the pieces of the puzzle fit. It's bothered me that Dad didn't insist on having his own mechanic check out the motor home when it became obvious that our trip was definitely on. But what if he were taking a whole different approach that ruled out any worries about a breakdown?"

"You told him where we took the motor home to be serviced. He might have talked with the mechanic there."

"He might have," Lindsey agreed, still on her own wavelength. "Something else that I've wondered about and haven't mentioned are some brochures on RVs that I saw on Dad's desk in his study a couple of weeks ago when I stopped at the house. I had gone into his study to leave him a note," she explained.

Emily's cheeks were hot at the reference to Rye's study, which automatically tripped off the disturbing memory of those nude drawings he had made of her.

"Why would he have brochures on RVs?" she asked. "And how does that fit?"

"At the time I figured that he might be shopping for a new motor home for us to use. I kept waiting for him to come driving up in one or have it delivered."

"A new motor home costs a small fortune. He probably discovered how expensive they were and ruled out the idea pretty quickly."

Lindsey looked doubtful. "Dad wouldn't have let the expense worry him. He likes to get his money's worth, but he isn't a miser. If our bodyguard theory is correct, he could have been looking into buying or leasing a motor home that the guy he hired could use. After all, the fellow would be staying in the same campgrounds where we stay. It would be necessary for him to travel in an RV or pull a camper, unless he planned to pitch a tent."

"Lindsey, you're getting carried away!" Emily scolded. "This sounds like a plot in a novel, for heaven's sake! Rye wouldn't go so far as to have a flunky tail us across several states."

"We'll know by noon tomorrow," Lindsey predicted. "I'm betting that we look out the side mirrors and see the same vehicle behind us, mile after mile."

"If we do, I'll pull over to the side of the highway, flag the fellow down and tell him to get lost," Emily declared.

Lindsey grinned at the picture her mother had brought to mind. "It's too bad that we don't have a souped-up engine in the motor home," she lamented. "Then we could have a wild chase scene, like in the movies."

"A ten-speed bicycle could probably keep up with us," Emily pointed out dryly.

"If only we'd zeroed in on Dad's plan earlier—if that is his plan—just think of the confusion we could have created. For example, we might have painted the motor home a different color, hidden it somewhere and sneaked away."

It was impossible to resist her daughter's lighthearted attitude. A smile tugged at Emily's lips as she accused indulgently, "You're going to be disappointed if this all turns out to be nothing more than a flight of fancy."

Lindsey's shrug was a sheepish admission. "You have to admit, Mom, that it could be a real kick. Plus there are certain practical advantages to having a big, strong male tagging along. If my roommate Sarah were here, she'd be seeing all the romantic possibilities. Depending on the guy's age, maybe one of us could have a mad affair with him. Wouldn't *that* serve Dad right!"

"I doubt that either of us will want to take retribution quite to that extreme," Emily objected. She was getting glimmers that Sarah wasn't the only romantic.

Tomorrow they would laugh at this whole silly notion. Emily was certain that Rye wouldn't do anything so ridiculous as hire a bodyguard-escort. And it gave her immense satisfaction that he hadn't succeeded in putting a damper on their eve of departure after all. If anything, he'd caused it to be more memorable, something mother and daughter would remember and laugh about years later.

Thanks to him, the trip to Florida would start out as that much more of an adventure.

Emily didn't set the alarm, relying on her inner clock to wake her about six-thirty the next morning. They would brew a pot of coffee, pour it into a thermos and have their first cup of coffee on the road. Lindsey had already appointed herself first driver with no argument from Emily.

The whole schedule was thrown off when Emily overslept, after a night of crazy cloak-and-dagger dreams. It was quarter of eight when Lindsey woke her with the news that the coffee maker wasn't working. Sure enough, it was totally unresponsive to jiggling the knob and plug. Emily even smacked it a time or two before she trudged out to the motor home and got the drip pot that she used when she camped somewhere without an electrical hookup.

"Damn you, Rye," she muttered under her breath. It was his fault that she hadn't had a good night's sleep and didn't feel up to coping. The fact that he even came to mind was highly irritating.

"Dad will be happy that the coffee maker has bit the dust," Lindsey remarked, revealing that her father was in her thoughts, too.

"Maybe I'll send him the bill for a new deluxe model, instead of waiting until I find another used one," Emily grumbled. She'd been planning to take the coffee maker, a lightweight portable model.

"He insisted that I get you a new one at the same time that I went out and bought you a new stove."

This was new information for Emily. "Buy. Spend. That's his formula for happiness," she mumbled.

"No, Dad likes things to function."

It was almost nine by the time they got off, after a dispute over whether to bring the coffee maker anyway on the chance that it might start working again. Lindsey had won, and the coffee maker was left behind.

Then the motor home hadn't seemed to want to start. Emily's nerves were thoroughly jangled by the time they were finally pulling out on the graveled country road after a bumpy ride along her driveway, which seemed to have developed more potholes during the night.

It didn't improve her humor in the least to have Lindsey think aloud in a wistful, worried tone, "I hope Dad isn't too upset with me." She had tried calling Rye again that morning and concluded that he must have gone out of town on business without telling her.

Emily managed to hold back a sharp, unsympathetic reply as she busied herself pouring coffee into two mugs and spilled hot liquid on herself.

The weather had been cold and dreary the past few weeks, with frequent rain and gray overcast skies. It seemed more an affront to Emily than a good omen when the sun broke through on the interstate and shone so brightly that she squinted at the unaccustomed glare.

The sun stayed out, and her spirits had lifted by the time she poured them each a refill, this time with a steady hand.

Just as she'd expected, in the light of day last night's brainstorming session about Rye's Plan C seemed a total figment of imagination. Neither of them made mention of it, although they both did keep a casual watch to determine that no vehicle was following them.

They had crossed over the state line and were in Mississippi before they even spotted another motor home, a large, new-looking RV pulled over on the shoulder of the interstate highway.

"Do you think those people are having mechanical problems?" Lindsey asked her mother, easing her foot on the accelerator. "Should we stop and see if they need help?"

"I don't see a sign of anyone," Emily replied. "A fancy, expensive motor home like that one probably has a telephone."

They drove past slowly, giving their fellow travelers ample time to appear and signal for help.

"Oh, look, it's pulling out on the highway." Lindsey's voice was relieved. "They might have been changing drivers. It was a Louisiana license plate," she remarked. "I wonder if they're headed to Florida, too."

"It often happens that another RV passes me on the highway and then I see it at a campground and meet the people," Emily said.

They drove along in comfortable silence, each glancing occasionally at the side mirrors. After a few minutes Lindsey spoke up, "There must be some problem that that motor home is going this slow and staying behind us."

"It looks brand-new. Possibly the owners aren't used to driving it," Emily suggested. "And the speed limit for RVs is fifty-five. We're almost up to that speed ourselves."

"I'm going to slow down to fifty," Lindsey told her mother.

The motor home stayed behind the same distance, but when Lindsey speeded up, it fell behind farther.

"They evidently are having a mechanical problem and are just taking it slow," Emily said.

Lindsey didn't say anything. At Waveland she took the exit from the interstate. She and Emily were in agreement that they would still take the slower but more scenic route along the Mississippi Gulf coast, with its miles of pristine sand beaches and gracious old summer mansions.

Crossing the bridge over Bay St. Louis, Emily gazed appreciatively at the view and caught sight of the RV in her side mirror. A quick look over at Lindsey confirmed that she knew it was back there, too.

"Biloxi probably has an RV service center," Emily commented.

Lindsey nodded. "I guess there's no reason a motor home couldn't be an office on wheels, with a computer and a fax machine," she said thoughtfully.

Emily blinked in befuddlement. "A motor home with a fax machine?"

"What you said earlier about a new RV coming equipped with a mobile telephone started me thinking," her daughter explained. "Mom, this is probably nothing more than just a half-baked idea, but that could be Dad following us in that RV."

"Rye?"

Emily stared at her and then stared at the side mirror, murmuring, "It can't possibly be him."

"Probably it isn't," Lindsey said soothingly. "Are you about ready to have some breakfast? I am."

"I was starting to feel hungry," Emily replied, "but you've about killed my appetite."

"It'll come back when I stop up ahead in Pass Christian and that RV goes on past us."

Minutes later she put on her right-hand turn signal and pulled over into a parking bay along a stretch of deserted beach. Emily opened her door and jumped down to the ground to stretch.

Lindsey didn't budge. "He has on his turn signal," she reported. The plural *they* had changed to *he*. "Mom, I think we may be having company for breakfast."

Emily froze in position, her arms up over her head. "You don't seriously mean..." The words died in her throat at the crunch of tires. Lowering her arms, she turned in slow motion, some part of her mind noting the smooth, powerful hum of the RV engine before it was switched off.

The door on the driver's side opened, and Rye stepped around into view as Lindsey was announcing with a jubilant note, "It's Dad, all right, big as life!"

Emily rested her hands on her hips in a belligerent stance and walked toward him, emotions churning inside her.

"Of all the *nerve,* Rye Keeler! You can just climb back behind the wheel of that...that—" Words failed her. "And head back to Baton Rouge!"

"Dad, you stinker!" Lindsey had gotten out and come to greet him. She kissed him on the cheek. Then she stepped back, demanding, "How long have you been plotting this?"

He shrugged. "I decided that it was about time for me to take a vacation."

"Well, don't let us keep you," Emily spoke up caustically. "I'm sure you have an itinerary all planned, and you won't enjoy your trip if you don't stick to your schedule."

"My itinerary is the same as yours," he replied calmly. "I plan to tag along with you and Lindsey. By the way, why were you so late getting on the road?" The question was directed at his daughter, not Emily. "I was about to call the state police when you finally came along."

"Mom and I overslept. The coffee maker conked out, and that caused another delay. We had to boil water and make coffee in a drip pot. Then we had a debate over whether to bring the coffee maker. The motor home got into the act and was cranky about starting," Lindsey explained cheerfully.

"I hope you won the debate and left that damned coffee maker in the trash can," Rye said. "I have a good coffee maker. We can use it."

"*We* are not using your coffee maker!" Emily informed him furiously. "*We* are not on this trip together!"

He raised his hand, palm out, as though to calm her down. "Relax, Emily. Let me rephrase that. I have a good coffee maker in my motor home that is available, should you and Lindsey want to make use of it. There's also an ice maker. If you need ice, you can help yourself. The bathroom has a full-size shower with plenty of hot water."

"All the comforts of home," she said sourly. "Depending, of course, on whose home we're talking about."

"Would you like to see inside it?" he asked, including both her and Lindsey in a gesture of invitation.

"No, I would not," Emily refused.

"Mom and I skipped breakfast. We stopped to have something to eat," Lindsey explained, her tone casually informative.

Rye glanced at his watch. "I ate breakfast, but it was early. I guess I'll have a bite of lunch myself."

"What are you having? Lobster salad? Smoked salmon?" Emily inquired sarcastically. "Personally I hope you choke on it, whatever it is." With those churlish words, she wheeled around and marched to the side door of her motor home, which looked old-fashioned and shabby compared to his, despite the bright camouflage of yellow paint.

Inside she jerked the curtains closed on the sight of father and daughter in conference and plopped down on the dinette seat, fighting tears of helplessness and outrage. Hadn't Rye done enough to her? Was there no end to it? Why did he have to seem so invincible? Emily wished that for once she could have the upper hand and come out the winner, but she was hampered, as always, by consideration for Lindsey's feelings.

It was the same old story.

But this chapter defied belief. Emily would never have credited Rye with being so devious. Why all the secrecy? As upset as she was, she was also nonplussed that he was acting out of character. It would have been more his style to announce his intentions and camp in her driveway in his luxurious motor home.

Emily was afraid that once her temper cooled, she was going to be intrigued. A part of her couldn't fail to appreciate the element of melodrama. Parting the curtain a tiny crack, she peered out.

Rye and Lindsey had finished their conversation evidently, and he was standing there, looking resigned and calmly resolute, but not especially pleased with himself. In fact, from his expression he was feeling excluded.

Why did he have to be so attractive? Emily asked herself, exasperated by her pang of empathy. What made standing up to him such an ordeal was that she was at war with herself, too, trying to curb her female response to his masculine good looks. Of all the men she'd ever met, why did he have to appeal to her more than any other?

Hearing the door of the motor home opening, Emily hastily dropped her hand and averted her head.

Anxiety was written all over her daughter's expressive features, so like her father's. She came over and sat opposite Emily, then, without any ado, matter-of-factly filled Emily in.

"Dad isn't bluffing, Mom. He means to stay right with us the whole trip. He'll keep in touch with the managers of his frame shops, but otherwise he's on vacation. He's been doing some painting the last few weeks and plans to do more on this trip. It seems that there are outdoor market shows that are held in conjunction with some of the juried art-and-crafts shows that you're entered in. He was able to get into a couple of those shows at the last minute, and will sell his paintings."

With Emily's permission, Lindsey had given Rye the list of shows in which Emily was an exhibitor.

"I've never heard anything so ridiculous!" Emily exclaimed, trying to hide how pleased she was at the news that he had started painting again. "Why would he want to sell his paintings? As though he needed the income!"

"Maybe he wants to find out if being an artist can be profitable." Lindsey shrugged to indicate that she was only conjecturing.

"Naturally he would want to explore the financial angle before he made any rash decisions to devote himself to painting," Emily said in a scathing tone that was pure self-defense.

Lindsey sighed. "I've really made a mess of things for you this winter, haven't I, Mom? Honestly I never dreamed that I would be setting off the sequence of events that have happened like a domino effect.''

''None of it is your fault, darling.'' Emily reached over and patted her cheek. ''You got right in the middle, didn't you?''

Her daughter went on ruefully, ''The whole situation is so ironic. This trip would have been like a dream come true once upon a time, even with you and Dad traveling in separate motor homes. Now I realize that it will be a nightmare for you. All you have to do is say the word, and I'll go back to Baton Rouge with Dad. Oh, sure, I'll be disappointed. I won't lie. But I'll understand, and it won't be the end of the world for me.''

Emily had a fleeting image of herself in the driver's seat of her motor home, driving away alone while Rye and Lindsey drove off in the opposite direction, back toward Louisiana. Loneliness clutched at her heart.

''No, indeed!'' she declared vehemently. ''If Rye wants to tag along, let him. As long as he keeps his distance, I'll just ignore him.''

''And I'll keep strictly out of it,'' Lindsey promised with a buoyant note. She wasn't hiding how happy she was to have her offer refused. ''I can't choose sides.''

''Of course not. You have to be impartial.''

Lindsey's grin was conspiratorial. ''As impartial as I can be, being female. Don't pull your punches on my account, Mom. Dad can handle himself. As long as you two don't come to blows, I'd rather have my parents fighting with each other than holding back and not clearing the air. It was never healthy for either of you that you didn't communicate—or healthy for me,'' she added, gently candid.

''Something tells me that the three of us will be extremely healthy by the time this is over,'' Emily replied with grim humor.

Before she got up to start breakfast preparations, she opened the curtains across the rear window as wide as they would go. Let Rye see them seated there, having their meal, if he cared to look.

"Dad's having tuna salad sandwiches," Lindsey volunteered as she got up, too. "He had them made up by a deli that makes great sandwiches, and he ordered enough for you and me."

Emily cast a baleful glance at Rye's motor home. "He knows that you love tuna salad," she said disgustedly.

"So do you," Lindsey reminded. "He said for me to come over and get them for our lunch if we wanted them. Otherwise they'll go to waste."

Emily couldn't abide wasting good food. "Then go and get them," she bade her daughter, who needed no urging.

The sandwiches were delicious. Try as she might, Emily couldn't keep from enjoying hers. After they'd eaten, it was a temptation to go walking on the beach, one she probably wouldn't have resisted, despite being behind schedule, if there hadn't been the likelihood of Rye's joining them.

She needed to get her hackles up again, for self-protection, and having to forgo the pleasure of a walk because of him did the trick. Emily nursed resentment as she took her turn driving, glancing often into the mirror and seeing Rye's motor home following along.

The day wasn't the kind that provided a good climate for ill will, though. The sun shone brightly, making the gulf water sparkle. Riding on the ocean side, Lindsey rolled down her window to let the fresh, tangy sea air into the cab. She was more talkative than usual, not seeming to have a care in the world.

Emily just didn't have the heart to be a wet blanket. She let her spirits rise to match her daughter's. Life was too good at moments like these for negative emotions.

A little nagging voice said that she was adjusting much too easily to an appalling state of affairs, but another voice answered that she had always been both volatile and resilient.

Past Ocean Springs, where the view of the open water was lost, she got back on Interstate 10. At Pensacola they would drop down to the coast again and take Highway 98, slower, but not so monotonous as interstate driving.

Rye dropped back farther, putting more distance between them, she noted. And when she stopped for gas an hour or so later, he pulled around to an island on the opposite side of the big station, even though there was room on the same side.

Emily couldn't explain why she was so annoyed that she wouldn't have to avoid looking his way. While she was manning the gas pump, Lindsey walked around to talk to him and came back in a couple of minutes with a message.

"Dad's reserved two spots at a campground between Fort Walton Beach and Panama City. He figures that we'll be ready to stop for the night by then. He wants to know if that's okay with you. If not, he'll cancel and find something either closer or farther along, whatever you say."

Rye was obviously handling Emily with kid gloves. She was irked over having nothing to be irked about.

"I guess it will be okay," she said. "Tell him to get campsites as far apart as possible."

At the campground, sure enough, he was located several campsites away. Lindsey went over to visit him, promising that she'd return shortly and make her portion of dinner, chili beans with frankfurters. Emily got out salad makings and started tearing off pieces of lettuce with a vengeance. She knew darned well that her daughter would have liked to invite Rye to eat with them.

She had been prepared to refuse, prepared also to turn down any invitation from him.

Lindsey returned in about fifteen minutes, full of compliments about the interior of Rye's RV. From the way she went into detail describing it, she seemed to be assuming that Emily wouldn't ever see it herself. The assumption was certainly a good one. Emily had no intention of setting foot inside the RV.

"It sounds very plush," she commented sourly. Trust Rye to make her home on wheels seem barely adequate and modest in comparison to his up-to-the-minute model.

"It is, but not homey like this one," Lindsey replied. "Dad's grilling himself a steak for dinner. He offered to throw a couple on for us in exchange for a helping of salad. I told him that he could have the salad, either way. I hope you don't mind."

Here was the maneuver Emily had been expecting.

"Why don't you take over a salad for both of you and have dinner with your father?" she suggested. "I'm not terribly hungry, and I'll fend for myself. You've kept me company all day."

"Nope." Lindsey didn't even stop to consider. "I came on this trip to be with you, not with Dad. You and I will be eating our meals together, just as we planned." She got out a plastic container and filled it from the salad bowl.

"But, Lindsey, you'll have to have some of your meals with him. You wouldn't feel right, knowing that he was eating by himself three meals a day."

Emily's daughter shrugged off the protest. "I'll just run this over."

She didn't come back immediately. Emily was on the verge of going over to find out what the delay was all about when Lindsey appeared, bearing a platter with two thick, succulent-looking cooked rib-eyes and two steaming baked potatoes.

"Dad already had them on the grill," Lindsey explained. "I did the potatoes in his microwave while I was waiting."

Emily's mouth had started to water. "At this rate, I won't need to buy groceries," she said.

They feasted on the steak dinner. Emily thought several times about Rye eating his meal by himself and tried to feel spiteful. After all, she'd eaten many meals alone through the years when he was sitting down to the table with their little girl.

But spitefulness wasn't a part of her personality, and she ended up feeling empathy for him. If Lindsey held out, Emily would have no choice but to have him join them occasionally, for dinner at least.

"Dad was going to make a pot of decaf. I don't care for any, but I'll go over and get you some in the thermos," Lindsey offered as they sat back.

"A cup of coffee would hit the spot," Emily said. "But it wouldn't kill me, I suppose, to go over to Rye's RV for a half hour."

Lindsey didn't blink an eye at that huge concession. "You can take his platter back and compliment the chef," she suggested lightly.

"I meant, of course, that I'd go with you, not by myself," Emily hastily informed her.

"If you and Dad need a buffer, sure, I'll go. But otherwise I'll stay and wash these few dishes and relax with a magazine."

Emily's heart had started beating fast. "No, we don't need a 'buffer,'" she replied. "I just assumed that you'd want to go over and visit him yourself." How could you tell your eighteen-year-old daughter that her divorced parents needed a chaperone?

"No offense, Mom, but I could use a half hour of my own company. I've visited with Dad a couple of times today."

Short of insisting, Emily could either do an about-face and decide against going over for coffee or she could venture over alone.

In truth, her yen for a fragrant, steaming hot cup of coffee had faded, but to back out would be cowardly.

And anticlimactic.

The last thing Rye would be expecting was her to pop over and pay him a call tonight. The thought of taking him completely by surprise appealed to Emily's impulsive instincts.

Chapter Nine

Rye had eaten only half of his steak. He wrapped the rest of it in plastic, not knowing what else to do with it, and put it in the refrigerator. Unaccustomed to washing dishes, he felt awkward standing at the sink, running water and squirting dish detergent.

Before this trip was over, he'd be used to being his own cleaning woman, he reflected as he scrubbed his plate squeaky clean. It had been years since he'd changed the sheets on his bed or done his own laundry. His experience with most household chores, like vacuuming and mopping floors, was minimal.

Growing up as a foster child, he'd done lots of menial jobs; mowed lawns, raked leaves, cleaned out garages and sheds, fed farm animals—all of it "men's work," as opposed to "women's work." The roles of male and female had been clearly defined in his mind. The woman of the house bore the major domestic responsibility. She shopped for groceries, cooked, cleaned, did laundry, took care of children. It fell to the man of the house to keep the family car running, to repair a leaky faucet, to be in charge of home maintenance, in other words. His main role, though, was that of provider and head of the family. He brought in a paycheck, asserted his authority and had the final word.

Rye realized with hindsight that he had been rigid and chauvinistic in his thinking when he met Emily. During their brief marriage, he'd considered himself as *helping* her when he picked up groceries at the supermarket or did laundry, even when he changed Lindsey's diaper or bathed her.

Emily hadn't taken any feminist stand. She'd gone along, cheerfully at first, never balking at assuming her duties, but never performing them with any proficiency, as far as Rye was concerned. Had he been hypercritical?

He conjured up a view of their efficiency apartment at its tidiest. A basket of unfolded laundry sat on the floor. Emily had never folded clothes at the Laundromat. She rarely got around to folding them once she'd brought them home, but fished out garments for the two of them to wear, and after Lindsey was born, tiny garments to put on Lindsey. The clothes were badly wrinkled, needless to say.

Rye let his mind's eye rove on around the apartment. There was clutter on all the surfaces of the tables and the dresser and chest of drawers, but not haphazard clutter. Emily had obviously "straightened up," to use her term. The bed was made up, the bedspread hanging just slightly askew with a bit of sheet showing.

It wouldn't do to linger over the inspection of the bed. Rye came back to the present to discover that he'd finished washing up the few dishes, including Emily's plastic bowl, which had contained the salad. He let the water out of the sink, rinsed it and dried his hands while he picked up his train of thought.

Emily had tried in her own way. Maybe he had been a demanding jerk. But her failings as a mother had been the real cause of their breakup, he reminded himself. He hadn't blown those out of proportion.

Or had he?

Before Rye could make another trip back in memory to try to answer that question honestly, someone rapped smartly on the door of his RV. It would be Lindsey, bringing back the platter.

"Just a minute," he called, and went with a quick step to open the door. He was more than a little glad for the interruption. After a whole day of his own company, he would have welcomed a stranger in for some conversation. If necessary, he would play on his daughter's sympathy to get her to stay awhile.

"I was hoping you'd take pity on me," he said, pushing the door outward gently in case she was standing in the way.

"Actually I came for selfish reasons," Emily's voice answered. "Lindsey said that you were serving coffee to freeloaders."

"Emily." Rye spoke her name in surprise and invited, "Do come in."

"Also I'm returning your platter," she said as she climbed the aluminum steps. Inside she handed the platter to him. "Thank you for the steaks. They were superb. Lindsey and I pigged out."

"I'm glad you enjoyed them." Rye hesitated before reaching to close the door. "Is Lindsey coming, too?"

"No, just me." She took several steps inside, looking around with open interest. "Am I interrupting you?"

"Not at all," Rye assured, trying to adjust to her presence, to the fact that she was paying a visit by herself. "Please. Have a seat."

She strolled over into the kitchen area instead. Her admiring glance took in the hallway that led to his capacious cabin at the rear. "Very nice," she declared, sounding sincere.

Rye had followed her. He got cups and saucers out of an upper cabinet and poured the coffee. She came over close enough to take hers from him and then led the way past the dinette into the living-room area behind the open cab.

They sat at opposite ends of the full-length sofa, which made up into a queen-size bed. She sipped her coffee, murmuring, "Mmm. This tastes good."

He tasted his and agreed. His fervent note seemed to heighten the tension. She took in a breath, lifting her breasts. "What a day," she pronounced, stroking the textured upholstery of the sofa with her free hand.

Rye's senses were so acute that he imagined that he could hear the faint abrasive sound. His whole body responded to the stroking motion.

"I could play some music," he suggested, realizing that it was dead quiet in the RV. He'd had the stereo on earlier and turned it off, the music seeming to accentuate his solitude.

"Yes, why don't you?" Emily's reply came with too much alacrity. Avoiding meeting his eyes, she sipped her coffee.

It occurred to Rye as he got up that music might not be such a great idea. The radio stations that came in clear were slanted toward teenage listeners with a lot of disc jockey talk. His selection of cassette tapes and CDs was mainly recording artists from the sixties and seventies, the same music that had played in the background when the two of them were together.

A Beatles classic was in place on the CD player. Rye started to replace it with a Beethoven symphony, which wouldn't have any associations. Instead he turned the player on.

"What wonderful sound!" Emily exclaimed after a moment. Her voice had an envious note. When Rye looked at her questioningly, she said, "If I do well in Florida, I'm planning to get a CD player. I've wanted one since they came out on the market. Now, of course, they've gotten much less expensive."

"I couldn't wait until they came down in price. I bought one when they first were available," Rye admitted. He would gladly have bought one for her, too.

"Lindsey mentioned it at the time."

"When I heard the sound quality, I couldn't resist."

"Why should you have? You've worked hard and made a lot of money. You may as well buy whatever you want."

Her tone didn't convey even grudging commendation. Stung in spite of himself, Rye sat down again, picked up his cup and took a big swallow of coffee.

"I have worked hard," he said when he trusted himself to speak. "And it feels good to have buying power, but that's not my only satisfaction in my career. There are others, like the knowledge that I'm contributing to the economy, providing employment and training and job benefits, promoting artists in my own way, and making it affordable for middle-income people, as well as the wealthy, to hang artwork in their homes. In the process of turning a profit, I affect a lot of lives in a positive way, like any responsible businessman does." Rye downed the rest of his coffee.

"Lindsey said that you had started painting again," she said.

He stared at her a long second, frustrated that she intended to make no reply to his long speech. "Were you even listening to me just now?" he demanded.

She sipped her coffee, testing his patience almost beyond its limits. "I heard every word. What exactly do you want me to say?"

"Something to the effect that maybe I have made something worthwhile of myself. But you'd never be convinced of that, no matter what other career I'd gone into, would you? Not even if I'd become a doctor or a scientist who did medical research. I couldn't be anything other than an artist to be a success in your eyes."

"My opinion isn't important, anyway," she pointed out, not making any denial. "You have plenty of admiration from other sources. Do I have to be a member of your fan club?"

"It wouldn't bother you if I thought you'd wasted your time and talent?"

"I haven't."

"I agree with you."

She searched his face, suddenly vulnerable. "You do, really?"

"Really."

"I haven't been very successful, monetarily speaking."

"No, but that wasn't a case of wasting talent." His wry tone took any bite out of the remark. "You don't have a business head. Unless you've changed, you're not the best manager, either. I learned pretty quickly not to turn my paycheck over to you."

"Or leave the checkbook in my possession," she reminded without any bitterness. "I have gotten better, but I still don't find it easy to stick to a budget."

"Do you have a budget?"

She smiled. "I use the word loosely."

Rye smiled back at her, and the attraction flared up so strongly that it burned away the friendly amusement.

"More coffee?" he asked, clearing his throat.

She drew in a breath, looking down at her cup. "I'd better not. I should be getting back."

"Don't go yet. Stay awhile and talk to me," Rye urged.

"Just a few more minutes, then." She handed him her cup. "If I stay too long, Lindsey may think we've knocked each other out cold."

Rye sat closer to her on his return from the kitchen. She had kicked off her shoes and curled sideways.

"The last thing I would have expected was for you and me to be sitting here tonight, drinking coffee and listening to the Beatles," he remarked. "I was prepared for a lot more fireworks from you."

"If I had raised enough sand, would you have turned around and gone back to Baton Rouge?"

"No."

She shrugged. "Then why waste the effort? What it all comes down to is that I have no choice except to make the best of things. You're Lindsey's father, and she loves you. Although she hasn't said as much, I can tell that she's pleased as punch at the idea of your coming along with us."

Rye wasn't satisfied with that answer. "There's more to it than that, isn't there? Would you have adjusted as fast if Lindsey hadn't told you that I had brought my painting paraphernalia along? I think not. For the sake of art, you're willing to tolerate my presence."

Her defensive expression told him that he'd hit on the mark.

"Was that whole business about starting to paint again true or not?" she demanded.

"It's true," he said. "I would offer to show you my efforts, but they're back in my bedroom."

"Can't you bring them out here?"

He stalled. "You'll be able to see them better in natural light."

"You haven't let anyone see them yet," she guessed. "Lindsey would have mentioned it if you'd shown them to her."

"I'm sure you can remember that vulnerable, exposed feeling."

"*Remember* it? I still experience it, every time I exhibit my pottery." She swung her feet down and scooted to the edge of the sofa. "How do you think I felt unloading my kiln with you standing there? If you're planning to try to sell your paintings in Florida, you can't be thin-skinned." She stood up, but not to leave. She would accompany him back to his bedroom, if necessary.

Rye got up, too. "Strangers' comments won't bother me a great deal," he said.

"I won't make any comments if you prefer."

"You won't have to," he replied.

"Are you afraid that I'll think the paintings are good or that I'll think they're just mediocre?" she asked. "I know ahead of time that they aren't awful."

"I don't know exactly what I'm afraid of except that what you think seems so damned important."

Her blue eyes widened at his sober admission. She looked so frightened that Rye wanted to put his arms around her and reassure her. But once he did, he knew that he would do more than comfort.

"Part of me hopes that I'm disappointed and your paintings show little evidence of talent," she confessed.

"Part of me hopes the same thing."

Rye reached for her cup and saucer, and she handed them to him.

The tension was thick as he deposited both cups and saucers on a counter in the kitchen and led the way. In the corridor to his bedroom, the door to the bathroom on their right was open, affording a glimpse inside. On the left was storage behind paneled doors.

The rear bedroom compartment extended the full width of the motor home and had a queen-size bed and built-in chests and dresser. Rye gestured for Emily to sit on the bed, and she perched on the edge while he slid open a closet door.

"You must have paid a fortune for this motor home," she remarked. "It's the most luxurious one that I've ever been inside."

He told her the price, giving her a rounded figure on the low side.

"That much?" she gasped, horrified. "You have done well for yourself financially, Rye," she said. "I have to give you credit."

This time there was grudging admiration. Rye was appalled at how much it meant to him.

"It was very important to me that Lindsey would grow up with the benefits of being from a well-to-do background," he stated brusquely. "I wanted her to be proud that I was her father and not a 'nobody.' "

"Lindsey could have been proud of a father who was an artist," she argued. "You wouldn't have been a 'nobody,' except in your own eyes, just because you didn't make the pages of *Money* magazine."

Rye welcomed the anger he felt flare. "Okay, so I was ambitious. If I'd stayed single and hadn't had a wife and child to care for, I still wouldn't have been happy in any profession that required me to scrimp and live the way you have. I had my stomach full of being a have-not, growing up as an orphan bastard.''

"You weren't a bastard!'' Emily protested. "Your parents just weren't legally married. I think this is all a lot of after-the-facts rationalizing. What I don't understand is why you channeled your interest into art in the first place. You were smart enough, even in high school, to know that most artists don't have a lot of prestige or become millionaires.''

Rye squatted down in front of the open closet, but didn't reach inside. He rested his arms on his thighs, letting his hands dangle between his legs as he answered unemotionally.

"If I'd had a better self-concept and been a more well-rounded high school kid, I doubt that I would have gone in the direction that I did. The art department was a place where anybody could gain acceptance. You didn't have to be outgoing or popular or well dressed. I was badly in need of some strokes to my ego, and I got them as an art student.''

"You got them because you were talented,'' Emily put in. Her tone was a mixture of accusation and sympathy.

He shrugged. "Even as a child, I could draw well. I won poster contests in grade school. But I obviously had other latent talents and abilities that I didn't develop because of lack of confidence. I could probably have enjoyed being on the debate team in high school and participating in student government.''

Emily made an impatient gesture. "I could probably have enjoyed being homecoming queen if I'd been prettier and been sent to modeling school, like Rosemary Quinton was.''

Rye couldn't help but smile at the notion of her as homecoming queen or modeling-school attender. She glared at him and then reluctantly smiled back.

He could feel the magnetic pull between them. The desire to give in to it was so powerful that he had to tense every muscle in his body. The strain caused an ache in his chest and in his groin.

"You'd better show me those paintings, so I can go," she murmured nervously.

Rye breathed in audibly. "Yes." He reached and got three framed paintings from those stacked in a cardboard box. "I used a quarter page," he explained unnecessarily, since she could judge the size for herself. He handed one to her. "That's Molly, my housekeeper. She's the most dour woman I've ever met. I tried to capture that quality with as little photographic realism as possible. I matted and framed these myself," he added irrelevantly.

Emily gazed long and hard and said nothing. Then she handed it back to him in exchange for another. Rye launched into another uneasy narrative. "This is the door of an old building in downtown Baton Rouge. The word *portal* has always come to mind, and it always seems to be in shadow no matter what the time of day. I had photographs of it that I'd taken and I painted the door from them."

She sighed and returned it to him.

"Seen enough?" he asked.

"Yes," she said, keeping her hand extended.

"That bad?"

"They're wonderful."

"They're not 'wonderful,'" he objected, giving her the third painting. Her pronouncement was as disturbing as it was deeply pleasing. "Technically they leave a lot to be desired. That one, of course, you recognize."

"My screen door." She gazed in frowning absorption.

"I was relying on memory and may have taken artist's license," he said, not able to read her reaction.

"Your memory is excellent. I'm just noticing how big those cracks are at the top and the bottom," she replied musingly. "No wonder the mosquitoes come in, in droves."

Rye was swamped by tenderness mixed with bafflement and amusement, an old, familiar blend of emotions, more potent than he remembered because of the yearning that welled up, too strong to curb. He rose to a crouch and moved swiftly over to sit beside her on the bed.

"How could you not have seen those cracks?" he demanded, his husky voice a dead giveaway.

"I saw them, but I didn't see them," she stammered. "You know what I mean. Or, no, you probably don't." Her fingers went lax, and she let him take the painting from her hands. "Is that all of them?" The question came out almost a whisper.

He leaned and put the painting on the carpeted floor, propping it at a safe angle against the nearest piece of built-in furniture. "No, there are six altogether."

"Six in three weeks! You have been busy."

"Four weeks," he corrected her, touching her hair. It formed a vibrant halo around her face, a darker red than in the sunlight, but still shot with gold. "I got out my sketch pad on Monday night after I was at your farmhouse. The next day I came home at noon and got out my easel and paints and brushes. It was a kind of natural progression. Making those sketches that you saw stirred up the urge to paint again."

She bit into her bottom lip, mulling over what he'd told her. Watching, Rye felt a jolt all the way to his toes, as though her teeth had nipped his mouth.

"You haven't painted from those sketches of me?" she asked.

"No, I haven't felt up to the challenge. And I didn't need the frustration." He brought his thumb to her mouth and massaged the spot she had punished with her teeth.

"We really shouldn't do this. We'll both be sorry." She spoke barely above a whisper, her breath warm on his hand.

Rye made the transition with no trouble. "I don't have enough willpower left," he explained, sliding his palm along her cheek and tilting her face up. "I've used it all up staying away from you all these years."

She whispered his name as he brought his mouth to hers, allowing her ample time to pull back or turn her head aside, but she moved to meet him instead. Her arms went around his neck as Rye's arms closed around her.

He had wanted to taste her lips, savor the texture and shape, but passion welled up, consuming more-delicate needs. He kissed her hard and hungrily, and she returned his bruising pressure, making little urgent sounds in her throat. Her mouth opened for his tongue, and the kiss became deep and moist and ravenous.

There was no ending it. Rye's breathing became labored, and his heart pounded in his chest. He pressed her backward on the bed without taking his lips from hers, thrust his hand up under her loose cotton pullover sweater and found her bare breast.

Once again part of him wanted to take a gentle possession with strokes and caresses, but his sharp-edged pleasure was too great for gentleness. He gathered up the warm, satiny fullness and squeezed and kneaded. She arched her back and moaned with her own pleasure. Her palms stroked his shoulders, and her fingers dug into his back, clearly impatient with the cloth separating her from his body.

Suddenly the desire to be naked with her gained precedence over all the other clamoring desires that had overwhelmed wisdom and reason. Rye ended the kiss with difficulty. His lips and tongue didn't want to part with hers. His hand didn't want to release her breast and withdraw. It was only the thought of taking off her clothes that made him relinquish his treasure with reluctance.

Rising up, he jerked his heavy cotton pullover shirt free of his jeans and stripped it off. His hands moved immediately to unsnap his jeans, but then stopped as he saw that Emily was ridding herself of her clothes just as frantically. She had scooted into the middle of his bed and was on her haunches, tugging her sweater up.

While he watched, she stripped it off with a fluent, quintessentially feminine motion, her back arched, her breasts lifted and thrust forward. The artist in Rye was as stimulated by the sight of her as the man in him was aroused. As much as he wanted to kiss and caress every lush curve, taste the pink aureoles of her breasts, suck and bite her hard, erect nipples, he also wished that he had the talent to paint her and capture somehow all the sexual promise in this moment.

She paused in the act of unsnapping her jeans, realizing that he was gazing at her with admiration and lust. Her split-second moment of shyness was quickly gone as she looked at his body, bared to the waist. Her expression was rapt, a blend of her own female lust and artist's pleasure in the male human form.

"Take off your jeans," she ordered him in her husky, sexy voice.

Rye stood and obeyed. He pulled down his snug briefs with the jeans while she unzipped her jeans and tugged them down past her hips, all her attention for him. Still on her knees, she presented another alluring sight as she paused, her own undressing forgotten, to look with una-bashed feminine interest and womanly vanity at his freed tumescence.

She reached to touch him intimately as, naked, he joined her on the bed, facing her, on his haunches, too. Rye had meant to finish taking off her clothes. At most he would allow himself to comb his fingers through her thatch of auburn hair between her thighs, to caress her rounded but-tocks, to slide ever so briefly between her legs to discover whether she was hot and wet for him.

But restraint was lost as she stroked him and captured him as familiarly as if they had made love only yesterday. He reached and claimed her just as familiarly, fitting her mound into his palm, squeezing hard. She writhed and closed her legs, trapping his hand, murmuring aloud words of frank need that excited him as much as her response. Her hand sheathed him less gently in an erotic pantomime of the lovemaking she wanted.

Rye lost all control, and Emily, completely without in-hibition, fed his frenzy to bury himself inside her. Kicking and tugging, she helped him get her legs free of her cloth-ing. Then she pulled him down to her, urging him all the while in her husky, sexy cadences to hurry.

As he plunged deep, she wrapped her legs around him, arching and welcoming the full impact of his entry. There was a split second of completion before urgency rose to new heights.

Time and place had no relevance. Nothing on earth mattered except being coupled with her, kissing her, mat-ing his tongue with hers, tangling his fingers in her glo-rious hair that seemed charged with electricity like the rest of her, shocking him and inflaming his desire.

Existence was sensation and emotion intermingled. There was no separating the wild, driving pleasure from a fierce possessiveness, from a satisfaction that she was with him for the journey and he would take her all the way.

Speech was uncensored. He had no more control over what he said than he had over their abandoned lovemaking. His vocal cords, like hers, were an instrument for uttering sounds of primitive enjoyment, sounds of desperate need, but also for forming words of love that they had spoken to each before, in years past.

Rye hadn't spoken those words to anyone since and was exultantly certain that she hadn't, either.

Her climax triggered his own, and they shared ecstasy in a realm where separate identity was shattered and they were melded into one.

He lay slumped on top of her, awash in satisfaction, when she murmured with vague alarm, "Oh, my God!"

Rye made an enormous effort and propped himself on his elbows, looking down at her. "What's the matter?" he asked, his tenderness at war with his instinct to put up a guard.

She gazed up at him, stricken and defensive. "Neither of us gave a single thought to birth control. That's what's the matter," she blurted out. "I'm not on the Pill, and I didn't come over here expecting to have sexual intercourse."

Rye's curse was directed at himself. "There isn't anything you can do after the fact?" he inquired.

"Nothing reliable. And the bathroom in my motor home is tiny, with just a shower. Lindsey is there."

He nodded, not needing her to elaborate on the practical difficulties of flushing his sperm from her body.

"Don't you have condoms?" she demanded.

"Yes, of course I do. There was no excuse. It was a case of total irresponsibility on my part."

"On mine, too," she said, willing to take her share of the blame once it was clear that he was shouldering his.

Rye hadn't made any move to withdraw throughout the discussion, nor had his tumescence subsided greatly. He started to pull out slowly and felt himself harden and swell with awakened desire. She closed her eyes on a little intake of breath, the silken sheathing of her body tightening to hold him inside her.

"I'm forty years old, not twenty-one," he reminded them both. "And you're probably not as fertile now."

"It's not likely," she agreed, caressing his shoulders. "I doubt that it would be easy for me to get pregnant now if I were trying."

She pulled his head down to kiss him, her fears allayed that they might repeat history.

Rye made love to her again without bothering to use protection. They were increasing the risk that already existed, but she didn't seem concerned, and he was willing to gamble with nature, he realized. Otherwise he wouldn't have gotten carried away and forgotten about birth control the first time.

If tonight resulted in a brother or sister for Lindsey, that might be the simplest solution for dealing with a future fraught with complications.

Chapter Ten

"Could I see the rest of your paintings before I go?" Emily asked as she came out of Rye's bathroom, where she had hurriedly washed and gotten dressed.

She didn't know what kind of explanation she would give her daughter for staying so long, but another couple of minutes weren't going to make that much difference.

"Oh. Sure." Rye took a second or two to answer. He had put back on his clothes and was squatted down in front of the closet, replacing the three paintings that he'd shown her.

Emily dropped down on the carpet near him. She peered curiously into the closet, noting that there were more than six frames in the cardboard carton and another carton besides.

"You brought along other framed artwork?"

Rye glanced at her keenly. "Yes, all original watercolors that I've taken on a consignment basis to sell in Florida."

"Why?" she demanded.

"'Why?'" he repeated. "Why did I take them on consignment rather than buying them outright? It's not an unusual practice. These particular artists were glad to get a broader market exposure."

"My question has nothing to do with consignment or the artists. Why is it necessary for you to make money on this trip?"

"It isn't *necessary*," Rye denied. "Not from a financial point, nor am I compulsive about earning money, if that's what you're driving at. I had plenty of space. Through my business, I have contact with a lot of artists. In Florida I'll have time to kill and a ready-made climate." He shrugged. "It just seemed made-to-order, especially since I was prepared to be persona non grata and thought I might need to occupy myself. Obviously I don't have enough paintings of my own and wouldn't be able to produce a sufficient number, traveling."

"What's wrong with occupying yourself with sketching and painting?"

"Nothing would be wrong with it if I wanted to devote myself to sketching and painting. I plan to do some of both."

She sighed. "You're on a treadmill and don't want to get off."

"I'm not on any damned treadmill!" he denied. "The reason that I'm a workaholic, aside from the fact that my personal life isn't all that satisfying, is that what I do isn't drudgery for me. It's nerve-racking at times, admittedly, but challenging."

"Like a drug you're hooked on," Emily summed up for him gravely, reaching out her hand.

He regarded it, frowning.

"I can't stay here all night, arguing with you," she said. "Just show me your paintings."

"Okay, for chrissakes," he muttered. "Just tell me one thing that I really don't want to hear. Would tonight have happened if there hadn't been any paintings for you to see?"

She countered with her own question. "Did you have any other purpose when you set up your easel other than rousing my interest and getting me into bed?"

"That's a hell of a good question," he said soberly. "As soon as I know the answer, I'll share it with you. Here." Without any ceremony, he plunked his three other paintings on the carpet and left her in the bedroom.

Emily was tempted to get up and march out and make a dramatic exit. But her pride was no match for her curiosity. Though *curiosity* wasn't the right word. It didn't convey her eagerness or her lack of choice in the matter.

She had *had* to see his paintings from the moment she heard about them. Why, she didn't completely understand, but comprehended that in her own way she was acting compulsively herself.

These were as good as the others. She examined them one by one, trying hard to be objective. Rye's first efforts after years of not painting probably weren't technically the best, but his talent shone through. Emily felt the same swell of pride that she'd felt when she was his girlfriend and then his wife. Tears of regret spilled down her cheeks as she put the paintings in their box.

"Aren't you finished looking at those?" Rye asked from the doorway.

"Yes." Emily stood up, wiping at her cheeks and sniffling.

He murmured a curse and demanded in a gruff voice, "Why on earth are you crying?"

"You know how close to the surface my emotions are," she answered defensively. "Among other things, it makes me sad to think about all the wonderful paintings that you might have painted and didn't.''

He shook his head slowly and drew in a long breath. When he spoke, he sounded bleak. ''Before you came tonight, I was doing some soul-searching about our marriage and wondering if I wasn't almost totally at fault. After all, you were very young, and I was neither patient nor understanding. Youth was some excuse for me, too, and I had all sorts of hang-ups. But looking back, I realize that I tried to find fault with you because I couldn't face up to the real truth—you didn't fall for *me*. You fell for an art student. Our relationship now will hinge, once again, on whether I make myself into the man you can admire and want.''

''I loved you with all my heart and soul!'' Emily cried. ''I've never stopped caring about you, even though I've tried to hate you.''

He glanced at the bed, and she knew that he was remembering, too, the words of love they'd said to each other in the heat of passion.

''You're the only woman I've ever loved,'' he said, utterly without joy. ''I'll walk you to your motor home.''

''Don't be ridiculous,'' she objected miserably. ''It's only a short distance. You don't need to escort me to my door.''

He didn't argue, but merely stood aside and gestured for her to precede him. She didn't lodge any further protests when he followed her outside and walked beside her. The truth was that she hated to part company with him.

''Would you like to have breakfast with Lindsey and me?'' she asked, turning her mind to the next day. ''If you would, I'll have her come over and get you when we wake up.''

''What time will that be?''

''About seven, if we don't oversleep again. I'd like to get a fairly early start.''

"I'll come at seven, then, and if you aren't up, I'll knock and wake you."

"Okay. Bring some coffee if you have it made."

They made plans, and her sense of hopelessness eased. At the door of her motor home, she paused to say good night to him. The thought of going inside and facing Lindsey filled her with reluctance.

"Do I have guilt written all over me?" she inquired, keeping her voice low.

Rye stepped up close to her and drew her into his arms. Emily willed herself to resist, but her arms went up around his neck.

"Do you feel guilty about our making love?" he asked.

"No, not really *guilty*," she admitted. "Embarrassed. How about you?"

"My only guilt comes from being selfish."

"Selfish?"

"Yes, I can't help thinking that if Lindsey weren't along, we could sleep together."

He kissed her, and when he started to raise his head, Emily pulled his lips back down to her.

"Mom! *Dad...*" At the sound of Lindsey's shocked voice, they drew apart. She had opened the door and stood regarding them. "I thought I heard voices out here."

Emily pushed against Rye's chest. He let her move out of his embrace, but kept an arm around her shoulders.

"Your mother and I have been making a trip down memory lane tonight," he said. "We discovered that the old spark is still there, along with all the old differences."

"Excuse me for interrupting." Lindsey was obviously as delighted and intrigued as she was apologetic. "I'll just say good night to you both and go to bed. Mom, be sure to lock the door. See you tomorrow, Dad."

She pulled the door closed.

"Well. So much for discretion," Rye remarked.

Emily pressed her hands to her hot cheeks. "You don't suppose that she suspects we went to bed, do you?" she murmured.

"If she does suspect, she evidently doesn't disapprove," he pointed out.

"Don't you feel awkward?" Emily demanded.

"Of course I do. But Lindsey realizes that she wasn't brought by the stork. The awkwardness will wear off." He hugged her shoulders. "Now, you'd better go in."

"Yes."

He dropped his arm and took a half step back.

"Good night," she told him.

"Good night," he replied.

"This reminds me of your bringing me back to my dormitory. Remember how many times we would kiss good night?"

"There was a real sense of déjà vu when Lindsey opened the door. For just a moment I was taken back in time and thought that housemother of yours had emerged in her robe and curlers." Rye added his own ironic recollection, and they smiled at each other.

"Miss Potter. She used to give us girls lectures about 'getting ourselves into trouble,' nice language for 'getting ourselves knocked up.' I felt sorry for her because I doubted that she had ever had a love affair."

"A pretty safe assumption, I would say."

"Well, good night." Emily held out both hands, and he took them, giving them a squeeze.

"Sleep well," he said.

"I'll try." She drew her hands away as reluctantly as he let them go. "Rye?"

"Yes."

She hesitated. "You didn't *seem* any less virile than you were when you were twenty-one. You really aren't worried?"

"I didn't feel any less virile," he answered. "But, no, I'm not worried about anything except spending the night out here."

They smiled at each other again, said good night again, and Emily finally went in.

Emily heard a thumping from a long distance and burrowed her cheek deeper into her pillow. She drew the covers up over her head to shut out the sound of voices and drifted back into a sound sleep.

"Mom, time to rise and shine. Dad's here for breakfast."

The cheery announcement from Lindsey roused her. She opened her eyes and quickly squeezed them closed as memory flooded back.

"I told him seven o'clock," she mumbled.

"It is seven o'clock," her daughter assured her. "You know Dad. Always prompt. Just slip on your robe and come on out. I'm not dressed yet, either."

Left alone, Emily rolled over on her back. It had taken her forever to get to sleep the night before. Then she'd had dreams...erotic dreams in which she and Rye had been making love. She hoped she hadn't talked in her sleep.

Now he was out there. She could hear him and Lindsey talking, as though nothing were at all unusual about his coming over for breakfast. Emily didn't feel up to coping. She hadn't really expected him to show up. The breakfast invitation had been issued before Lindsey had opened the door on her parents' good-night kiss. In his place, Emily would have conveniently taken a rain check.

Dragging herself up, she followed her daughter's instructions and put on her robe rather than getting dressed.

Lindsey was bustling happily around the cramped kitchen area, playing hostess. The dinette table was set for three. Rye was seated on one side of it, looking clean-shaven and showered. Emily felt a wave of feminine pleasure at the sight of him. She was certain she could have caught a whiff of his soap and after-shave if the delectable aroma of fresh-brewed coffee hadn't been competing with another mouth-watering food aroma.

"Good morning, all," she greeted them, a smile curving her lips. She sniffed and inquired of her daughter, "What are you cooking that smells so divine?"

"I'm heating up some scrumptious blueberry muffins that Dad brought over. They should be just about ready. Sit down, Mom. I think everything else is on the table."

Emily sat across from Rye. "This is a nice way to start the day," she remarked lightly but sincerely. "I could get spoiled."

"I'll gladly supply coffee and food any time for this kind of service and company," Rye declared in the same vein.

"Isn't it a hoot, though?" Lindsey demanded, adding her own similar sentiments in youthful vernacular. "You want to pour the orange juice, Mom?"

She deposited a basket of muffins on the table, filled their coffee cups and took her place next to Emily. The muffins were huge and moist and as delicious as they smelled and looked. In addition to low-fat margarine, Lindsey had put out a dish of apple butter and another of strawberry preserves, both homemade from the kitchen of Mabel Peabody.

Emily savored every bite of food, every swallow of tangy orange juice and rich black coffee. Her own enjoyment was increased by her perception that her daughter and Rye were enjoying their breakfasts equally as much. The conversation centered around their travel plans for that day. There was harmony without any effort on anyone's part.

All in all, it ranked as one of the best meals Emily had ever eaten and was one of those low-key, quietly happy occasions when time and place and circumstance all just happen to be perfect. There was enough novelty to provide a pleasurable level of stimulation and yet enough complacency to prevent tension. With weeks of leisurely travel ahead, they would have many more meals together.

While Emily and Rye were lingering over third cups of coffee, Lindsey excused herself, announcing that she'd like to make use of her father's beautiful, big bathroom and take a shower before they got on the road.

"She is definitely your daughter, in looks and personality," Emily commented fondly when she and Rye were left alone.

"Yes, she is a lot like me," he admitted in a voice full of paternal pride.

"I enjoy her company. She has your dry sense of humor and is a wonderful conversationalist. We've talked about anything and everything these last weeks, including men and sex."

Rye frowned. "She hasn't confided in you..." he growled.

"Your little girl's still a virgin," Emily reassured him, reaching over and touching his hand. "One of the pressures that had gotten too much for her was to follow the example of the majority of her college girlfriends and make sexual intercourse a part of the dating relationship with a steady boyfriend. She's too strong-minded, like you, to cave in and needed to examine her personal standards and decide for herself whether to change them."

"That kid Eric was insisting that she go to bed with him," Rye deduced grimly. He had laced his fingers with Emily's. "What conclusion has she come to?"

"That she still wants her first experience with making love to be that—making love." Emily smiled with tender amusement. "Besides which, she isn't having any of getting laid in the backseat of a car or in an unmade bed with dirty sheets, the two most common options for campus sex. You've instilled an appreciation for the finer things in life. Your daughter wants to be seduced in style, with some romantic ambience."

"You didn't tell her that she might have been conceived in the backseat of a car?"

Emily's smile turned apologetic. "She wanted to know all about our love affair."

Rye grimaced. "I was fairly conscientious about changing my sheets, even if the bed wasn't always made. That apartment was a pigsty, but I shared it with three other guys."

"You were far more fastidious than I was. I remember how impressed I was when we went to the Laundromat together and you took hangers along for your shirts and folded the rest of your clothes so neatly. I didn't have the heart to point out that folding clothes hot out of the dryer only puts creases in them."

"As opposed to wrinkles. So that was why you never folded our laundry." His mild irony was teasing. "You never explained that theory to me."

"It would only have led to discussion of whether the laundry couldn't be folded and put away in drawers after it was cooled," Emily explained sheepishly. "I always had good intentions of doing that, but before I could, the basket was empty and the clothes all dirty again."

"I could have folded them and put them away myself," Rye pointed out.

She nodded, agreeing. "But that never occurred to me. I wasn't much of a feminist back then."

"Now if I asked you to get me clean underwear, you'd direct me to the laundry basket?"

"More likely the dryer. I never minded bringing you clothes to put on, especially underwear," she confessed. "We weren't married long enough for the intimacy to wear off and for seeing you naked to become ho-hum."

"I wasn't such a chauvinist that I expected you to hand me my clothes, piece by piece. It was a good excuse." Rye made his own confession, squeezing her hand.

"Speaking of unmade beds," Emily said reluctantly. Lindsey would be returning, and the conversation had become provocative. She was aware that she was dressed in her nightgown and robe.

"The less mention of beds the better," he replied ruefully. "I already feel like doing more than holding hands."

"So do I."

She pulled her hand free. "We can't have an affair right under our daughter's nose."

"That would be setting a very poor example as parents."

"Plus we don't want her to be put in the position of being a fifth wheel."

"Certainly not."

"We're not a couple of oversexed teenagers anyway."

"Hardly that."

Emily sighed. "It seems like we're in agreement. Which means there's a chance of world peace, I guess."

"Who said that the two of us would never think along the same lines?" he said with an effort at lightness.

"You," she answered.

He smiled at her glum tone, and she smiled back. Then they both noticed that they were holding hands again.

The whole day progressed with the same leisurely quality. When Emily wasn't smiling or laughing, she felt on the verge of doing one or the other. The sun shone brightly, and the temperature grew warmer the farther south they traveled along the western coast of the Florida peninsula.

There were frequent stops, for gas, for lunch, for changing drivers according to a schedule that Lindsey devised and labeled musical motor homes. They would all take turns driving both motor homes, all have stints of driving solo. She grinned in response to teasing accusations that she had figured out a way for her to tool down the highway in her father's modern motor home, with the cruise control turned on and the stereo playing loud.

"I am ready to hear some Bruce Springsteen," she admitted.

As he had the previous day, Rye made reservations at a campground. There was no discussion of whether the sites would be adjacent, as they were.

Dinner was a cooperative affair. Rye cooked barbecued chicken on his portable grill that he set up outdoors. Lindsey made a rice dish, and Emily a green salad.

They ate outside at a picnic table and afterward went inside Rye's motor home to play a trivia board game that Lindsey had brought along and to enjoy his stereo. At nine-thirty, Lindsey stretched and yawned.

"It's not the company," she said, "but I think I'll go give myself a manicure and then read awhile."

"I should go, too," Emily declared conscientiously.

"Then I'll feel like a party pooper," Lindsey objected. "Stay and play another round with Dad. We can all sleep in tomorrow morning."

"It's early," Rye put in. "I'll bend the rules for you and give you two turns to my one." He and Lindsey had easily come out the winners in the three-way competition.

Emily indignantly seized his challenge as an excuse for staying. "You don't think that she was making herself scarce, do you?" she asked when Lindsey had gone and she and Rye sat, looking at each other and sharing the knowledge that they were alone.

"If she was, it was strictly her own idea," he replied. "Neither of us wanted her to go."

"No, she couldn't have picked up any vibes because there were none." Reassured, Emily sighed. "I guess we have to play this stupid game. She'll ask tomorrow who won. Or rather, she'll confirm that you won," she added, making a face at him.

"You're not competitive."

His indulgent tone took any criticism out of the insight.

"No, I never have been. I guess I'd like for everybody to be able to win and nobody to be a loser."

"The world doesn't work like that."

They were sitting on the sofa, far enough apart that Lindsey could have sat between them, although she had chosen the carpeted floor instead. Rye stretched out his arm along the back of the sofa and was just able to reach Emily's shoulder.

"Maybe we should make this game more interesting," he suggested softly. "Something along the same lines of strip poker."

"You'd have me in my birthday suit after three points and you'd still be fully clothed," Emily retorted. "Then what?"

"Then I'd start forfeiting points." He caressed her shoulder with his fingertips.

"Rye!" she admonished him weakly. "Have you forgotten our discussion this morning at breakfast?"

He sighed and looked rueful. "No."

"Out of the two of us, you're the one with the self-discipline."

"Sorry. I'll try to exert it. Can we handle sitting closer and touching?"

"Sitting closer, yes. As for touching, we'd have to stick to the nonerogenous zones, of course," Emily answered regretfully.

She was already scooting over, and he was sliding toward her. Tonight he was wearing lightweight slacks instead of jeans. Emily had been conscious of the way the khaki fabric pulled slightly across his thighs and crotch as he sat with his legs comfortably open. Now she couldn't fail to notice that the pants had gotten tighter in the past couple of minutes.

"You don't really expect me to sit next to you and hold hands when you're...you're—" She completed the sentence with a meaningful glance. "That's not really cooperating, in spirit."

"Neither is letting your nipples get hard and poke against your blouse," he replied with his own meaningful look that didn't correct the problem one bit.

Emily folded her arms across her breasts. "I have no control over that happening. Any kind of stimulation causes a tingling sensation, and I can feel them hardening into rocks."

"Thanks for that explanation," Rye said ironically. "Believe me, I can empathize. Why don't we change the subject and get our minds on something besides sex? Then maybe our bodies will get back to normal."

Emily sat in the circle of his arm. "What shall we talk about?"

"We can talk about books, movies, world events."

"Books."

"That wasn't multiple choice," he teased, making her smile.

"Let's see. Did you happen to read...?" She pretended to search her memory and mentioned the title of a technical volume on ceramic glazes. "It came out about three years ago."

"No, I didn't see that among the selections of any of the book clubs," he replied. "Did you happen to read...?" He named the title of a bestselling book about Japanese business management.

"I was waiting for that to come out in paperback," Emily said. "But then I never happened to see it at any garage sales."

"I have it in hardback in case you want to borrow it."

"I have the Robin Williams book in hardback, too. Well, let's see. Did you read...?" This time she mentioned a fiction blockbuster that had recently been made into a movie.

Rye had read the book and started to discuss it with her.

"I haven't read it or seen the movie," Emily told him. "I just wondered if you had. Feeling any better?" she inquired, managing somehow not to answer the question for herself with a downward glance.

"No, not 'better.' You make it sound as though I were suffering from a malady of some sort."

She chided, a smile in her voice, "You know what I meant. Are you feeling more comfortable?"

"The situation is stable, if not noticeably changed. How about you?" He kept his dark gaze on her face.

"The same applies. What exactly constitutes 'having an affair'? Does it involve arranging an opportunity to have sex?"

"Emily." He groaned her name in protest. "We can't rationalize our way into bed."

"You're lucky. You can at least take a cold shower. I've always heard of that as a remedy."

"Before you leave, you're welcome to take one yourself."

They could take a cold shower together. The thought was so mutual that Emily didn't know whether it had formed in her mind first or not. She could feel the shock of cold needles of water on her skin, coursing down her body. Her shiver was pure excitement.

"Movies," Rye said hoarsely. "What good movies have you seen...?"

Chapter Eleven

"Emily. So you did make it here from Louisiana!" exclaimed a stocky brunette woman.

"Bev! Hello!" Emily stopped in the middle of setting out her pottery and walked over, arms open, to embrace her friend from Georgia. "It's great to see you. How is Amos?"

"As antisocial as ever. We kept an eye out for your motor home on the way down here and didn't see hide nor hair of you. Did you just roll in to Naples this morning?"

"No. I've been here several days. I'm staying in a different campground this year," Emily explained.

"Don't tell me you found a cheaper rate and didn't come and round us all up."

"No, it's not cheaper, by a long shot. My daughter is traveling with me." Emily looked around and smiled at Lindsey, who glanced up from unpacking a carton. "Come and meet my friend, Bev Humble. She's a weaver, and her husband, Amos, is a painter.''

Lindsey rose and came forward to be introduced. After exchanging a few remarks, she got back to work. Bev stayed and chatted for a few minutes, passing along tidbits of news. As she was about to leave, she asked the name of the campground that Emily had chosen this year.

Bev's eyebrows rose in surprise when Emily disclosed it rather reluctantly. ''The pottery business must be good,'' she commented.

''I'll be down later to say hello to Amos,'' Emily promised, evading any further discussion.

Rye had chosen the campground, which was the nicest and the most expensive in the exclusive Naples area. Emily had gone along without argument, even though she'd cringed a little at the expense. If she'd made an issue of the cost, he would only have insisted on paying.

Emily hated to wreck the harmony. It was just easier to be outvoted, as she was at every turn. Rye and Lindsey both were accustomed to living well. Economy wasn't a factor in their everyday lives as it was in hers.

On their arrival Wednesday, Rye had promptly rented a car so that they could go sight-seeing. They'd spent the next day seeing Naples and nearby Marco Island and had eaten lunch and dinner out, in good restaurants. He'd picked up the checks. Driving around, they'd spotted marinas with pontoon boats for rent and had idly discussed that it would be fun to have a day's outing on the water.

Before Emily had known what was happening, definite plans were in the making. Rye had turned the car around to head back to a marina, put down a cash deposit to reserve a boat for the next day and also arranged for a cooler of drinks to be on board.

She had been aghast at the rental fee, but just as excited as Lindsey. They'd departed from the marina early on Friday morning, wearing shorts and shirts over their bathing suits, motored southward within sight of land to Marco Island, then circled it, stopping at tiny, uninhabited islands to swim and sunbathe.

To everyone's utter delight, they'd several times sighted schools of dolphins frolicking. Adding a picturesque element were the sea eagles' nests that formed scraggly caps on the pilings that bore channel markers.

At noon they'd gone ashore on Marco Island, a retirement paradise for the wealthy, and had a gourmet lunch, then motored back to Naples, taking turns at the helm. A sea had kicked up, making the ride more adventurous. Ending the perfect day, they'd showered and changed back at the campground and gone out to dinner, sporting their suntans, at another marvelous restaurant.

It had to stop. Emily felt as if she was on an expense-paid vacation, but she didn't know quite what to do. What bothered her, among other things, was the nagging suspicion that she could adjust to luxury with a little practice.

On the other hand, she had to wonder if Rye could gear down to a less affluent life-style.

As much as she had enjoyed the past two days, the thought hadn't been far from her mind that he could have gotten in some sketching and painting. He had brought along his camera both days, but not a sketch pad.

Was there any real possibility, she wondered, that he would devote himself seriously to painting?

This trip would tell the tale.

If the interest and the creative urge were really there, he would apportion some time to his art once they settled down into a leisurely routine. Emily didn't expect him to spend whole days working, but at least a couple of hours or so daily. He could set his easel up outdoors or even rent studio space, given his resources.

If Rye wanted to paint, he would. It was as simple as that.

"Mom, I'll go park the motor home now that we've finished unloading your pottery." Lindsey broke into Emily's thoughts. "Then I thought I'd walk over to the market show and see Dad's setup."

The unjuried market show that Rye had learned about and managed to get into, at a late date, was within walking distance.

"You've been awfully quiet this morning," Emily remarked.

"You've been pretty quiet yourself," her daughter pointed out.

"I guess I have been lost in my own thoughts. You don't have to rush back. Walk around. Or go shopping." Emily had noticed her daughter casting longing glances at the upscale stores in downtown Naples, which reportedly had as many wealthy inhabitants as Palm Beach.

Lindsey brightened at the suggestion. "Maybe I will browse in a few stores. Also it's Saturday morning. I thought I might use Dad's phone and call Sarah and find out what's going on at school. I may give Eric a call, too."

Emily offered no advice, pro or con, since none was requested. "I can take care of things here," she reassured.

She watched her daughter walk off with her elegant, leggy stride. Something had apparently brought on an attack of homesickness. Lindsey had seemed perfectly content these past weeks not dating or socializing with young people her own age, but Emily had known that she would eventually become dissatisfied.

There had been the likelihood from the outset that her daughter wouldn't last the entire trip. Emily had been prepared for that eventuality until Rye had showed up.

If Lindsey decided to return to Baton Rouge, he would, too, obviously. The prospect of being abandoned by both of them was unendurably bleak.

Her poor sales did nothing to lift her spirits. She had sold only a few lower-priced items when Lindsey came back at noon to relieve her for lunch. After Emily had eaten, Lindsey went off again to resume her shopping spree. The afternoon went better, but was still disappointing. Experience, however, had taught Emily not to lose heart. One good customer could show up the last half hour and make the difference, and there was always tomorrow. Sunday could be a great day.

Emily put on a cheerful face.

Around four o'clock Lindsey returned, all her earlier moodiness having vanished. She'd found some fabulous buys, she claimed, and described her purchases, which included a blouse for her mother. She didn't volunteer any prices, and Emily didn't ask, able to figure out for herself that Lindsey must have spent far more than she herself had taken in.

Emily also didn't inquire what kind of success Rye was having at his market show. She could deduce that he was doing well from what Lindsey said, with offhanded pride. ''I visited Dad on my way back here. You'd swear that he was an old pro at this. Of course, it doesn't hurt that he knows a lot about displaying things to advantage. His setup is eye-catching and stops everybody going by.''

It also didn't hurt that he had gone first-class, naturally, and purchased the best canopy on the market. Unlike the majority of the artists and craftspeople, he wasn't having to improvise and use ingenuity to design a booth setup, either. Once again he'd opted for quality and bought panels that could be easily arranged in a variety of configurations, easily taken apart and stored without requiring much space.

Promptly at closing time, Emily let down the side curtains on her own canopy, which she'd acquired secondhand. The art association sponsoring the outdoor show provided good security. The area would be cordoned off and patrolled by guards during the night, and she, like the majority of the exhibitors, planned to leave her booth intact.

That morning Rye had been leery about doing the same. Emily didn't know what he'd decided. She agreed with Lindsey's suggestion that they might go and see if he was in the process of dismantling his booth. If he was, they could give him a hand.

A number of people were still in evidence at the market show, browsing in booths, including his. He obviously hadn't closed up shop yet, but was so involved in conversation with a very attractive blond woman about Emily's own age that he didn't even notice her and Lindsey walk up.

The woman looked familiar. Emily thought that she must have seen her previously. She had a country club tan and could have modeled her chic, casual skirt-and-blouse outfit at a charity fashion show luncheon. When she gestured with a manicured hand, Emily was pleased to note that she wore a whopping big diamond and a wedding band.

She wondered jealously whether Rye had taken note of the fact that the woman was married. He was smiling at her and nodding, hanging on to her every word.

After his exposure to the sun yesterday, he was a whole shade darker and looked fit and glowing with health, not to mention handsome and virile. It was absurd of Emily to feel a strong pride in his appearance, a fierce possessiveness, as though he belonged to her. She was his ex-wife and had no claim to him, legal or otherwise.

They weren't even lovers, conscience having ruled out an affair.

While Emily hung back, nursing her insecurity, Lindsey stepped up and caught her father's attention. He greeted her and immediately glanced beyond her. The welcoming light in his dark eyes as he saw Emily boosted her morale higher than it had been all day.

"Come and meet Bonnie Wright," he urged.

The introduction revealed that Bonnie was a local shop-owner in Naples. She ran a gallery/frame shop and had been out that day scouting for artwork. The reason she had seemed familiar was that she had stopped by Emily's booth and, according to her, admired Emily's pottery.

She and Rye had been talking business, apparently firming up a transaction that involved several paintings. Emily could sense that he was exhilarated beneath his calm, and was excited for him. She assumed that the paintings were his own and waited impatiently until Bonnie had left to hear the details.

Her face fell as Rye corrected her error. Bonnie hadn't been interested in his paintings, it turned out, but in those of a couple of the artists whose work he had brought along. He had made her a package deal, where she outright bought two paintings and took two others on consignment, with him acting as the artists' agent.

He didn't show any disappointment, but looked and sounded thoroughly pleased. There was no hint of under-lying discouragement when, in answer to Emily's tentative inquiry, he admitted that he hadn't sold a single one of his watercolors, but had already exceeded his goal for sales for the entire show before Bonnie had come along.

"I hope you don't mind sticking around on Monday," he said, explaining that he wanted to personally deliver the paintings to Bonnie's gallery on Monday afternoon.

Emily replied that she was in no particular hurry to get to Tampa, their next destination. Her good mood had quickly fizzled. Pleading fatigue, she went back to the campground alone, leaving Lindsey with him.

It wasn't a case of sour grapes. She wasn't resentful that Rye had had a profitable day and she hadn't. She just wished that a different kind of success had gotten his adrenaline flowing.

If he'd been selling his own paintings, she could have related to the thrill of having strangers come along and want to own a piece of artwork that he'd produced. But to get excited over selling other artists' work, she would have to have a personal stake, like wanting to give their careers a boost so that they could earn a living. There could be no joy in the transaction itself, an article exchanged for money.

Emily was dismayed by her intuition that it was the business aspect that gave Rye his thrill.

Pushing that thought away, she tried to look on the bright side. At the rate he was going, he'd soon run out of his stock. Plus the novelty would probably pall after a couple of shows. There was no real incentive. The money he could take in was peanuts for him, not worth his time and effort.

Lindsey's shopping bags were strewn around the motor home, another jarring note. Emily could judge by the quality of the bags themselves, as well as by some of the store names, that the merchandise inside was expensive.

Her daughter wouldn't mind if Emily looked at her purchases. Liking pretty clothes as well as the next woman, Emily peeked inside one bag and saw that it contained a blouse made out of a gorgeous paisley material. The price tag dangled in sight, and she peered at it, her eyes widening at the sum. It would have had to be slashed in half and then reduced again before Emily would have taken the blouse off a sales rack.

She closed the bag, some instinct telling her that she'd happened upon the blouse that Lindsey had bought for her.

Deciding that she'd have a glass of iced tea and sit outside and unwind, Emily had gotten down a glass before she happened to think that Rye's motor home, with his ice maker, wasn't parked next to hers. Her little refrigerator didn't have a freezer compartment. She poured the cool herb tea from the jug and sipped it with very little enjoyment.

Outside, the scent of food cooking on grills brought thoughts of dinner. She should have stopped at a supermarket, but she hadn't. And she doubted that Rye and Lindsey would, either. They'd be all for going out to get something to eat.

Emily's stomach was growling by the time Rye's motor home drove into the campground. She was not only hungry, but stubbornly resolved.

Lindsey acted as spokesperson, announcing the dinner plans that had been made without consulting Emily. "Dad has a reservation for us at one of the best restaurants in town. Bonnie recommended it. We'll need to get dressed up a little. You can wear the blouse I got you today. I'm dying to see it on you."

"I'd much rather not get dressed up tonight," Emily replied. "I was going to offer to take the two of you out for pizza. It's definitely my turn to treat."

"Pizza?" Lindsey repeated in unison with Rye.

"Couldn't you take us out for pizza tomorrow night?" he suggested.

"Tomorrow night I had in mind throwing some hamburgers or hot dogs on the grill. I've been sitting here smelling good barbecue smells."

"I had my mouth all set for lobster tonight," her daughter cajoled.

"Why don't you and your father go out to dinner, then? I'll order a pizza and have it delivered."

"But we wouldn't enjoy ourselves without you!" Lindsey protested, exchanging a glance with her father and asking him wordlessly to add his persuasion.

"I'll call and cancel the reservation," he said flatly, then added to Emily, "It's your party."

"Now, just a darned minute!" she objected. "I've been going along meekly, letting you play the big spender. I refuse to be made to feel like a wet blanket. Unlike Lindsey, I'm not your dependent."

"I haven't been 'playing the big spender,'" he denied, anger in his voice. "I've been enjoying the hell out of myself and was under the impression—apparently a wrong one—that you were enjoying yourself, too."

"I *have* been enjoying myself!" Emily claimed heatedly.

"If we've definitely decided on pizza, I say let's go and find a pizza place," Lindsey intervened with a pleading note. "I'm starving."

They climbed into Rye's rental car and had a tense, silent drive, the only discussion pertaining to their choices of pizza restaurants. He and Lindsey both left the final decision up to Emily.

She picked one that was a local establishment, not a chain. Its crowded parking lot attested to its popularity on a Saturday night. The interior was attractive, with Mexican tile on the floor and tables and booths made of dark-stained wood, not Formica. The atmosphere was casual, but comfortable and inviting, not noisy or brightly lighted.

"This is nice, Mom," Lindsey said with sincerity, and Rye seconded the approval.

Everything else measured up. Their beverages were served in frosted mugs. The service was cheerful and prompt. The pizza looked appetizing and tasted good. They did justice by it, conducting polite conversation that steered clear of any sensitive issues. The waitress brought the check to Rye. He glanced at it and handed it to Emily.

Conscious of him watching her, she counted out money, adding a tip. They got up and trooped out. The trip back to the campground was made in complete silence, each of them buried in separate thought. Gone was the earlier tension, the only currents of emotion a quiet disappointment and hollow resignation.

Emily didn't know when she'd felt at such a low ebb. She wanted to say, *I'm sorry,* and yet what was there to apologize for? All around them tonight, families had been enjoying a relatively inexpensive night out.

Was she supposed to apologize because she couldn't afford to take her daughter and her ex-husband out to a fine restaurant? Didn't she have a right to some pride?

Rye told Emily and Lindsey good night and went straight inside his motor home without inviting them to join him, without mentioning seeing them the next morning or the next day.

Emily was battling tears as she tried to unlock the door to her motor home. The key didn't seem to want to fit.

"Here, Mom, let me," Lindsey said in a dispirited tone. "Or would that be infringing upon your independence?"

The remark, as gently spoken as it was, cut to the quick. Emily handed over her keys, not trusting herself to make a reply until she had her voice under control.

"You think that I'm overly sensitive?"

"Only where Dad's concerned." Lindsey sighed, leading the way up the steps. "I'm not choosing sides, but I have to be fair."

"Of course you do. I've never ever asked you to choose sides or tried to undermine your good opinion of your father." Emily defended herself.

"No, you didn't. I wasn't suggesting that you did," her daughter quickly assured. She cleared her packages out of the way, and they sat opposite each other at the dinette. "Mom, I can sympathize with your position, but I can also sympathize with Dad's. What do you want him to do? Be a tightwad? The fact of the matter is that he can afford to give us and himself a good time. Is it such a big deal to let him?"

"In other words I should swallow my pride and not worry about my self-respect so that he can have the pleasure of spending his money. Why does a 'good time' have to cost a fortune?"

"It doesn't have to cost a fortune, but it also doesn't have to be free. Dad hasn't spent an excessive amount, especially considering that this is a vacation for him. He doesn't throw money around for show. You really hurt his feelings tonight. I felt sorry for him."

"I didn't mean to hurt his feelings or seem unappreciative."

"The idea of being appreciative doesn't even enter into it." Lindsey looked over at the shopping bags that she'd dropped onto the floor. "I didn't buy a blouse for you today because I wanted you to thank me. I bought it because I got a real lift, thinking about showing it to you and seeing the look on your face. I just knew you'd love it and enjoy wearing it."

"I peeked into one of your bags and saw a beautiful paisley blouse," Emily confessed. "Is it by chance the one you bought for me?"

Lindsey answered affirmatively and reached for the bag without any enthusiasm. She brightened when Emily raved over the blouse and jumped up to try it on, making no mention whatever of the price. At her mother's urging, she modeled her purchases for herself, confessing what Emily already knew—that she had been down in the dumps that morning.

"You didn't mention whether you'd called Eric this morning," Emily said, opening the door for more confidences, which were forthcoming. Lindsey had called him. She recounted the conversation, which had ended with the near certainty that she and Eric would patch things up.

"Naturally he wanted to know if I couldn't cut my trip short," Lindsey said.

"My guess is that you told him you were considering that very thing," Emily answered gently.

"How did you know?"

"Just intuition. You've had a break and you're ready now to tackle your own life again."

Her daughter nodded. "I thought I'd stay through next weekend, help you with the Tampa show and then fly home. I want to get a job right away as a salesclerk in a women's clothing store, for the experience. Today it came to me that I'd like to study marketing and becoming a buyer." She smiled ruefully. "I guess you could say that it's a career I've been training for subconsciously for a number of years."

Emily managed a brave smile. "Are you in that big a hurry that you won't drive back with your dad? It's only a two-day trip, at the outside."

"If Dad were heading back to Baton Rouge, of course I would go with him."

"You were his whole reason for coming in the first place, and he wouldn't hear of your living by yourself at home. Neither would I," Emily added.

"I can easily make arrangements to move in temporarily with a friend's family." She shrugged, dismissing the whole problem, and rose gracefully to her feet, ending the heart-to-heart talk, as well. "Good night, Mom. I think I'll pop over to Dad's motor home and have a cup of hot chocolate with him, if he's still up."

She didn't invite Emily along.

"Dad, I haven't been totally honest with you lately."

"No?" Rye replied, and waited quietly for his daughter to bare her guilty conscience.

"When I led you to believe that I might major in art, I wasn't being truthful. I've never had any interest in pursuing a fine-arts degree." She smiled ruefully, holding up her hand to show him a broken nail. "For one thing the life of an artist is death on long fingernails."

"When you tossed out the idea of being an art major, I wondered whether you were ready to sacrifice your long polished nails," Rye said with a dry, indulgent note. "The required ceramics and sculpture classes are especially hard on pretty hands like yours."

"Dad, I deliberately misled you. The same applies to my hinting very broadly that I might follow in Mom's footsteps. I can't see myself as ever being happy living her kind of life-style. You've spoiled me too badly. It's fun to visit Mom, kind of like roughing it at camp, but I like my creature comforts."

"That doesn't necessarily mean you're spoiled."

"Dad, have you been hearing me? I played a part, like an actress."

"You mean you pretended to be unhappy with school and confused about your goals for yourself? If you're that good, I'll send you to New York to go on stage," Rye scoffed. None of what she was telling him was coming as that great of a surprise, he realized.

"No, all that was legit. Everything was, up to the point that I got the brainstorm to end the cold war between you and Mom. You gave me the inspiration yourself by over-reacting instead of trusting me to work out my problems in a levelheaded manner."

"I didn't handle the whole situation very well," he conceded.

"Not from the start. You didn't handle *me* well. You've never put your foot down before and given me ultimatums. Is it possible, Dad, that at least subconsciously you wanted to square off with Mom?"

"In retrospect, very possible," Rye said. "To use your cold-war analogy, I think I was probably ready for a shooting war after so many years of diplomacy. In any case, you shouldn't feel bad for any part you've played, knowingly or unknowingly. The new state of relations between your mother and me is an improvement over the way things were. Don't you agree?"

"From my point of view, it is. I guess I just wanted to hear that you thought so, too. I worry about Mom, but I also worry about you in a different way."

"You shouldn't ever worry about me," Rye chided gruffly. "And from now on, you can leave worrying about your mother to me. I intend to look after her, whether she likes it or not."

She looked immensely relieved, as well as pleased. "Good. You've taken a weight off my mind. Now I can go home to Baton Rouge, make up with Eric and start job hunting."

Before Rye could recover from his surprise and question her, she went on enthusiastically, filling him in on her plans for her future, both immediate and long-range.

Rye listened with fatherly interest, putting in sincere words of support and encouragement, but a part of his mind was busy assimilating the information that in another week he and Emily would be left alone together.

They could make love, sleep together, be intimate. The prospect made him eager, but apprehensive, too. He now knew without a doubt that he loved Emily and wanted to try again to make a life with her, but was she willing to compromise and meet him halfway?

The weeks ahead would tell the tale of whether they could get along on a day-to-day basis and forge a relationship strong enough to survive personality differences and conflicting philosophies. If they weren't compatible traveling together here in Florida, they didn't have a prayer of making a go of it when the trip was over and they returned to Louisiana.

"Mom assumes that you'll be cutting your vacation short and going back to Baton Rouge, too," Lindsey commented just before leaving. She had outlined several acceptable possibilities for temporary living arrangements on her return home, and Rye had left the final decision to her.

"It's easy to understand why she would make that assumption," he replied. "I know I've tended to be a little overprotective as a father."

"A *little* overprotective!"

He smiled ruefully. "Okay. I admit it. A *lot* overprotective. It's time I let you grow up. Just don't expect any overnight reform. I'll still want to touch base with you often during the next few weeks." His voice was gruff with emotion as he added, "No matter how old you are, you'll always be my little girl, you know."

"I'll always want to keep in close touch with you and Mom both," Lindsey said, blinking hard. "It's going to be so great to talk to you and her during the same phone call and know that you're together, keeping each other company."

Rye wished that he could promise his daughter that she could depend on her parents being together permanently. He wished that he were more confident of that outcome himself.

Rather than raise false hopes, he kept his own hopes to himself.

Chapter Twelve

"You've decided to sell that big jar, after all?" Lindsey's inquiry was more of a protest than a question. "Why don't you keep it? You know you love it."

"I'm sentimentally attached to all of my pottery," Emily replied, clearing a place for the big jar where it would be the focal point of her display. "Even the ugly ducklings. If I kept every piece that I loved, I'd have to have a warehouse."

Lindsey persisted. "I still think you should keep it. You said yourself that if you never did another wood-firing, you could be satisfied, because of that jar. And maybe I'd like to inherit it some day when I have a home of my own."

Emily was swayed by the last argument, even though she had sense enough to know her daughter was just giving her justification to be impractical.

"I'll put a ridiculously high price on it to discourage anybody from buying it."

"How much? More than that," Lindsey insisted when she heard the price, which was twice that of any other large piece. "I think you should ask more for all of your pottery. It seems to me that you're selling it too cheap for the work you've put into making it."

"But that's why I'm selling my pottery like hotcakes," Emily wisecracked. She wasn't having any better a day on Sunday than she'd had yesterday, which was the reason she'd decided to bring out the jar. "Okay, we'll make this jar five hundred dollars even. Is that outrageous enough?"

"By comparison I guess it is," Lindsey capitulated. "I don't mean to be critical, Mom, but somehow your pottery just doesn't show up as well in your booth as it should."

"There's just so much that you can do with folding tables," Emily pointed out, not offended. She had enough objectivity that she realized that her booth wasn't slick and commercial. "I figure that my pottery has to sell itself on its own merits. After you become an expert on marketing techniques, you can help me out."

"Dad could help you out now if you'd just ask his advice. He could probably pinpoint the problem in a minute."

"No doubt, he could. But he's busy making sales. And I wouldn't be likely to ask his advice, anyway," Emily admitted honestly. "I could take criticism from anyone else better."

"Mom, you make your living from selling your pottery, not just from making it. It deserves to be shown to best advantage."

Fortunately Emily's booth filled up with a small crowd of lookers, bringing an end to the discussion. Lindsey didn't resume it when there was a lull. She glanced at her watch and announced that she was going to stretch her legs and walk over to the market show.

When she was out of sight, Emily glanced around at her display and then walked out to the front of her booth, trying to see it with an objective eye. She did some rearranging, but wasn't satisfied that she'd improved the overall effect.

It was just coincidence, she knew, that she had a small flurry of sales within the next fifteen or twenty minutes. Busy with a transaction, she didn't see Rye approaching her booth. All of a sudden she glanced out, and he was there, standing out front.

He smiled, and she smiled back, flustered and then immediately defensive. Lindsey must have made a beeline and sent her father to offer his retailing expertise.

With the normal ebb and flow, her booth emptied, and he stepped under the canopy, glancing around.

"My daughter didn't waste any time dispatching you," Emily said by way of greeting.

"She didn't 'dispatch' me," he denied. "I came straight here when I learned that you'd put out this jar that I like so much." His dark gaze rested on the jar admiringly. "If you're going to sell it, I want to buy it."

Emily was flooded with new suspicions, as well as a little thrill of pleasure that he might really want the jar for his own collection.

"If you're buying the jar for Lindsey so that she can give it back to me, that's not necessary. The chances of anyone else buying it at that price are highly unlikely."

"I don't happen to agree with you. And I'm not buying it for Lindsey. Is my credit good, or shall I pay you now?" He reached to his hip pocket.

"Don't be silly!" she chided. "If you seriously want the jar for yourself, I'll give it to you at a more reasonable price."

"That is a reasonable price. If I paid less, I'd be stealing from you."

Two well-dressed women in their sixties entered the booth. Rye moved over to one side, getting out of their way. They headed straight for the large lidded jar, exclaiming over it. Emily flushed with pleasure over the complimentary remarks that were being spoken in his hearing.

"Wouldn't this look just stunning on the hearth in my library in the New York house?" one of the women inquired of the other, who agreed and urged her friend to buy the jar.

"Excuse me, madam." Rye spoke up politely. "I couldn't help overhearing. I'm sorry, but the jar is already sold."

"Rye!" Emily murmured, still not absolutely certain that he had been truthful with her about wanting the jar for himself.

He ignored her and went over to pick up a vase, approximately the same size, that was sitting on the ground. "Did you notice this vase?" he inquired of the woman who had been on the verge of making the purchase. "It's quite handsome, too, and has similar flashings."

"Flashings?" the woman repeated.

Rye looked questioningly at Emily, inviting her to step in and take over.

"No, you're doing fine," she said with an ironic undertone.

The two matrons listened with interest as he explained that all the pottery in the booth was wood-fired and that flashings occurred when the flames actually roared through the kiln, branding the vessels, so to speak, with rich, subtle colors and patterns. From their comments, they revealed that they hadn't even realized her pottery had been fired in a wood-burning kiln.

"That's fascinating," declared the woman who coveted the jar. "I do like that vase almost as much. But why is the price so much lower?"

Rye peered at the sticker. His eyebrows shot up. "Er, the pricing of artwork by an artist tends to be rather subjective." With his tone, he managed to suggest that the pricing was probably an error.

"If you don't want the vase, I think I'll take it," the prospective purchaser's friend decided.

"No, I definitely want it. I'm sure this gentleman can help you find something else on the same order."

"Certainly," Rye assured.

Emily enjoyed being an observer on the sidelines, despite an instinctive disapproval. Good salesmanship was too much a con game for her liking.

Both women paid with checks after first taking out credit cards. As she explained that she accepted payment only in the form of cash or personal checks, Emily stole a quick glance at Rye and caught him shaking his head. She mentally prepared herself for being put through the third degree about her reasons, and took her time swaddling the two large vases in newspaper.

"I should pay you a commission," she remarked as the women walked off after stopping to thank him for his invaluable assistance. "That was quite a demonstration of selling technique."

"There's not much selling technique involved in helping interested customers make a selection of merchandise they're predisposed to own. I didn't mean to overstep my bounds, but I hated to see those two ladies get away. It was written all over them that they have megabucks."

While he answered her, he was taking it upon himself to rearrange her display to fill in the gaps left by the two missing vases.

"I was going to put out a couple more pieces," Emily said. She had pottery stowed out of sight underneath the draped folding tables.

"Don't you think you have enough out?" he replied.

"I take it that you do. Or was that a roundabout way of telling me that I have too much out on display?"

"It wasn't a roundabout way of telling you anything. Don't read something into my words that isn't there. If you want to know my opinion of your display, then ask me outright."

"Lindsey did ask you to come and see my booth, didn't she?" Emily demanded.

He shrugged. "She mentioned yesterday that she wished that I would take a look. I told her that you wouldn't welcome any constructive criticism from me."

"So, what is your opinion?" Her voice was grudgingly curious.

"This setup would work better for the type of pottery that looks good in profusion. Your pottery is more the type that can be appreciated in a sparse display. Each piece stands on its own and begs to be admired individually."

"This happens to be the setup that I have." Emily threw up her hands. "Maybe next year I can come up with something different, although I can't quite imagine what."

"Do you have a piece of paper and a pencil? I'll make you a rough sketch of what I have in mind."

She handed him a paper bag and a ballpoint pen. A small crowd of people drifted in, and he retreated to a far corner, out of the traffic, and stood with frowning concentration, drawing with quick strokes. She could sense, though, that he wasn't missing anything that was said, including her negative answer to an inquiry about whether she took Visa or Mastercard.

"May I ask why you don't take credit cards?" he asked when the crowd thinned out without her having made a sale.

"It's too much rigmarole. I would just rather not go to the bother. People who really want something and can afford it will write a check or pay cash."

"Research indicates that a great deal of the impulse buying is done with credit cards."

"That doesn't mean that I have to encourage it."

His pen stopped momentarily.

"Just now I didn't notice that you were encouraging any buying at all," he commented when he had resumed the movement of his hand.

"I'm a potter, not a high-pressure salesperson," she informed him. "I smile and say hello, and if a customer has a question, I answer it. I treat my customers the same way I prefer to be treated when I go browsing in a store."

"A lot of people may not know what questions to ask or they may be a little afraid of sounding ignorant. Even if you don't make a sale, you can still pass along some knowledge."

"I guess I never looked at it from that standpoint," she admitted.

He had finished drawing. Emily walked over, curious and glad of the excuse to go up close to him.

"What do you think?" he asked.

She gazed a long moment at his sketch of a booth, complete with canopy. Instead of the more usual tables or shelves, pedestals of varying heights were arranged in a semicircle. On top of each one, he'd drawn a pottery vessel, all of them recognizable as her forms.

"I think it's great," she praised, inhaling the scent of his after-shave lotion. "You have such a knack for drawing. Your scale is perfect and so is the perspective. It's all the more impressive since you were just visualizing it in your mind's eye."

He was looking at her oddly.

"What?" she asked.

"Do you like the display idea?"

"Why, yes. A booth like this would probably catch the judges' eyes and win best of show. But those pedestals would take up a lot of room in my motor home. I'd have to have them built out of wood. That would be expensive, and they'd be heavy." She stopped. He was shaking his head.

"They could be made out of fiberglass and the sizes varied slightly so that they would stack one inside another."

"It's certainly an ingenious idea," she said to placate him. She took the paper bag and held it out. "I'd love to see you do a watercolor of this sketch. I would trade you the jar for it."

"I'm buying the jar," he replied. "You'll have to offer a different incentive."

"I wasn't offering you any incentive," she denied. "You either have the urge to paint or you don't."

"Don't kid yourself or me, Emily," he said quietly. "You're offering me a very powerful incentive—not to paint in my spare time, but to *be* a painter. What if the urge isn't there or what if I have other, stronger urges? What excites me about making that sketch is visualizing the display itself and knowing how effective it would be." He sighed. "But I will make a painting of it for you. Not this coming week, while Lindsey is still with us, but after she leaves. There's a condition, though."

Emily stared at him, not quite believing she'd heard right. "You're not leaving, too?"

"I'm here in Florida for the duration. Do you mind?"

"Mind?" she breathed, trying to take it in that he was staying with her, not returning to Louisiana. Joy was coursing through her and must have shown in her face, giving him his answer.

He bent and kissed her on the lips. They hadn't kissed since that night they'd somehow resisted making love. Emily closed her eyes at her own surge of response and opened them to look into his face.

"The condition you mentioned..." she muttered, and he smiled.

"It's not that. I'm taking for granted that I'll be able to get you into bed."

"Such confidence," she accused huskily, and still holding the paper bag in one hand, put her arms up around his neck and drew his head down for another kiss.

He hugged her hard and then held her in a close embrace. "The condition is we don't keep track of who's paying for what. I'll restrain myself and not flash a big roll of hundred-dollar bills."

Emily made a sheepish face at his indirect reference to her having called him a big spender. "That was uncalled-for, my attacking you like that last night. Okay, I'll agree to your condition. But I won't take money for the jar."

"Would you take a couple of my watercolors off my hands and give them a home?"

"You know I can't resist and say no. I would have bought them all if I could have afforded them."

"Then take all five that's left."

He had evidently sold one. Emily was as pleased as she was dismayed that some stranger would own his painting. "Which one did you sell?" she asked.

"I didn't sell any. Lindsey has spoken for the one of your screen door. The rest are yours." He kissed her lightly and released her. "You have customers, and I should get back and mind my booth. I'll take the sketch and do some more work on it."

Emily hesitated slightly before handing the bag over to him. "I think the composition is very good, just like it is."

Before the words were out, she realized, from his expression, that she wasn't on the same wavelength with him.

"It's the setup I'm going to work on," he said with patience. "Not the sketch itself. I want to figure out dimensions."

"Why waste your time?" She tried to match him in patience. "I love the setup, but it isn't feasible."

"Yes, it is feasible," he disagreed. "Take my word for it for now."

Emily sighed. "I'll take your word for it, period. Rye, let's get one thing straight. That 'condition' I just agreed to about letting you pay more than your share on this trip doesn't extend to your providing me with an expensive setup. You're not my own private finance company."

"Emily, you can't see the forest for the trees. If you improved your display and joined the twentieth century in your business attitudes, you could support yourself more than adequately."

His criticism, even phrased tactfully, stung. She wanted to strike back, as well as defend herself. "In other words I could take you and Lindsey out for a steak or lobster dinner instead of out for pizza."

"That's right. Pick a fight and cloud the whole issue," he said tersely. "If it's so damned important for you to be financially independent, why not take some free and available advice from someone with a track record? Haven't you punished me long enough, living below the poverty line?"

Emily gasped with indignation. "Of all the egotistical, *insulting—*"

"Er, excuse me." A deep masculine voice with a hint of stern reproach intruded.

Emily transferred her attention unwillingly to a tall giant of a man in his late fifties, standing beside a petite woman. He was bald headed and, even dressed as though he might have come off the golf course, carried himself with authority.

"Yes, may I help you?" she asked.

"My wife would like to know whether you use lead in your glazes," the man rumbled.

"No, I don't," Emily answered.

"The problem with lead glazes only pertains to functional pottery that is used for cooking or serving food," Rye spoke up. "Isn't that right, Emily?"

She glared at him. He was prompting her.

"Yes, it's perfectly safe for decorative pieces to be covered with a lead glaze, although not very safe for the potter. I mix all my own glazes and prefer not to handle toxic ingredients."

The tiny woman held up a chalice in her be-ringed hands. "How do you get this wonderful streaked effect?"

"That's what potters call 'a gift of the kiln,'" Emily explained, moving over toward the couple. "I'll see you later on," she told Rye pointedly, and he took her hint, slipping out the back of her booth.

A younger couple were listening interestedly to her conversation with the huge man and his wife. They interrupted apologetically to ask if she took Visa and then walked off. Emily hoped that Rye was out of earshot by then.

The information didn't deter the diminutive woman from purchasing the chalice. Her husband took out his wallet and extracted a crisp hundred-dollar bill.

"Would you mind my asking a question?" Emily asked on impulse. "Kind of consumer research."

"No, not at all," the woman replied.

"If I had had someone tending my booth who couldn't have supplied information about my pottery, do you think that you would still have bought that piece?"

"No, as much as I liked it, I would have been uneasy, not knowing whether the glaze was safe."

"So, once I'd put your mind to rest on that point, you were ready to buy?"

"Oh, yes. I just love this piece and have the perfect spot for it. But it'll be that much more special after meeting you and getting some insight into your work. Next year I'll be looking for your booth."

It wasn't the first time, of course, that Emily had heard the same sentiments. On a selective basis she chatted with strangers with whom she formed an instant rapport, but this couple certainly wouldn't have come in that category.

Yet she was left with a nice feeling as they left, a feeling that was more than being glad that she had their money in the till. Maybe she should make herself more approachable, strike up conversations with customers as Rye had suggested, not merely to sell pottery, but for the human interaction itself.

Emily still couldn't stomach the idea of a sales pitch.

She thought about the interrupted quarrel with him and got indignant all over again, recalling his words, *Haven't you punished me long enough, living below the poverty line?*

The implication was absurd that she'd lived her life with any notion whatever of disturbing his peace of mind or causing him any guilt. While because of Lindsey he wouldn't have been able to blot out her existence completely, any more than Emily had been able to blot out his, she hadn't been under any illusions that she mattered in the least to him.

If Emily wasn't a success financially, it was purely and simply because she didn't have a business head and wasn't motivated to make a lot of money. In other areas besides finances, she wasn't a failure. She had friends, good relations with her neighbors, a rewarding career, a life-style that afforded her many enjoyments.

For Rye to write all of that off as "living below the poverty line" was a sad commentary on his sense of values, as well as a blow to her pride. He equated happiness with a bank account, and, since her bank account was only in four figures, wanted to make her out as miserable.

Well, Emily wasn't miserable, darn it.

Or at least she hadn't been when he went slumming and barged into her life. Now he wanted to take her on as a project and turn her into a success story, raise her standard of living to suit him.

Was that why he was staying in Florida, to put her through his own personal business-training program while he was having an affair with her?

Whatever the answer and despite her hurt pride, the knowledge that he was staying made her glad, deep down in her heart.

"Bye, Mom." Lindsey gave Emily a farewell hug. "Bye, Dad." She kissed Rye on the cheek. Backing away, she smiled at them. "Take good care of yourselves."

"We will. Don't worry," Emily assured her daughter in an emotion-choked voice.

"Have a safe flight," Rye said gruffly.

He put his arm around Emily's shoulders, and she leaned against him. They watched their daughter stride away down the ramp. Before she disappeared into the tunnel, she turned and blew them a kiss.

The tears Emily had been keeping back welled up in her eyes and rolled down her cheeks. She wiped at them.

"I'm going to miss her like the devil," she said. "These weeks with her have been such a delight."

Rye's arm tightened around her shoulders, and Emily turned toward him. He put both arms around her and held her close. She hugged him around the waist, realizing that he was seeking comfort as much as giving it.

"She's been the light of my life, and I have you to thank for her," he said with a kind of tender fervor.

A strange pain gripped Emily's heart at the unexpected words, spoken in the tone a man uses to address his wife, who has born him a much-wanted child. She pushed back from him abruptly. His arms loosened, but didn't drop away.

"I've wanted to say that to you for a very long time," he told her. "Tell you how rotten I feel about a lot of things, including the way I reacted to the news that you were pregnant."

Emily swallowed hard. "Your reaction was understandable under the circumstances. There's really no point in feeling rotten now. It's all past."

"I can still see you so clearly. As much as you were dreading breaking the news to me, you looked as though you had a wonderful secret."

"I was thrilled that I was pregnant with your baby." Emily's voice came out a choked whisper. "In my naïveté and stupidity, I actually expected you to be excited, too, once you recovered from the shock. Of course, you never were. I think the worst was when the baby had started to kick inside me. I put your hand on my stomach, knowing you *had* to be glad when you felt the movement of this new little person.'' Tears were flowing down Emily's face again. ''But you jerked your hand away.''

''I wasn't rejecting you or our baby, even though it must have come across that way,'' Rye protested. ''All my life I had been the victim of circumstance, and now suddenly my freedom and my options were snatched away. Whether I wanted to be or not, I was the head of a family and had responsibilities thrust on me that I could never shirk. I felt trapped, resentful.'' He sighed. ''None of which excuses me.''

Emily twisted free of him. ''You had every reason to be resentful,'' she said.''And I knew that you couldn't help reacting the way you did. I felt terribly guilty for messing up your life. I suppose I always will feel bad, even though I could never regret having had Lindsey.''

''But you didn't mess up my life. You did me a favor. My only regret concerns us, Emily. I wish I hadn't been so hard on you. I wish I hadn't given up on our marriage.''

''There's no going back and changing it now, Rye.''

''I want to make amends somehow.''

Emily nodded dully. ''I know you do. That's why you're here in Florida.''

Chapter Thirteen

The subject of the past seemed to have been ripped open in the airport. Emily felt as though she had been ripped open, too. On the drive back to the campground, she bared her soul with a relentless honesty, while Rye did the same. It was painful for both of them.

"You undermined my confidence in myself as a good mother," she accused him. "I more than half believed you when you insisted that you were better capable of raising her than I was."

"I sincerely thought that I was." Rye met her gaze, his dark eyes full of regret for what he had to add next. "If one of us had to have the primary responsibility of raising her, I still do think that I was better qualified to be a parent then. You loved Lindsey, but you had no concept of establishing a healthy routine for her."

"You have no idea how it hurts to relinquish the role of being a mother."

"You didn't ever stop being her mother. She spent quality time with you, talked to you on the phone often. Look at the relationship that you have with her," he pointed out with a note of pleading. "You two are closer than the majority of mothers and daughters are."

"Yes, we are close," she agreed. "You're very close to her, too. She admires you and respects you, as well she should. You've been a good father, Rye. That's what has kept me from being bitter and allowed me to go on with my life, accepting things as the way they were. There was a comfort in knowing that my little girl wasn't lacking for anything, including love and attention."

"She missed out on growing up as a part of a close-knit family." Rye's voice was full of regret. "Her only experience with family activities came from visiting the homes of her friends."

"You were married to Claire for five years," Emily reminded him, jealousy creeping into her tone.

"It seemed longer than that," he reflected. "I married her because I hoped she'd be a good stepmother for Lindsey, as well as the kind of wife I thought I needed. On both counts I was disappointed. The divorce came as a relief to all three of us, Lindsey and Claire and myself."

"That period was a real test of what kind of person I was," Emily recalled. "Part of me wanted your marriage to fail. I naturally felt threatened and jealous because Lindsey now had a stepmother, who might crowd me out. The less selfish part of me wanted whatever was best for Lindsey, which would be for you to be happily married to a nice woman who would mother her. When Claire got pregnant, Lindsey was so excited about having a baby sister or brother. To my credit, I was genuinely sorry when Claire miscarried."

"Lindsey was excited about having a half brother or half sister, all right." Rye glanced over at Emily with a pained expression. "You know she planned right from the first to take her sibling along on weekends or holidays that she spent with you. That went over very big with Claire, as you can imagine."

Emily nodded. "I remember Lindsey telling me about those plans and about the negative reaction from you and Claire. I have to admit that it did my heart good that Lindsey wanted to share me with her little brother or sister."

"She adored you and had a wonderful time with you. I had a battle with myself not to be jealous because she always came back more animated and talkative than she was normally. Even though I worried about her safety—I won't lie about that—I knew that you were good for her. That you supplied something vital to her development that I couldn't give her."

His words were a thrill and a comfort to Emily, and yet they had been too long in coming to mean what they once would have. "I appreciate your telling me that, Rye," she said. "All I did was try to enjoy every precious moment that I had with her and yet not smother her with love."

"Between us, we've raised a terrific young woman. I couldn't be prouder of her." Rye took his right hand from the wheel and extended it toward her, palm up.

Emily gave his hand a brief squeeze. But when his fingers tried to link with hers, she pulled free and returned her hand to her lap. She couldn't hold hands with him. After a second or two, he dropped his hand to the console between them.

"I'm very proud of her, too," she stated. "I feel very fortunate to be her mother."

Rye took in a deep breath. "Can you possibly forgive me?"

"I already have forgiven you," Emily replied, her truthfulness easing some of her regret for having to rebuff him. "You weren't intentionally cruel. You just did what you thought was best for Lindsey."

"Where do we go from here? Can you give me a second chance?" He looked over, searching her face.

She shook her head slowly. "I don't think so. I doubt that I could ever trust you again. You hurt me too badly."

"But I care about you. I never really stopped caring. You're the only woman that I've ever loved."

"I care about you, but we're still no more right for each other than we were when we first fell in love. In fact there are more obstacles now," Emily went on with sad wisdom. "Before, we were both dirt poor, a couple of college kids getting through school on loans and grants. Both of us orphans. Both art majors. For a lot of years we've lived in two entirely different worlds, striving for different goals."

"We have a daughter in common." Rye reached out his hand tentatively. This time Emily gave him hers. They held hands in heavy silence. There didn't seem anything left to say.

It was early afternoon on Monday, following the second show on Emily's schedule, in Tampa. Their next destination was Orlando, an easy day's drive that they would make the next day. Somehow Emily didn't doubt for a moment that he was still committed to staying in Florida. Some kind of pact had been made between father and daughter, she sensed.

Despite everything, Emily was glad.

"I need to do laundry," she stated as Rye pulled into the campground, which conveniently had a Laundromat. "If you want, I'll do yours, too."

"I'll go along and do mine," he replied. "It'll be like old times when we went to the Laundromat together."

"You're just afraid that I'll bring them back all wrinkled," she accused.

He grinned and didn't deny it.

Feeling one hundred percent more cheerful, Emily went inside her motor home and collected her dirty clothes. She also stripped the sheets from the bunks. Rye was waiting for her when she emerged. He carried both their laundry bags, one slung over each shoulder, and they strolled through the wooded, parklike setting to the complex that housed the campground office and a grocery store, as well as the Laundromat.

Rye had stripped his bed, too, Emily saw as they were stuffing washing machines. She watched him surreptitiously, amused that he was applying himself to his task, separating his clothes. He glanced over and caught her smiling.

He smiled back sheepishly, and Emily's mood got even lighter. Anticipation curled through her at the thought that she and Rye had the whole rest of the afternoon and the evening before them.

They took a walk in the opposite direction from their campsites while their clothes were washing. Rye took her hand, and they held hands casually. He kept track of the time and headed them back to transfer the loads into dryers.

While their laundry spun round and round, they sat next to each other in molded plastic chairs, thumbing through dog-eared magazines.

"What do you want to do about dinner?" he asked.

"I don't care," Emily answered.

"We can decide later."

"Yes."

They looked at each other, the sense of leisure laced with awakening urgency. Emily had a provocative flashback of herself at eighteen, sitting on Rye's lap in a Laundromat near the LSU campus. If there hadn't been people present today, she would have been tempted to turn back the clock and climb on his lap and neck with him the way she had years ago. She was every bit as attracted to him now.

"Remember how turned on we used to get, doing laundry?" she mused. "I was shameless in public, couldn't keep my hands off you."

"How well I remember," Rye answered softly. From his tone and the expression in his dark eyes, she thought he might be seeing his own flashbacks. "I was either turned on or on the verge of being turned on most of the time when we were together. It took all of fifteen seconds for me to be ready for us to make love."

"That's about how long it took my body. But the foreplay was so good for me that I tried not to rush you."

"It was good for me, too," he said, his eyes dropping to her breasts. "You weren't exactly passive or shy."

Emily's breathing had quickened, and her nipples were contracting under his intimate gaze. "What you're saying very tactfully is that I was a bold little hussy," she murmured protestingly. "And I really wasn't, or hadn't been before then. You were such a good lover at twenty-one."

"After all these years, it swells my ego to hear you say that," Rye admitted. "And not just my ego." He glanced downward. "Could we discuss laundry detergents and pick up this subject after we've finished up here?"

"I hope you don't take forever folding up your clothes. You'll probably just put the same sheets back on your bed," she speculated. "That's what I'll do."

"My bed is already made up with clean sheets."

She blinked in astonishment. "You changed your sheets in that amount of time? That has to be a record."

"I changed them this morning, the same time I put out fresh towels."

"Monday housecleaning," Emily mused. "Did you vacuum and all that?"

"My motor home is spick-and-span, ready for company."

"Mine isn't. You're far more efficient than I am, as always."

They had been talking in low tones for the sake of discretion. Rye waited until a stout woman with two children had walked past them, making her exit with her folded laundry.

"I'm not only efficient," he warned Emily. "I'm horny. With that combination, I can have you naked and in my bed faster than you can imagine."

"Oh, don't forget. I have a vivid imagination," she reminded him. "About laundry detergents. I usually buy the large economy size of the cheapest brand."

He went along with the change of subject without a pause. "Your most economical buy would be the detergent with the least inert material that adds bulk. Do you ever read the small print on the box to find out what the ingredients are?"

"No. I'm very partial to those brands with colored granules," she confessed.

"The colored granules are probably nothing more than that, granules tinted with dye," Rye pointed out.

"But white laundry detergent is so blah."

"Why do I get the impression that you're not putting me on?" he demanded ruefully.

Emily's laugh was an admission that she was revealing her buying idiosyncrasies. "I'll bet you buy one of those concentrated laundry detergents that aren't sold in supermarkets."

"Actually I do. They end up being more economical since you're paying for cleaning agents, not bulk."

"You don't do laundry, of course."

"No. Most of my clothes go to the cleaners."

"I gathered that much," she said. He looked at her questioningly, and she explained, "I have Lindsey save me the plastic coverings from her dry-cleaned clothes. It's perfect for using to wrap my pottery when I want to keep it from drying too quickly. From the quantity that she brings me, I figured out that some of it had to be coming from your closet, too."

"It does," Rye confirmed. "I'm instructed not to discard any of the plastic and not to tear it. I suggested to her that she could get you a roll of it from the dry-cleaners, but she said you would much prefer the used stuff."

"She was right. The used stuff works just as well, and it would be a waste to throw it away."

Emily felt odd with this new knowledge that Lindsey had enlisted his cooperation. He would have had to give Emily an occasional thought when he was taking garments off the hangers, being careful not to damage the protective plastic.

In the process of dressing, he might not have been wearing more than his underwear.

"What?" Rye asked, reading her expression.

"Just that it was nice of you to be so tolerant, a busy man like yourself. You must have things on your mind when you're getting dressed. The natural thing would be to rip the plastic off."

"I do sometimes."

She was intrigued by his tone. "You forget or just get impatient, I would imagine."

"I don't forget," he denied. "I can't drive past a damned dry-cleaners without thinking about you."

"If it's any consolation, I can't wrap up a pot without wondering if the plastic covered a jacket of yours... or a pair of pants."

"More likely the first. The plastic over my pants tends to get rougher treatment."

"A few of those must get put in with the rest. Every now and then there's a piece that's really mangled."

They smiled at each other, enjoying the humor and finding the disclosures they'd made highly provocative. Emily had invaded his private world, and he had invaded hers.

"Hell, those clothes must be dry enough," Rye said recklessly. "If they aren't, we'll bring them back later."

There were curious looks in their direction as they opened the doors of the dryers and hastily crammed the contents into their laundry bags, then left in a great rush, Emily's laughter blending with his. She had to make two running steps to his one on the way to his motor home.

Once they were inside, Rye tossed the bags onto the floor and opened his arms wide. Emily ran into them. He lifted her up against him, hugging her tight, and twirled her around. She hung on for dear life, laughing, caught up in his mood of exultation.

Their lips met, and he came to a standstill, still holding her so that her feet didn't touch the floor. In moments they were both breathless with the depth and passion of the kiss. Rye groaned as he slid her down his body.

They undressed, helping and hindering each other, attending to themselves by turn and kissing all the while. It seemed to take forever to shed their clothes. There were delays as they both gave in to the temptation to stroke and fondle and claim intimately bared flesh.

Finally they were naked together. They embraced, celebrating and sharing their excessive pleasure in one another's bodies. Desire sharpened as they voiced their male and female needs, so different and yet compatible, his to be inside her and hers to welcome his penetration and sheath him.

"Now," Emily urged.

"Here? Standing?" Rye was carrying out her command even as he questioned it, lifting her and coupling them in the union that they both wanted.

There was no separating or stopping, not even when one of them—Emily wasn't sure afterward which one it had been—remembered that they hadn't taken precautions.

"I hope I didn't sound guilty."

"You sounded like yourself," Rye assured her.

They had just hung up his mobile telephone after talking to Lindsey.

"I felt embarrassed, carrying on a conversation with my eighteen-year-old daughter after spending the whole afternoon in the sack with her father."

"Not the whole afternoon," he objected. "And it took us a while to get to the bed."

His tone and smile were complacent.

"Don't you feel a little red-faced yourself over the way we acted?" Emily asked, intrigued with his whole manner. "We left the Laundromat almost at a dead run and were practically tearing off our clothes as we got through the door."

"A man my age feels no embarrassment over a repeat performance," Rye confessed with a candid grin. "Today probably set my mid-life crisis ahead another ten years."

She hesitated, hating to bring up a worrisome subject. "This is a more fertile time of the month for me than when we had our previous sex orgy. We shouldn't let ourselves get carried away again."

"We won't. And it was just the first time we made love that we weren't careful today."

"All it takes is one sperm, and somehow I have trouble believing that yours aren't vigorous."

He kissed her lightly on the lips. "I'll take that as a compliment. Ready to go?"

They were dressed for going out to dinner. Emily had suggested just going to a fast-food place, but Rye had been in favor of trying an Italian restaurant that they'd driven past that day.

She answered that she was ready to go, assuming that the discussion of their foolhardiness was being dropped with no signs of anxiety on his part.

In the car, though, he continued the conversation in an oblique sort of way, half-asking and half-stating, "If you were to get pregnant, you would have the baby."

Emily didn't have to stop and consider. "Of course I would."

"You didn't have any complications with Lindsey and didn't complain much at all."

"I felt great."

"As I recall, you had a relatively easy labor."

"I was in the delivery room only three hours."

"But you're twice the age you were then," he pointed out.

"I wouldn't have any serious qualms, from a health standpoint, if I were in my forties," Emily replied. "If I slipped up and got pregnant, it wouldn't be the pregnancy and childbirth that would concern me, but taking care of a child."

"You mean that it would be a major adjustment to take on the role of being a mother to an infant, changing diapers and breast-feeding and all that."

"An adjustment certainly, but one I think I could make without a lot of difficulty. A bigger problem would be financial. I couldn't work the hours I do in the studio. Or travel to shows. Supporting myself as a single mother would be very difficult. It's a hypothetical situation that I've confronted once or twice when my period was a day late and being pregnant was a possibility."

Rye frowned. "Every baby has a father."

"Yes," she said flatly.

He looked at her searchingly.

Emily didn't keep him in the dark. "I made myself a promise, Rye, that if I should ever have another child, there wouldn't be any custody fight hanging over my head."

"You wouldn't stigmatize a child with being illegitimate?" His voice conveyed his horrified skepticism.

"I was illegitimate, and it didn't cause me any hang-ups. Society is even more liberal now than when I was growing up. Not that it's an ideal background that I would deliberately choose for my son or daughter. If it were, I probably would have been a lot less careful than I have because I would have liked to have had another child or two."

"Emily, your son or daughter would be a man's son or daughter, too. Doesn't he have any say or rights in your mind?"

"This all goes back to our conversation that we had coming from the airport, Rye. There would have to be an awful lot of trust for me to share parenting."

"I understand," he said quietly. "And I won't be careless again. Because for starters I couldn't live with myself if I allowed a child of mine to be born illegitimate."

"We'll take double precautions, to be extrasafe."

"When will we know for certain that it's not too late for precautions?"

"A couple of weeks. But I'm sure I'm not pregnant," Emily scoffed. "Let's not worry in advance about a problem that we won't have to face."

She spoke more confidently than she felt.

Neither one of them suggested abstaining from sex and not having an affair. That night they didn't make love, although by unspoken agreement Emily slept with him in his motor home. The next morning, though, she awoke to the delicious sensation of his caresses.

Later, after they had made love, showered together and gotten dressed, she got her first glimpse of him in his businessman persona. He was engrossed in his own thoughts as they fixed and ate a simple breakfast.

"You seem a thousand miles away," Emily commented.

"About that distance," he admitted. "I hope you aren't in any big hurry to shove off. I need to make some phone calls and touch base with my store managers."

"No, I'm not in any hurry. Why don't you go ahead, and I'll take care of these few dishes."

He took her up on the offer at once. Emily dawdled over a third cup of coffee, watching and eavesdropping surreptitiously. After he had hung up following his conversation with a man he addressed as Barry, he explained that he'd been talking to Barry Bordelon, the manager of his Baton Rouge frame shop. Then he also briefly filled her in on the particulars of several matters that he'd discussed with Barry.

While Emily was quietly cleaning up, he placed his second call and talked to a woman named Bernice, using exactly the same tone, friendly but brisk. Again the social chitchat was kept to a minimum. From his end of the conversation, Emily was able to surmise that there was a problem with recently acquired machinery.

"That was Bernice Telefono, who manages one of the Houston shops," he said, hanging up.

"I'm glad to hear that you have a woman manager," Emily remarked. "How old is she?"

"Thirty-five. I think you'll like her. She has an art degree and is a very talented photographer." He went on, as he had following the previous phone call, and explained the gist of his conversation with Bernice.

Emily wondered whether she was giving him the impression of being curious. While he was punching out a new set of digits, she slipped out of the motor home, disturbed that she was torn between wanting to stay and wanting to leave him to make his calls alone.

Had he even realized that he'd used future tense, *I think you'll like her,* as though she were likely to meet Bernice? It was highly unlikely that she would meet her or Barry or any of his other managers.

She had no desire to meet them, Emily told herself, and was even more disturbed to realize that that wasn't entirely true. During the past thirty minutes, an unwilling kind of interest had been kindled.

Rye's own vital interest in his business affairs was like a force she found difficult to resist. Never would she have expected to find him so appealing when he was immersed in the occupation that had stolen him away from a career as a artist.

Vaguely depressed, as well as upset, Emily went inside her motor home and applied herself to cleaning chores.

An hour and a half later Rye came over to say that he was ready to take off when she was. It was obvious from his voice and manner that he felt thoroughly invigorated after two hours of conducting business on the phone.

"You drive my motor home, and I'll drive yours," he suggested.

Emily declined. "No, thanks, I'll drive my own."

"We'll switch every hour, then. I insist. Otherwise you'll be all tired out when we get there." He kissed her, undermining her independent spirit.

"If I'm tired, I'll have plenty of time to rest before this weekend. Today's only Tuesday."

"That gives us Wednesday, Thursday and Friday to see Epcot Center and Disney World." He kissed her again, more persuasively, and then gave her a playful pat on her fanny. "Don't be stubborn."

Emily relented.

"Okay, we'll switch."

It ended up with her doing the majority of her driving behind the wheel of his motor home, enjoying the music from his stereo. The next three days would be fun. There was no doubt of that. After the week just past, when she'd played tourist with Rye and Lindsey, Emily had given up worrying about the money he was spending for her entertainment.

Obviously he wouldn't get around to doing any painting in Orlando, not with the sight-seeing plans that he had. Next week they'd be traveling on to St. Augustine, which had its own attractions for visitors. Emily was doubtful at this stage that Rye would feel any strong urge to get out his easel there, either.

Seeing him and hearing him as he talked to his managers this morning, she had realized that he wasn't going to change occupations. He thrived on what he was doing. In all probability he wouldn't pursue painting in his spare time, either. A perfectionist, he couldn't derive satisfaction from producing paintings that didn't measure up to his standards, and the motivation wasn't there to devote the best part of him to art.

Rye wasn't and never would be an artist.

After so many years of inner protest, Emily was oddly at a loss to discover that she had reached a calm acceptance. It was as though she had suddenly discovered that her commitment to a major cause she'd long espoused was gone.

Rye was a familiar stranger, someone she had known intimately and didn't know at all.

Chapter Fourteen

Emily didn't normally keep track of her menstrual cycle to the extent of marking the dates on the calendar. When she'd indicated to Rye that they would know in a couple of weeks that she wasn't pregnant, she'd been making a general estimate. The next day or so, she'd looked at a calendar and counted off days.

Her period was due the middle of the week following the Orlando show, which meant that her correct answer to Rye would have been, "A week and a half." Emily was just as glad that she'd given herself a few days' leeway, in the event that he was keeping track. The more relaxed she was about her body's female schedule, the better.

She mentioned nothing to Rye about consulting a calendar, and soothed her vague uneasiness with the knowledge that there was very little chance that she was pregnant.

Married couples who wished to start or increase their families weren't usually successful in a single month. It stood to reason that Rye, at forty, wasn't as potent as he had been at twenty-one, and she wasn't as fertile at thirty-seven as she had been at eighteen. Emily had always held the theory that she'd probably been more at risk because she was taking birth-control pills and forgetting occasionally.

If she and Rye had used some other method and slipped up a few times, she might not have gotten pregnant.

Emily put out of her mind the possibility that she might, for the second time in her life, be the mother of Rye's child. She didn't want to grapple, even imaginatively, with how she'd react and deal with such an eventuality.

For one thing she was too busy falling in love with him all over again to worry and mope. He kept them on the go after they arrived in Orlando. They visited Epcot Center and Disney World and had a marvelous time. While he was playing tourist and enjoying himself, the businessman in him was taking in the design and operation of the famous amusement park and the futuristic center of scientific knowledge.

Emily found she was no longer bothered that his business acumen was an integral part of him. It was stimulating to be in his company, as well as fun. They laughed and carried on teasing conversations and also had more serious philosophical discussions. While agreeing more often than not, they almost inevitably arrived at a consensus by entirely different thought processes.

Rye applied logic and cited data, while Emily relied on her instincts and personal experience. He was analytical, and she was intuitive.

They argued and differed with each other, but somehow weren't at odds. Emily sensed that he accepted the fact that her mentality was unlike his. On her part she admired his intelligence, which, coupled with a sense of humor, made him a wonderful companion.

"You know what?" she confided on Friday when they had left one building at Epcot Center and were strolling hand in hand toward their next destination. "I think I'm really falling for you."

He looked pleased by her remark, which had been teasing and yet sincere. His reply was in the same vein. "I hope so, because I'm knocking myself out to impress you and give you a good time. I'm considered a good catch, you know."

"I'll bet that you are. You're bright and personable and good-looking and rich."

"That depends on your definition of rich," he demurred, and then grinned because he hadn't contested her other compliments.

Emily smiled back. "How about 'well-heeled'?"

"We're getting along very well," he observed, giving the conversation a serious turn.

"Yes, we are, but this isn't exactly like real life."

"No, it isn't."

"You don't have to agree with everything I say just to prove your point," she said with an irritable note. "A little friction keeps a relationship from being boring."

Bringing them to a standstill, he kissed her and replied, "I don't think there's much danger of our having a boring relationship."

Emily's ill-temperedness disappeared as quickly as it had materialized.

The weekend was a test of sorts that they passed with flying colors. Rye wasn't in a market show, as he had been during Emily's two previous shows. He helped her set up early Saturday morning. She was using his nicer canopy, at his suggestion.

Emily was expecting him to show more initiative in putting her pottery out on display. But he had obviously decided in advance not to overstep his bounds. He was there to take instructions and assist, not supervise.

Finally she chided him, "You don't have to handle me with kid gloves."

He smiled. "I'm not taking any chances of getting thrown off the premises in the next two days."

"I wouldn't worry about that."

At her invitation he rearranged the pottery she'd set out and completed the display to his satisfaction. Emily was sincerely complimentary when she walked out in front of her booth with him when they were finished to survey the overall effect.

"That looks great!"

Rye was more critical, asking her to stand there and render a verdict while he made several changes.

The show was Emily's most successful, so far. She knew, though, that the number of sales and the praise from customers weren't responsible for her flush of happiness.

It was Rye's presence in her booth that kept a smile on her face and a lilt in her voice. They might have been doing shows together for years, so well did they work together. After several customers had tried to pay with credit cards, he asked her if she'd like to run charges, using his machine and imprint, and Emily said yes without any compunction.

When the show had closed on Sunday afternoon and they were dismantling her booth, she remarked on her diminished stock, adding, "If we do this well next week in St. Augustine, I may not have enough pottery for the Jacksonville and Tallahassee shows."

The plural, "we," had slipped out.

"Do you have more pottery that we can have packed up and sent?" Rye inquired.

"What I didn't bring is mostly seconds, with some slight defects, and not of a high-enough quality."

"Then it sounds like we may be heading back to Louisiana a week or so earlier than planned," he commented cheerfully.

From his tone Emily could infer that he wasn't exactly upset over the idea of cutting the trip short.

"If you start to feel antsy, you can always head back whether I do or not," her pride compelled her to point out.

"In another week I will have had enough of this being on the road, I suspect," he admitted honestly. "But I'm sticking with your itinerary."

"Did you promise Lindsey that you would finish out the trip with me?"

"Not in so many words." He glanced at his watch. "Let's hurry and get finished here and call her before we go out for dinner."

Emily speeded up. "Dinner is on me tonight," she said. "You pick the restaurant."

"I haven't had an offer better than that in a long time," he replied agreeably, and smiled a warm indulgent smile that melted her urge to assert her independence.

She was prepared for him to choose a family-style restaurant or claim that he was in the mood for pizza or Mexican food, but he chose a restaurant that he might have picked if he were paying. It had nice atmosphere and a promising menu with prices that Emily would have considered high a few weeks ago, but had begun to regard as the norm.

Rye ordered what appealed to him and acted as though tonight were no different from any other night that they'd dined out and he had picked up the tab. Emily wondered if he had some idea about insisting on paying himself when the check came.

But instead he gave pleasant instructions for the waitress to give the check to Emily and showed no discomfort when Emily counted out money for the total and a tip. Two weeks ago he had squirmed and gazed off into the distance at the pizza place in Naples.

"Am I leaving a big-enough tip?" she asked, taken aback by his whole casual attitude. More than anything else, she wanted to get to the bottom of it.

"I don't know. How much is the check?"

Emily told him the amount and also the extra that she'd added.

Rye shrugged. "That's fifteen percent. I usually tip twenty when I'm pleased with the service."

She added additional money, remarking, "Well, this has certainly been more relaxed than the other time that I bought you dinner."

"Very relaxed," he agreed. "But then I'm a lot more relaxed than I was two weeks ago."

"You needed a vacation."

"I needed this trip, not just a vacation. The time with both you and Lindsey was special. Then I've had the best time of my life here in Orlando with you." He reached over and squeezed her hand. "It's immaterial to me whose money we spend, yours or mine, as long as I have your company."

"I've had a wonderful time this past week, too," Emily said, deeply flattered but still not satisfied. "You've given me a vacation."

"We'll take some real vacations together," he promised.

"I'd better start saving my change in a jar."

Her lightly sarcastic remark drew a smile. "With the kind of vacations I have in mind, you'd better tuck in a few dollar bills." He pushed back his chair.

Emily pursued the conversation on the drive back to the campground. "What kind of exorbitantly expensive trips are we going to take? A cruise on the *QE II*?"

"I think a cruise might be fun. Don't you?" he answered.

"Where? In the Caribbean?"

"It depends on the time of year. In the winter a tropical cruise would be nice. If we were taking a summer cruise, I'd love to see the fjords in Norway."

"So would I! Those travel posters of Norway have always caught my eye."

"Good. Then that's one trip we'd both like to take. I'd also like to go to Europe."

"Which countries?"

"Either France or Italy. I'm not really keen on the whirlwind tours. I'd rather just see one country, rent a car and drive through the countryside. Do some sight-seeing, but also get an idea about how the people live."

"That's a tough choice, France or Italy." Emily deliberated briefly. "Italy gets my vote."

"Italy it is, for our first trip to Europe. We can visit France another year. Then there's the Orient, China and Japan."

"If I visited Japan, I'd want to go to some of those little villages with famous potteries."

"I'm sure we can work that into our itinerary. It's a foregone conclusion that you'll be dragging me to the studios of potters in any country that we visit. How about Africa? Could I interest you in taking one of those safaris for camera buffs?"

"Absolutely. Africa has wonderful native potters."

They outlined travel plans that would take them well into the twenty-first century. Emily knew it was all fantasy, like speculating on winning the lottery, but she had always delighted in making up her own fairy tales.

When she returned home to Louisiana, she'd deal with reality.

"How about angling these tables to form more of a V, like this?" Rye inquired.

"Use your own judgment," Emily answered tersely, shaking out a tablecloth. She stood with her back to him and didn't turn around.

"What's the matter?" he asked, his tone patient and concerned. "Why are you so edgy?"

"I'm not edgy," she denied, giving the tablecloth a brisk pop.

"Yes, you are." He came over to stand behind her and put his arms around her waist.

Emily held herself stiff, resisting, and then relaxed against him. "I'm sorry," she apologized. "I guess I am irritable."

"Are you feeling okay physically?" His palm slid down to stroke her abdomen gently.

She bit her lip to keep from blurting out the truth. She felt fine physically, as she had all the previous week. That was the problem. So far she hadn't experienced the first symptom that announced her period, overdue now since Wednesday.

"I'm not sick, if that's what you mean," she said.

"That was a roundabout way of asking if you're having menstrual cramps," he chided.

"I seldom have cramps," she evaded. "I'm fortunate that way."

"You never complained. But I remember that you were cranky and moody. You'd cry at the drop of a hat. And weren't your usual energetic self."

"That hasn't changed."

He hesitated. "So we're out of danger?"

Emily swallowed and then got out the lie. "Yes. You can rest easy."

"It is a big relief, under the circumstances." He hugged her gently. "Why don't you just take things easy and let me set up?"

"Really, I'm fine," Emily insisted, her voice husky with tears that welled up in her eyes and spilled down her cheeks. She wiped at them with the tablecloth.

Rye turned her around and regarded her with a tender expression. "That's conclusive proof that it's 'that time of the month,'" he teased, and kissed her on each damp cheek.

Emily closed her eyes with the unbearable sweetness mixed with panic and despair.

Subterfuge was totally alien to her nature, but she had to buy time, confirm that she was carrying his baby, and then figure out what to do.

It jangled her emotions even more that he was so kind and loving all weekend, treating her as though she were fragile and precious. Emily let him take charge of running her booth on Saturday and Sunday of the St. Augustine show.

The sales were as good as they had been at the Orlando show, further depleting her stock. She hardly had enough pottery left for the Jacksonville show. After she'd sold a few pieces, her booth would look bare.

"Let's head home tomorrow," Rye urged on Sunday evening. "According to Lindsey, spring has already come to Louisiana. The azaleas are all budded out and will be bursting into bloom. I'm ready to get back into my nine-to-five working routine,'' he admitted candidly.

Emily hedged. "I'll decide in the morning what I want to do."

He started to say more and then didn't.

The next morning when Emily awoke, he wasn't in bed. She smelled the aroma of coffee brewing and felt faintly repelled. It could be nerves, she told herself, but she remembered how she hadn't been able to abide the smell or taste of coffee all during her pregnancy with Lindsey.

It wasn't nerves.

She was pregnant.

For a few panicky moments, Emily was eighteen years old again, scared and thrilled. *Oh, my God, what is Rye going to say when I tell him? Will he be furious? Is he going to hate me?*

"Are you awake? I've brought you a cup of coffee."

Rye's voice brought her back to the present, but dispelled none of her panic and uncertainty.

Nor did it dispel the same thrill that she had experienced the first time when she knew that she was carrying his baby inside her. Emily curled up on her side, hugging her stomach.

"Yes, I'm awake," she said, not opening her eyes. "But I don't want any coffee this morning. I've decided to lighten up on the caffeine."

She could sense his surprise. "Would you like for me to make some decaf?"

"No, when I get up, I'll have some orange juice."

He had sat down on the edge of the bed. Emily heard the light clunk of the mug of coffee and wrinkled her nose at the stronger aroma.

"Are you feeling okay? You tossed and turned all night."

He was stroking her back.

"Did I talk in my sleep?"

"No. Why do you ask? Is there some deep, dark secret that you're keeping from me?" His tone was tender and indulgent.

"Yes," Emily blurted, and turned over on her back. When he reached to smooth her hair away from her face, she caught his hand and held it against her cheek. "It's not a secret that I can keep indefinitely, anyway," she said, filled with dread and yet bursting with eagerness to tell him.

He rubbed his knuckles against her cheek as he regarded her thoughtfully. His gaze dropped down to her abdomen and then flicked over to the built-in bedside table, where he'd set the mug.

Emily felt his hand go lax and knew that he'd put all the clues together. He'd watched her diet like a hawk when she was pregnant with Lindsey and would remember that she'd stopped drinking coffee.

"Let's hear it," he ordered her gently but with his own note of eagerness.

"Unless I'm mistaken, Lindsey is going to have that little brother or sister that she wanted." His fingers tightened on hers, and his expression made Emily's heart swell until she thought she would burst with joy. "Don't look so doggoned proud of yourself that you might have knocked me up again," she chided him happily.

He didn't smile or come back with a teasing rejoinder. His reply was sober and earnest. "I hope you aren't mistaken. I want us to have another child. This time will be so different, Emily. The birth of our baby will be a happy event." Laying his free hand on her abdomen, he bent and kissed her on the lips. "I hope I'm not mistaken, too," she admitted. "Even though I do wish that having a child was something that we'd planned, not another accident that forces your hand."

"It's an accident that I welcomed happening, partly because it would speed up my getting back together with you. A baby imposes certain time limits on getting married again." His hand on her abdomen rubbed gently. "Less than nine months, to be exact."

Emily sighed. "Another shotgun wedding. Of course, we don't have to rush out and apply for a marriage license until we know for sure that I am pregnant."

"If I propose to you here and now, and you accept my proposal, we wouldn't be having a shotgun wedding, regardless."

"You never proposed to me before," she reminded him wistfully. "Your exact words were, 'Well, we'll have to get married.'"

He grimaced. "To make up for that reluctant-bridegroom act, I'll have to go the whole route, won't I?" Holding her hand in both of his, he knelt beside the bed. "Emily, will you make me the happiest man in the world and marry me?" he asked with the utmost gravity.

"Yes, I will."

He kissed her hand. The moment was filled with emotion.

"You'll be marrying a businessman, not an artist."

"I know. I'm going to be a very proud wife, Rye." She smiled at him. "Actually the baby is all a ruse. I'm marrying you for your money."

He smiled back. "I'm really worried about that."

Emily flipped back the sheet as he got into bed with her. She cuddled against him as he held her close.

"Are you feeling queasy?" he asked.

"Uh-uh," she answered. "Just happy. I'm thinking about how pleased Lindsey is going to be. Of course, for now we'll just tell her that we're getting re-married."

"We don't have any other definite news, anyway," Rye answered. He was caressing her, rousing wonderful sensations and destroying her contentment.

"No, that's true." Emily moved languorously against him. "We don't know for certain."

"Well, I don't want to rest on my laurels, then."

"Evidently not." She could feel his body against hers, hard and aroused.

"In case we haven't been successful, I'm putting my order in for a redheaded kid with big blue eyes."

"A girl or a boy?"

"Either."

Emily made sounds of pleasure as his caresses became more intimate. "What if he or she has my personality?"

"That's a thought that might stop me in my tracks," Rye said as he got down seriously to making love.

*   *   *   *   *

Silhouette Special Edition

presents

SONNY'S GIRLS

by Emilie Richards, Celeste Hamilton and Erica Spindler

They had been Sonny's girls, irresistibly drawn to the charismatic high school football hero. Ten years later, none could forget the night that changed their lives forever.

In July—
ALL THOSE YEARS AGO by Emilie Richards (SSE #684)
Meredith Robbins had left town in shame. Could she ever banish the past and reach for love again?

In August—
DON'T LOOK BACK by Celeste Hamilton (SSE #690)
Cyndi Saint was Sonny's steady. Ten years later, she remembered only his hurtful parting words....

In September—
LONGER THAN . . . by Erica Spindler (SSE #696)
Bubbly Jennifer Joyce was everybody's friend. But nobody knew the secret longings she felt for bad boy Ryder Hayes....

SSESG-1